FOG CITY BLUES

Jan 2016

A MAX LeBLUE MYSTERY

For David

FOG CITY BLUES

With Love and Sorrow

Frank

by Frank Lauria

Rothco Press • Los Angeles, California

Published by
Rothco Press
5500 Hollywood Blvd., 3rd Floor
Los Angeles, CA 90028

Cover design by Rob Cohen
Cover image by Dewey Thomas

Rothco Press is a division of Over Easy Media Inc.

ISBN: 978-1-941519-32-5

Electronic ISBN: 978-1-941519-33-2

For Ellen Smith, a dreamer like me...

Chapter 1

The phone woke me from a sound nightmare

"Turn on the TV."

It took fuzzy seconds to place the voice. "Son of a bitch."

"The TV. Turn it on," Delaney said. Cool and easy, like an old buddy touting a sports event. Except in the real world Delaney coached the team trying to take me down for ten or twenty. Years not yards.

I clicked the big eye awake and stared at the screen, bruised brain struggling to focus on the images and follow the headlines streaming below. I switched channels. Same image no distracting headlines, clear, calm voice. I turned up the volume.

"The first jet crashed into the North Tower at 8:45 followed by a second jet that hit the South Tower at 9:05, ramming it with such force the airliner burst through the other side," the voice said. "We have a report a third jet has crashed into the Pentagon..."

"Jesus." I pawed the night table for a cigarette.

"You believe this shit?"

I didn't answer, alerted by Delaney's tone. Until now it had always been cold steel. Always, even when we worked together. But today he was whistling a warmer tune.

Whistling Dixie. I watched a rerun of the second jet blasting into the South Tower.

"This is fucking insane." I dragged on my cigarette waiting for Delaney to make his point.

He took his time. A real pro, even back in the day, when everybody else was frisky.

The TV voice announced people were leaping from the towers. "My God," I blurted as I finally grasped the enormity of what was happening. Both towers of the World Trade Center were billowing flames and black smoke, the passenger jets having rammed the upper floors. I could see people trapped above the blazing wreckage. I wondered if they could bring in helicopters.

"What about chop..." Before I could finish the thought the South Tower started to implode.

The structure fell in on itself in cinematic slow motion. Like a column of disintegrating dominoes it shook itself down one floor at a time until it exploded into roiling clouds of toxic dust.

"We're at war here, Sam."

Here it comes I thought, waiting.

"We need to talk, right away. Meet me at 51st and Lex in one hour, okay?"

Okay? That wasn't like the arrogant bastard I'd learned to despise.

"Ninety minutes." I hung up the phone, still staring at the screen.

The second building went down while I was taking inventory. I looked up from the open drawer in my night table, jaw slack with disbelief as I watched the North Tower collapse on itself.

"What the fuck is happening?" I said. Nobody answered.

I lit another Camel and watched a rerun of the planes crashing into the towers. There was limited footage of the first jet but the second hit was covered from various angles. I watched the airliner soar into view from below, appearing to accelerate before it slammed into the 95th floor. For a moment it vanished then burst through the other side spewing fire and horror.

The coverage cut to the Pentagon attack with aerial views of the burning wreckage. I looked over my inventory: two Valium, two Percodan, less than a gram of coke, a quarter of gourmet weed, a bag of smack for emergencies, a silver flask filled with absinthe, a crumpled pack of Camels, a deck of Bambu papers.

I extracted a leaf from the deck and rolled a J. Three tokes was all it took. An ease of mind oiled my stiff limbs as I rolled off the bed and stumbled to the kitchen.

Technically a studio, my downtown apartment had more space than most two-bedrooms. The foyer was large enough to serve as an office, the living room large enough to split into a bedroom, it had an eat-in kitchen, and walk in closets with interior lights.

It was also rent-controlled. I would never leave. Yeah, right, I would never learn.

I downed two glasses of water then went to work preparing breakfast. I grabbed a variety of fresh fruit from the fridge; cantaloupe, watermelon, papaya, mango, the works. Then I sliced the fruit and tossed it all into a blender along with some orange juice.

The mixture went a long way to restoring my energy. But it couldn't repair the damage of a thousand bad nights. I shook out some vitamin tablets and washed them down with more juice. Then I ducked into the bathroom and brushed my teeth. I doused my face and hair with cold water and I was good to go.

Pulling myself together, I kept my eye on the screen. Every two minutes they showed a replay of the towers crumbling.

Think hard, I asked my reflection in the mirror, how does this even remotely affect the DEA? More mysterious, why was Delaney so damned clubby all of a sudden? Like he gave a shit about his ex-partner. Or anybody else. I tapped out a line of coke.

One line. Moderation. I snorted half a line in each nostril and screwed the small vial shut. The coke swept away the valium cobwebs. Moved by a rush of energy I put on fresh clothes, snatched my gym bag and headed for the door.

Everybody at the health club was gathered around the TV, watching replays of the disaster. I paused to check if there were any new developments then moved back to the lockers. I had long stopped working out but dropped in often for a tribathalon—jacuzzi, sauna, shower. Reasonably refreshed, I put on my dress clothes; grey flannel trousers, deep blue shirt, ancient madder tie, navy blazer with black buttons, very old school. On my way out, I paused at the TV. They were rerunning the South Tower collapse.

The baths had flushed the intensity out of the drugs I'd ingested leaving an alert glow. I was ready for a sit down with good old Al.

The subway was in chaos. The people crowding the platform stared like startled deer, shuffling anxiously. They all kept one eye on the tunnel and the other on the exit. A well-dressed business man looked at me and shook his head. "Jesus. This is horrible."

I nodded and turned away, still insulated by the drug glow. After fifteen sweltering minutes I bolted from the subway and headed uptown on foot.

The people on the street had the same stunned look as those I had left underground. They all walked more slowly than usual, moving around each other with exaggerated politeness, actually making eye contact, talking to one another. Many stood and watched the dirty grey cloud devouring the downtown sky.

I paused and considered my options. Technically I should have hung up the moment I recognized Delaney's voice. Alvin Delaney was New York director of the Drug Enforcement Administration—and the man directly responsible for my arrest.

The fact that I was working undercover cut no slack with Delaney. His boys found various uncontrolled substances in my apartment and my bloodstream. They also found my stash of automatic weapons, a Beretta Tomcat and a WWII Luger. At the moment I faced a buffet of federal charges, any one of which could destroy what was left of my life.

Even if I managed to beat the case, I was fucked. I was hopelessly behind on alimony payments, overdrawn, hyper-extended, maxed-out, and scuffling to pay my lawyer. Mostly because of Delaney. And today, of all days, he decides to have a friendly talk. It occurred to me the meeting might justify a mistrial.

I made a conscious effort to center myself and walked to the appointed corner. He was twelve minutes late. Standing there, I wondered why Delaney didn't have the meet at his office. Probably worried. The last time I visited his office was to turn in my badge. Actually I threw in my badge, shattering the frosted glass panel in Delaney's door. Fortunately he was out at the time, so the fallout was minimal.

Another nail in the coffin of my reputation.

My brain kept orbiting the enormous tragedy less than three miles away. It was still difficult to comprehend. Along the way, I had heard estimates of five thousand dead. Five thousand husbands, wives, lovers, families, all destroyed in less than an hour. My thoughts circled back to Delaney. Obviously this had something to do with the plane attacks. But the connection evaded me.

The energy I had managed to stoke up that morning was draining fast, leaving me with a slight coke depression and a thirst for scotch. I scanned the street for a bar. A black town car with tinted windows stopped beside me. The rear door opened and I glimpsed Delaney's face.

Show time.

I gathered myself and ducked into the car. It immediately pulled away. There was a closed partition between the driver and the plush rear compartment. Delaney sat in front of an ebony pull-down desk peering at an open laptop. He looked up as I settled in and our eyes met. Two gladiators behind iron masks sizing each other up.

Delaney had put on weight. His blue eyes seemed smaller inside the jowly face. But his mouth remained tight and nasty, like a snapping turtle. That, and his carefully-combed hair gave him a passing resemblance to the late, great, J. Edgar Hoover. I wondered what he'd look like in a dress.

"Hello, Sam. Good to see you. How have you been?"

The paternal tone annoyed me. Like the priest who walks you to the electric chair.

"Been better, thanks."

Delaney nodded somberly, trying to look as if he cared. Then he settled back and clasped his hands over his paunch. "As of today, everything shifts into high gear, Sam."

He inclined his head at the laptop. I bent forward and saw the now-familiar image of the tower collapsing.

When I leaned back, I felt the first pulse of a headache behind my eyes. "What the hell is going on?"

Delaney hunched his beefy shoulders. "Terrorists, Sam. Well funded, well organized, totally dedicated terrorists out to destroy democracy. It's that simple."

It's never that simple I thought but kept my poker face.

"Motherfuckers hurt us bad today," the director was saying, "worse than Pearl Harbor."

"That why you called? What am I, the fucking cavalry?"

The reflexive scowl on Delany's face was familiar. In that twitch I saw his distaste for the task at hand. Despite my swelling headache I felt better. I decided to take the high road. So did Delaney.

"In Chinese the character for the word crisis includes the character for opportunity," he said calmly. "I called to offer you an opportunity, Sam."

"I'm open to all suggestions, Alvin."

Delaney looked out the tinted window. "How would you like to be dead, Sam?"

"Haven't liked it so far."

Delaney's gaze swung around and fixed on me. "I'm serious. Think about it. One stroke and you're out from under all of it, trial, jail, bankruptcy, divorce, disgrace, the whole pathetic tragedy."

The word pathetic lit my fuse. I felt it searing through my headache. "I call it combat trauma," I said, eyes not budging from his. "You think somebody can go deep cover for three years without doing drugs? Get real, Alvin. It ain't like administration."

I clenched my jaw and looked away. I had already said too much. But at least it was out in the open; Delaney's distaste, my pitiful resentment. The headache expanded.

"Actually that's why we chose you," Delaney said. "We need someone with nothing to lose."

I turned. "Who is 'we'?"

Delaney's face was blank. "You report only to me. I'll be the only person who knows you're alive."

"And what, I'm supposed to trust you?" My emotions were still burning at *pathetic*. "I haven't recovered from the last time."

Delaney's disgusted scowl bloomed at last. "You were using and dealing drugs."

My laugh made the headache worse. "Duh, I was deep cover for the DEA, your office, that was my job."

"You were selling drugs to pay for your divorce."

"Big fucking deal. I was selling drugs at your behest. The cash came in the cash went out—money has no home. Let's discuss my conviction rate."

Delaney exhaled slowly and nodded. "Granted. Seventeen percent over average. That's exactly why we are offering you this opportunity, Sam."

"The opportunity to be nobody."

"To be anyone you want to be."

"You must have thought this up yourself."

"What makes you say that?"

"The first tower hadn't collapsed when you called. This deal isn't official is it?"

"If I want it to be—it's official."

"What if you have a fatal stroke?" I asked hopefully.

"Then you're up shit's creek. But you'll still be dead. It's a trade off."

I didn't answer, scanning for the loophole.

"You are facing jail time, debts up the ying-yang. This way your wife gets the insurance, you avoid all criminal penalties and you get a fresh start."

"As a drug dealer."

"Counter-terrorist, Sam. Think of it that way."

"I will still be dealing and using drugs won't I?"

"Yes to the first part, the second is your call."

"You sound like Nancy Reagan."

"You sound like a loser."

I smiled. "Thanks for the opportunity, Alvin. But no thanks."

Delaney's features sagged. I leaned forward to tell the driver to stop.

"Whoa, Sam, just wait a minute. I didn't mean it like that." He took a deep breath. "Just hear me out."

I sat back, headache eased by my newly discovered power to sway Delaney. I wondered how badly he wanted me to do this.

"We—*I*... am prepared to make concessions, Sam. I want you to know I will protect you. You will be informed of any surveillance or impending raids. I'll give you a number to call if you're arrested. What more can I do to assure you?"

I had already decided. "My apartment."

"What about it?"

"I'm dead. I can't go back. I'll need an outstanding rent-controlled place for the new me... if I agree."

"I'll see what I can swing, Sam..."

"And—if I agree—I'll need my weapons returned. Especially the Luger."

"Maybe." Delaney settled back. He was in his element. "What else?"

"Tell me, what's the DEA's connection here?"

Delaney leaned closer. "These Arab terrorists are extremely well financed. Much of their money comes from drugs. They use that money, or drugs, to buy arms, everything from AK-47's to rockets, grenade launchers, heavy ordnance of all kinds. We need to trace the drugs back to the Uzi's and Stingers. We need to identify the arms dealers behind the drug dealers."

There was a long silence. "And?"

"And what?"

"Once I identify these dealers you're talking about what am I supposed to do?"

"That depends, doesn't it?" He let the question hang between us.

"Get this clear, Alvin. I'm no assassin."

"Come on, Sam, you served with the Marines in the Persian Gulf and were a street cop before you went DEA. You telling me you never shot anyone?"

I didn't tell him that a judge had ruled I either serve with the Marines or serve time. A dumb pot bust in my senior year. When the Marines found out I had completed three years at Columbia they put me in computer school. In those days the computers still had stacks of cards. However, I did see some combat in the Persian Gulf.

After discharge, I joined the NYPD and finished my education at night. It took three years but I finally earned a master's in Physics. When my superiors found out about my academic achievements they immediately assigned me to the main computer. I never even heard a shot fired in anger.

Actually, I joined the DEA just to get a bit of action. And I got it—in spades. First year on the street, I had to kill two men, both of whom were trying to kill me. It was about then I stopped sleeping well.

"So why do you need the damn silencers?"

I looked out the window. "Noise pollution."

The town car had turned uptown and made a left on seventy-second. As we passed Park Avenue, I looked down the long sloping thoroughfare and saw a dark cloud billowing like a funeral veil above the Pan Am building.

We were entering the park when Delaney said, "In or out, Sam?"

I noticed that the joggers, bikers, and bench bums all had their eyes on the southern sky.

"I'll require a starter kit."

"What's that?"

"A pound of heroin and a kilo of coke."

"Done. You'll need cash. " Delaney reached into his pin striped jacket and extracted a thick, tan envelope. "Twenty thousand."

I waved off the envelope. "I haven't said I'd do it."

"What's your option? This way your debts and crimes are erased and you're free. The other way you are FFL—Fucked For Life. Face it."

I had faced it, alright, and knew damned well it was a suicide mission, hanging out there with nothing but Delaney's good will and a phone number.

"I'll need access to a sanitation unit," I said, stalling.

"What?"

"You know, clean up, mop up, whatever you guys do."

"Thought you're not an assassin."

"I'm not, but we're negotiating here."

"Look, there'll be no formal contract..."

"That's why I'll need a three year lease under my new name. Remember, someplace discreet, ground floor of a brownstone, that sort of thing, good neighborhood, dropped living room, big kitchen."

Delaney snorted derisively. "Why blow prime real estate on a dealer?"

"In the drug business it's location, location, location. But I still haven't agreed to anything."

"Then get out right here."

I stared him down. "See? That's exactly it. First obstacle, you people jump ship."

Delaney tossed the envelope on the leather between us. "You can stay at a hotel until we arrange another apartment."

"Can't get a hotel room without ID."

"There's a driver's license and credit card in the envelope."

"How much did you say is in there?"

Delaney knew I was in. He rolled the number off his tongue. "Twenty thousand dollars."

"I'll need another thirty, plus your cell number. All access."

"Hey, once you're dead, you're dead."

"Also a passport, a blank birth certificate and a social security card."

"Look, Sam, let's not get carried away here."

I had been waiting for this. I paused and caught his eyes. "You know what, Alvin? Those very bad men you want me to find have friends everywhere; the cops, the courts, even the fucking DEA. I need a bulletproof identity. I need total anonymity."

Delaney looked away. "Apartment, thirty grand, starter kit, bulletproof ID, that about do it?"

"Just about." I picked up the envelope. It felt good. I put the cash in my inside pockets and the documents in my shirt pocket. In my business neatness is survival.

"Where will you be staying?"

"Give me your cell number."

Delaney scribbled the number on his business card.

"Here's how it will go down," I said, bristling with confidence. "When my apartment is secure we will meet for the last time. You will deliver the required items personally. At which time I will be on my own, free to operate as I see fit."

"I'll require monthly reports," Delaney countered. "If you don't check in, we'll come looking for you—with extreme prejudice. We have a deal?"

I hesitated. One way or another, it was a set up. Delaney was using me as a pawn in some vicious chess game. But I was all out of options.

"Let me out here."

Delaney pressed a button on the console in front of him. "Pull up anywhere."

The car slid to a stop near the Columbus Circle exit in Central Park. I started to open the door. "I'll call you tomorrow."

"Close it."

When I pulled the door shut our eyes met. His were blue holes in a wall of ice. "Call me exactly at noon. Clear?"

"Crystal." I opened the door and stepped into the park as the town car rolled away

I experienced a profound sense of relief.

I was dead. *Oh that magic feeling nowhere to go*, said John Lennon.

Sirens were wailing from two directions. I looked around and saw a jogger approaching at half-hearted speed. Behind him a pair of bikers stood perched on their wheels looking up at the dirty sky. In the near distance I saw people milling aimlessly around Columbus Circle, faces blank. Without knowing why, I began walking west.

Somewhere off Amsterdam I spotted a bar called the Blue Shamrock and stepped inside. The permanent gloom was soothing. Three patrons sat in staggered positions along the bar glumly contemplating the TV. The bartender, too, stood watching the towers collapse yet again. I took a stool equidistant from the other drinkers. The bartender edged closer, head cocked toward the TV. "What'll it be?"

"A Jameson straight and black coffee."

The bartender nodded in solidarity.

As he moved off I finally took a deep breath. The quiet and minimal light made me feel like I was in a movie house. I patted my pockets and found the pack of Camels. I also felt the vial of coke. I shook out a cigarette and lit up.

When the whiskey arrived I drained it and signaled for a refill. While I waited I sipped my coffee and watched the TV. On the second whiskey I offered a toast: curse me for profiting from this misery.

The scotch, caffeine, nicotine, and solitude helped me sort this out. There I was. Nobody. I reached into my shirt pocket and peered at the name on my new driver's license. Philip Munson.

Philip. I weighed the name against my essential spirit, the whiskey having made me a philosopher. Munson was alright. Nondescript. A proper dealer's name. Of course, I didn't buy into Delaney's hypocrisy. I don't inhale bullshit. I was proud of what I'd accomplished. I had a goddamn outstanding conviction rate. And I coddled my various addictions like war wounds.

The way the whiskey burned deep into my belly reminded me I hadn't had a proper breakfast. I looked at my watch. Lunch time. Problem was the black coffee and whiskey had eaten my appetite. Get something anyway, I told myself and signaled the bartender.

I ordered a grilled cheese with bacon and tomato and ate in gloomy silence, watching the TV. Hundreds of firemen were dead or missing. A man at the end of the bar said, "they oughta nuke the bastards."

Food was a good decision. Fortified, I thought about where to stay. Normally I would have chosen the Chelsea or Gramercy Park but everything below fourteenth was cordoned off, which meant everything below forty-second would be chaos. I decided to try a hotel I'd visited a year before, the Exeter on West Eighty-Second street.

When I left the bar I lucked into a cab and headed uptown. It occurred to me I might be followed. Just to be sure I had the driver drop me on Eighty-Sixth Street. I walked back four blocks changing my route sporadically. If I was being tailed it didn't show. Alone at last.

The Exeter had a vacancy, many in fact.

"We need your credit card, Mr. Munson."

I leaned closer to the night clerk. "I'll be having drinks with a friend. If my wife sees the bill she might misunderstand. I pushed one of Delaney's hundreds across the polished desk. The clerk hesitated then picked up the bill.

A wave of exhaustion swept over me as soon as I entered my suite. It had a small sitting room, a smaller kitchen and a large bathroom. I showered and dove into the double bed. When I awoke it was dark. I checked my watch, ten-fifteen p.m. Time for breakfast. Before I went out, I made a list: toothbrush, razor, all the essentials.

The night air was crisscrossed with whining sirens. The streets were deserted and many stores were closed. Finally, I found an all night market but choices were severely limited. Hoarders had bought up the bread, milk, water and beer. Fortunately they'd overlooked the razors and toothpaste.

Not finding much in the way of food, I looked for a restaurant or café but New York had become a ghost town. I hailed one of the few cabs prowling the empty streets and went to the East Side. There was a die-hard bar on Seventy-Fourth; great burgers, eccentric clientele, good place to think.

JG Melon's was open, a beacon in a bleak sea. It was like walking into a cozy inn after a long cold trudge across the moor. The comforting sizzle of burgers on the grill mingled with the smoke and muffled conversation, I slid onto a vacant stool in the corner and ordered a bacon cheeseburger. As I ate, I reminded myself I was dead. No jail, no debts, no wife. Forget Ishmael, call me Munson.

However, I carried some heavy baggage, a stubborn memory and many bad habits. I remembered the vial of coke in my pocket. When I finished the burger, I ordered an Irish coffee figuring the whiskey would cut the cholesterol. I lit a cigarette and looked around.

The deck of tables up front and the large back room were both densely populated, as was the bar. The crowd was more subdued than usual, a cross section of brokers, lawyers, actors, writers, athletes, hookers, and gangsters. Everyone was speaking to each other quietly and earnestly, like mourners at a funeral. A group of regulars at the far end of the bar were conferring with a burly bartender. The other bartender brought my Irish coffee and paused to stare out the window. "My wife's brother is missing," he said, eyes on the street. "He's a fireman."

"Lots of confusion down there. He'll probably turn up."

"They got the city sealed off, nothing in or out below Fourteenth." He turned to serve another customer. I sipped my cream-topped coffee, savoring the hot breath of whiskey.

My mind kept circling back to Delaney. Goddamnit, why? Why had Delaney chosen me? As director, he already had certified assassins at his disposal. Why was he being so generous? The fatted calf routine, I decided.

I signaled for another drink, this time single malt scotch.

"Glenfiddich straight up," the bartender intoned. I watched him move listlessly away, body wooden. The patrons, too, had a certain physical numbness. Night of the Living Dead, I thought.

As if in response something flashed in the corner of my eye. I half-turned and looked out the window. A group of people were holding a candlelight procession. I watched them pause at a mail box, tiny flames bobbing in the darkness. When they resumed marching downtown I saw they had hung a leaflet on the mail box.

Right about then it hit me. I sat there, staring at the white patch on the mailbox across the street. With one deft move Delaney had shifted the entire weight of this colossal tragedy onto my shoulders. I'll confess, in the car with Delaney, I wanted a flash of coke to burn away the debris in my brain. At the moment I could feel the glass vial against my thigh. But I didn't need any more stimulants at the moment. My guts, brains, and what was left of my soul were seething with rage at myself, and at Delaney for using this hellish thing to manipulate me. What I needed was another drink. One hit of coke and I could conceivably kill someone. I was that wired.

"Do you have a cigarette?"

Five chords in a familiar song. Before I turned I checked her reflection in the glass. But it didn't matter. Those five words had spoken volumes. They said; lonely, experienced, exciting, and definitely trouble.

"Yeah," I said, extending the pack.

"You only have two left."

"One each, the math works."

She carefully extracted a cigarette and waited for a light. I took a matchbox from the basket beside me and handed it to her. With a slow smile she struck a match. The flare illuminated her face. Tawny eyes, dark curves under high cheekbones, wide, full mouth. She lit her cigarette then cupped the flame and lit mine. Nice gesture, I thought, leaning forward. But I had already decided to pass.

She exhaled and looked out the window. "Hell of a day."

"Still not over."

"Good point." She studied me over the rim of her glass. "They say the city is cut off."

"It is an island."

She sipped her drink, features veiled by cigarette smoke. I noticed the way she carried herself, long torso erect, chin high. One part Katherine Hepburn. What's the other part, I wondered.

I drank and watched the customers. More were coming in and nobody seemed to be leaving. The conversations remained subdued and the bartenders, waiters and cooks went about their business with resolute efficiency.

"Sad night for a lot of people," she said.

"Yeah, it is." I signaled the bartender who came over with the scotch bottle. "And whatever the lady is having."

"One Glenfiddich, one Absolut," he intoned.

When they arrived I lifted my glass. "To all those who died today."

She touched her glass to mine. "We all died today."

I liked her voice. And she had an attractive way of looking at me sideways. It was the flinty spark in her dark eyes that worried me.

I glanced around at the crowd. "Guess nobody wanted to be alone tonight."

"I don't."

It caught me by surprise. The speed, the candor, the need. I lied. "I'm married."

She gave me a tight smile. "I prefer it."

"Nothing like a bit of tension."

Her laugh sealed the bargain. We both knew it. Now it was just a matter of style. I took my time, telling myself I could enjoy the flirtation and leave alone if I so desired. But I was lying. And the booze swore to it. So I did the next best thing. I excused myself and headed for the restroom.

Along the way I paused to allow a couple to pass which gave me a second to scan the room. It rankled that I hadn't noticed the lady until she spoke to me. It stung my professional pride. Theoretically, I was supposed to have the instincts of a panther.

I checked the tables in the rear as I entered the tiny men's room and checked again as I came out. Slipping back through the crowd around the bar I gave the front room a careful look. No one had that predator vibe—except her.

Still she looked damned fine sitting there against the window. American grace, rangy elegance, sex and danger, a hero fit for me. But I wasn't Norman Mailer and my hero days were long gone. I trusted nothing, least of all the ruins of my nobility.

When I sat down I sensed an aura of return, *hi, honey, I'm home.* Her smile said she'd been waiting all day. I bought it for a moment, basking in the fragile illusion. Self-indulgent bullshit. I imagined Delaney scoffing.

But you can't crack a con unless you buy into it. That went for Delaney's death trap as well as this lady. It occurred to me I didn't know her name. It seemed uncool to ask. I waved at the bartender. She looked disappointed.

"By the way, I'm Brett."

I was impressed by the synchronicity.

"My father, he read a lot."

"I'm a Fitzgerald man, myself." I dropped a hundred on the bar and finished my scotch while I waited for my change.

"There's stuff to drink at my place."

I looked at her, trying to reconcile her rangy elegance with *stuff to drink.*

She flashed a sideways smile, as if we were both in on the joke.

"Sounds promising," I said.

The smile tightened. "No promises."

I swept up my change and left a ten on the bar. "I'm fresh out of promises myself."

We left quietly and walked two blocks uptown to one of those small apartment units that stand like tombstones between larger buildings. There wasn't much conversation. We kept glancing at each other with concern as if both listening to some dread newscast on the radio.

She opened the street door and I followed her up the steel staircase to the second floor.

I waited while she unlocked her apartment door. Inside, it was practically institutional. Two railroad style rooms with kitchen. And Brett had done very little to spruce it up.

Clothes, books, CDs, shoes, were strewn around the living room. The place had an impersonal feel, like a college dorm. There was an array of bottles on the kitchen table, wine, scotch, vodka, tequila, bourbon. At least Brett stayed on top of the fundamentals.

She flashed me a toothy smile. "Help yourself."

She moved into the next room. A light switched on and I could see an unmade bed.

I ambled to the makeshift bar, the Clash's musical quandary, *should I stay or should I go?* looped around my thoughts. I was under no illusion. Brett's invitation had nothing to do with my manly charms. It had everything to do with Brett's own demons. But it wasn't your ordinary night. There were demons everywhere.

I stayed with scotch and poured Brett a healthy vodka. When I opened the fridge for ice I found a number of ancient food containers that looked like lab experiments ripening on the shelves. Not a good sign.

I recalled a movie called *Repulsion* where young Catherine Deneuve lets her dead rabbit rot on a shelf while she slashes a number of prospective lovers. The French version of Elimidate.

"Pardon the mess, I just got back from Barcelona."

When I looked up, my reservations vanished. Brett had changed into a pale blue shift of some sheer material that outlined the shadowy curves beneath. Demure yet sensual. A hint of lavender. That and her plausible explanation of the chaos in which she dwelled dispelled my doubts. I handed her the vodka. "What were you doing in Spain?"

"Business, two full days. Vacation, three. That's okay, isn't it?"

"Very civilized."

We drank in silence. Then she moved across the floor. "Music. What do you want to hear? I don't have a big selection."

"Anything by Aretha Franklin, Bob Marley. After that it's your choice."

A for Aretha, B for Bob and C for *Chain of Fools*, which came, came, came, trooping out of the speakers. We smiled in recognition, drank a bit more. During that funky chorus, I leaned in and kissed her. We stood swaying in time in the kitchen, half dancing, half exploring each other, our drinks set aside, listening to Aretha straight through Dr. Feelgood.

Right about now you expect me to tell you what a great studly experience we shared but it wasn't like that. Someplace between *Heartbreaker* and *Say A little Prayer* it came down on me heavy. My salvation ransomed by four thousand lives. The horror—the sheer fucking horror.

Brett felt it too. I could tell. There was a sense of fragility about her. As if her bones were made of glass. I didn't know what particular circle of hell she occupied but it was definitely on my side of town.

We made our way to the unmade bed where I held her close, rocking her until I fell asleep. When I woke up I was still holding her. I gingerly extracted my limbs and padded to the window. A dirty grey haze smeared the pink sky. Quietly, I retrieved my clothes and slipped out.

It's always a bit depressing when you go home at dawn, the city silently reproaching as you crawl back to your lair, like a vampire. But this morning, a certain charnel smell hovered over the stillness. Cabless and chilled, I scuttled west to my coffin.

Chapter 2

I woke up at ten. In the bathroom I caught my reflection in the mirror. Dark circles around washed-out green eyes, alcohol flab around my chin, Philip fucking Munson.

Despite the name, the new man didn't feel that bad. Except for one line and a few scotches. I was relatively drug free. Didn't even need a Valium to sleep.

I called the desk, got the number of a local deli and ordered some food. Then I showered and dressed. I found a near-empty pack of Camels and lit up while waiting.

At exactly noon, I called Delaney's cell. The steely tone was back and his response was curt. "Tomorrow, fourteen-hundred, same place."

While waiting for the food, I switched on the TV. Reruns of the towers collapsing looped every channel while endless updates crawled below the hellish scenes. The networks pandering to the lowest human denominator for ratings. Sanctimonious grifters in designer suits selling Jesus, the flag, and Viagra to an under-informed, over-indulged audience. By the time my delivery arrived I had almost lost my appetite.

Almost. Mind clear for a change, I had ordered breakfast and lunch at the same time. For breakfast, there were two poppy seed bagels, lox, cream cheese, and three cups of black coffee. Lunch featured a turkey swiss on rye with mustard, a side of cole slaw, a Dr. Browns cherry soda, and a slab of cheese cake.

Nothing like New York deli. I wolfed down the first bagel before slowing down to savor the fresh lox and fragrant coffee. After breakfast, I carefully stashed the rest of my supplies in the hotel refrigerator and went back to bed.

I woke up three hours later feeling totally refreshed. I eased down to the carpet and began stretching. I'd managed to stay limber through my various binges, but today I began working out with a purpose.

Whatever game Delaney had devised hinged on my being a drug-dependent degenerate with a drinking problem. So my best defense was to clean up a bit. Cool out the drugs and drinking and concentrate on being a degenerate.

I worked out for nearly an hour then took a long shower. Afterwards I got ready to go out. While dressing I remembered the money Delaney had fronted me. Twenty grand. I had cut a small stack for walk-around and stashed the rest in a special pocket inside my custom blazer. Always stay mobile.

The special pocket was there, all right. But it was empty.

After the initial racing heart, flushed skin routine I settled down and ticked off the possibilities. Anyway I sliced it, Brett came up prime suspect.

Outside, the air smelled toxic. I looked south and saw ugly brown clouds rolling over the skyline. I took the long way across the park, pausing frequently to check for a tail. There were lots of people around, most of them wandering about with aimless expressions as if lobotomized. Others stood searching the grim sky for answers.

I had lots of questions of my own. Number one being, why would Brett take the cash since I know where she lives and she is far from stupid? I happen to be a devout paranoid and believe nothing of what I hear and half of what I see. It works for me.

Traffic was still erratic and the few passing cabs were full. I didn't mind walking. It went with my new life style.

It was cocktail hour by the time I reached the Upper East Side. Emerging from the park at Seventy-Second Street I was immediately struck by the vast patchwork of posters, flowers, votive candles and ribbons that quilted the usually staid neighborhood. Mostly they were photos of loved ones. Lost loved ones, the three saddest words in the universe.

As I approached Melon's I made a plan. One drink. If Lady Brett wasn't there I'd check her apartment.

The atmosphere inside the bar was solemn. I scanned the room. No sign of her. Probably out on a shopping spree. I had my drink, Glenfiddich neat, water back, and turned to go. That's when I saw her. She was sitting alone at one of the front tables with her back to the bar, reading a book. So much for my laser senses.

She glanced up when I neared and gave me that side-wise smile.

"I've been waiting for you." She set the book aside. Jane Austen.

I sat down. "You took my cash."

"I wanted to see you again."

Male Ego 101. I didn't bite. Still I had to admire her criminal mind.

"Well, I'm here, where's the money?"

Her voice got husky. "At my place."

Male Ego 102. But I had no choice. Go along, I told myself. Find out more about her. A polite drink, some witty dialogue, get the cash and leave. No sex, end of drama.

We walked slowly up Third Avenue not saying much. I was uncomfortably aware of the pedestrians on each side of the street moving as if underwater.

Everyone in the city was wired to the catastrophe downtown. Manhattan Island was virtually sealed off from America and nobody got below Fourteenth Street without a note from the governor.

Brett seemed to be taking things in stride. She had unusually good posture for a fallen woman, chin high and features set in a cool, compassionate smile. Her apartment was still a mess when we arrived, strewn possessions, unwashed glasses. The only thing that seemed in order was her bookcase.

"Pour yourself a drink," she said on her way to the bathroom.

Instead, I lit a cigarette and browsed the apartment. Like many New York flats there was a kitchen, dining alcove and living room. Beyond the living area was a small bedroom.

I leaned inside the bedroom and casually inspected the unmade bed and untidy dresser. My eye paused on some familiar objects in an open box. Standing at attention in Brett's jewelry case were six .38 caliber bullets.

I backed out and stared at the closed bathroom door. Was Brett going to come out shooting? Of course not, the bullets were in her jewelry box. In which case, her gun wasn't far away. I wasn't about to search her bedroom but scanned the place for possibilities. The piece could be in the freezer or under the radiator.

Then I had a rare flash of inspiration. For a bookcase to stand as an oasis of order in a junkyard it had to hold special significance. I recalled Brett was right-handed so I tried that side and scanned the shelves. There were several large volumes on the middle shelf about chest high. The first book I pulled was The Complete Shakespeare. There, nosing in the gap like a tiny shark was the snout of a .38. The rest of the revolver was hidden behind a leather bound edition of Hemingway short stories.

"You never struck me as the literary type."

I shoved Shakespeare back into place and smiled as I turned. My smile turned to jelly.

She was wearing a blue silk robe that hung partially open, revealing black stockings and long legs. Framed against the bathroom light she could have been a Modigliani.

Her expression said she enjoyed my admiration. "Make me a drink," she murmured, "and light me a cigarette."

Needless to say, Male Ego 102 prevailed. I did not have a polite drink and leave. In fact there was nothing polite about anything we shared that night. Hours later, Brett nestled in the warm hollow between my chest and shoulder, I dredged up the remnants of my willpower and refocused.

"There's still the matter of my money."

I felt her stiffen slightly. "Let's get this out of the way," she said briskly, rolling out of bed and padding to the bookcase. It occurred to me she was going for her gun. Too late.

By the time my feet hit the floor she had pulled out a large book on the right side. When she turned there was something in her right hand. An envelope. My envelope.

She gave me a cat smile and handed it over. "Count it."

I riffled through the stack. "Close enough."

"You never even told me your name... Philip." She spat out my new name as if that justified everything. She relaxed then, vindicated. "Are you leaving?" She pressed her smooth, naked skin against me. So much for willpower.

Later, while getting dressed I called her on it. "You have a permit for that gun?"

"Are you some kind of cop?"

"Are you?"

She flashed that crooked smile. "Something like that."

My belly froze. "Is that why you took the money?"

"I told you why." She leaned close and kissed me. "It worked didn't it?"

I did the math. No percentage in prying for details. I was out of there for good. She read my thoughts. "I won't see you again, will I?"

"I'm in town for a business meeting."

"Yeah, and I'm Ernest Hemingway."

"Funny you should say that." I kissed her goodbye with genuine regret.

Brett's choice of profession had made me extremely fucking paranoid. I kept checking for a tail every other block. It was about 3 a.m. and I was hoofing it back to my hotel when I saw a gypsy cab cruising uptown. Despite the hour there was a steady trickle of pedestrians and it was difficult to separate a tail from a stunned mourner.

On impulse, I hailed the cab. At the very least it narrowed the possibilities.

"Where to, please?" The cab hadn't started which suggested I'd be back on foot if my destination didn't qualify. The driver wore a turban and a gaudy green and yellow portrait on the dash matched his bearded face. The calligraphy beneath read "Sultan Gee." Much classier than a hack license. It took me a moment to decide where I was headed. Then I remembered.

"One Hundred Twenty-Seven and Fifth."

Sultan half turned. "Harlem?"

"Is that a problem?"

"Not for me, maybe for you."

"No problem, let's go."

Sultan sighed. "Why not. You're my last client tonight."

Client. Obviously Sultan was a man of taste.

"Busy night?" I asked.

"Busy day. You can't believe. Many subways are stopped. So many poor, sad people. Clients looking for loved ones. Nobody can go in or out of the city. Everybody going around in circles. I've been working since six this morning. "

Abruptly he slowed and stopped at the corner of eighty-sixth. "You're not going to rob me are you?"

"Not tonight. Your fortune is safe with me."

He started rolling. "I almost think I have bad karma making money while people suffer."

"Relax, Sultan, it's the essence of capitalism. The whole planet has bad karma. That's why UFOs won't land here."

He glanced at me uncertainly in his rear view. "Really. You think so?"

Did I think so? Somewhere out in space there's a big sign— *Drive by this planet. Inhabitants hostile, lethal, and meaner than junk yard dogs.* To Sultan I said, "We all have to survive."

Actually that said it all.

We didn't talk much after that, Sultan probably wondering if it was better to have a thief or a madman in his cab. On the way, my mind kept turning back to Brett. William Burroughs once said, 'Paranoia is having all the facts.' And over the years he's been spot on.

Fact: Brett lifted a bundle of cash from a secret pocket in my blazer. She claims I am so damned attractive she had to make sure I came back. And I stand still for it, buy it in a brain-follows-dick kind of way. Depressingly unprofessional.

On the other hand Brett might be a PI, a security guard, whatever. The .38 didn't mean that much. After all, it was in the bookcase not pointed at me. I weighed the evidence.

Fact: At this rate I wouldn't last more than thirty seconds in the espionage business.

It didn't matter I told myself. I'd never see her again.

I had other plans.

"One Hundred Twenty-Seven ," Sultan announced over his shoulder.

I checked the streets. "Keep going and make your first right."

Sultan made a smart turn and went halfway up the block. "Stop here."

He stopped. I extracted a fifty and passed it over. I was out the door and walking before Sultan could fold the bill.

I doubled back down Fifth. Sultan couldn't follow and there was nobody ahead. I knew the route exactly, which made it a breeze. I circled the block, ducked down a long alley and came out where Sultan had dropped me.

Confident I had shaken off any tail I walked around the corner to a three-story townhouse. I went down a stairway to a service entrance obscured by the shadows beneath the main stairway. I jabbed the button next to the door. Within seconds, the door buzzed open. I stepped into a steel cubicle covered by security cameras. The heavy metal door shut hard behind me and I knew I couldn't leave until I'd been scanned and identified.

Only a select few were allowed into the sanctum.

Interlopers were severely sanctioned.

Why was I so select?

Some years back I was working as a heroin dealer with a runner called Cuda AKA Barracuda. Cuda was a nasty piece of work but had sterling credentials as a junkie, his specialty being hooking young girls and turning them out.

My target was a Russian importer in Brighton beach known as Big Benny. The agency figured if they brought down Big Benny they could get him to flip. Or so they told me.

All I know for sure is that one night under the El in Coney Island I was staring at an Uzi held by a moon-faced man in a tight fitting blue suit that started as an Armani but wound up looking like a duffle bag.

"No offense," Big Benny said. "Just careful. You brought money?"

"He's got it," Cuda said.

The triumphant whine in his voice tipped it. A set-up.

I smiled. "Money is in the trunk of my car."

"We all go get it," Benny said.

I opened the trunk and took out an attaché case holding a hundred thousand dollars. I set the case on top of my roof. "It's all here, where's the smack?"

Benny shrugged. "First, we see money."

"Open it, man," Cuda said. He seemed nervous. It probably occurred to him that Benny might do us both. Junkie bird dogs are easily replaced.

"It's a combination lock," I said, jabbing the numbers. When the case opened I slid it across the roof, hard. It dropped to the ground spilling cash everywhere.

Cuda and Benny bent to scoop up the money. I did the same except I wasn't reaching for the bills. I came up holding the Beretta I had tucked in my ankle holster.

Greedy bastard that he was, Benny didn't notice right away, totally absorbed in the hundreds decorating the gutter.

"Drop it, Benny. No trouble."

My voice was calm but everybody panicked. Cuda yelled and dove aside as Benny swung the Uzi towards me, still clutching a fistful of hundreds.

The first bullet caught him square in the chest and he rocked back, Uzi spitting a few rounds in the asphalt before he fell. I looked up and saw Cuda running for a red Cadillac parked across the street. A large man emerged from the driver's side.

"He got Benny," Cuda shouted.

The large man lifted his weapon but Cuda was in his way. I had no compunctions about hitting either one. I fired two quick shots. The first stung Cuda's shoulder. As he dropped to one knee I saw the second bullet had hit the big man. He stood dazed, swaying from side to side. I fired again and he collapsed.

"You shot me." Cuda's hoarse voice sounded both shocked and accusing.

I kept moving toward the Caddy, weapon locked on the man in the back seat. The shadowy figure sat stock still as I neared. I kicked the fallen driver's weapon aside and squinted through the back window over the barrel of my Beretta.

A well dressed black man sat quietly, wrists handcuffed below his diamond cuff links.

He gave me a tight smile. "You got here just in time."

It was then I saw the attaché case beside the driver's seat. I reached inside and hefted it. It felt full of cash, like mine.

I turned and saw Cuda scurrying across the street for my fallen money. I followed him half-way and lifted the Beretta. "Bring it here, Cuda. All of it."

For a nanosecond he considered going for Benny's Uzi then reluctantly began stuffing the strewn bills into the case.

I backed up to the car and leaned inside. "Where's the key?"

"The driver."

Keeping an eye on Cuda, I went through the dead man's pockets and found a set of keys. Cuda limped back, one hand clamped over his arm and the other holding the case like a war trophy. I opened the rear door and unlocked the cuffs.

"You crazy?" Cuda said, sounding indignant. "Take the money, there in the front and let's split man. It's a heavy score."

I snatched my case from him and lifted the gun. "Disappear before I kill you."

Apparently I was convincing because Cuda melted into the pillars of the El. I never saw him again.

The man in the back seat hadn't moved. But his gold fleck-ed eyes burned in the darkness.

I looked at him. "How did he know about the money?"

"Cuda set me up, same as you. Two for the price of one Benny called it. Was fixin' to do us both, maybe the rat too. Heard Benny talking to the driver before you arrived."

"Alright, take off."

"What about my case?"

I weighed the options. If I took the money I would have to kill him, making me a bona fide murderer. Or I could do the right thing.

I heard a siren in the distance. "Keep it, I'm out of here."

"Wait."

He reached into his coat and for a second I thought he was going to shoot me. Instead he pulled out a grey business card. There was nothing on the card but a phone number. "Ask for Weary," he said. He slid behind the wheel, started the motor and zoomed off in Benny's Cadillac.

Since then, I have been on Weary's A-List which is quite a large perk.

Long off the streets, Deacon Weary now heads a powerful, tax-free ministry based in Harlem and his town house is home to the powerful, rich, and beautiful. Almost any night will find them gathered in Weary's salon transacting business or pleasure with equal abandon.

This night was different.

When I entered the main room I felt the heavy vibe. The conversations were subdued and the mood grave. Deacon Ezra Weary came over to greet me but his expression was hardly convivial. "Angel, my main man," he said, using the name he'd conferred on me. It suited me fine. Uptown, to Weary's flock, I was simply Angel. Delaney didn't know it, my ex-wife didn't know it, Brett didn't know it. The name gave me comfort.

"As usual, your timing is impeccable," Weary said as we hugged. "Can I get you something?"

Something meant anything from champagne to cocaine but I shrugged. "Just coming out of the rain."

Weary gave me a shrewd look with those gold-flecked eyes. He had the lanky elegance of a basketball player and something more; a brain that separated reality from emotion. That brain was probing me and noting the changes. In Weary's world changes were dangerous.

"What are you having?"

"Scotch good?"

My response seemed to reassure him. "Fine."

Despite the face that there were various knots of most-likely important people scattered about his luxurious den, Weary had a way of making you feel you were the only person worth talking to—and in my case he was right.

Weary poured two from a crystal decanter and handed me a glass. "Strange days," he said and we drank.

"Glenmorangie," I said appreciatively as the scotch warmed my throat.

"You were always a man of taste, Angel. And I'm sure your tastes are the same. Terry over there," he inclined his head toward a slender black lady I knew from other nights, "is holding a bit of cat pee, I understand."

"Thanks but I'm good for now."

Weary became more attentive. "So why are we graced with your visit at this auspicious hour?"

"Figured this was the best place to get the four-one-one."

He studied me for a moment. "It's not good. City's shut down tight. Nothing in or out. They got agents crawling all over everywhere busting anybody who's not blonde."

"We need to talk."

He nodded. We'd been through this routine before. He turned, I followed.

Deacon Weary always conducted his business in a private, windowless, lead-lined room that was swept twice daily for bugs. The private room had brighter light and I noticed the change in Weary. As always, he was perfectly groomed but his chiseled features seemed puffy and showed hints of age. Obviously he hadn't slept.

However the Deacon maintained his center. His voice was as smooth as a mother's lullaby. "How can I help you, Angel?"

Weary had risen to the rarified level of facilitator. Political favors, connections, introductions, sit-downs, all fell under his capable mantle.

I reached into my pocket, counted out five thousand-dollar stacks and pushed the money across the ebony table. "I need a customer who's also a source."

Weary ignored the cash. "What's your product?"

"Remember Brooklyn?"

"Okay—and the source?"

"Hardware."

His eyes searched my face. "Never knew you to be interested."

"I sense an upswing in the market."

A bare wisp of a smile floated across Weary's face. "That's the kind of vision that built America."

"I'll name the east wing after you."

"You know this is not an auspicious moment for a new hobby."

"That's the second time you've said 'auspicious' since I walked in here."

Weary's body tensed as he considered my request. "These are unusual times, bro."

"That's when it counts."

He suddenly relaxed, lanky body unfolding like a Japanese action figure. "Can't argue with the truth."

He gathered up the money in his large hands and it disappeared inside his jacket.

I waited. Once you've spoken the truth it's time to shut up.

"Okay." He reached down inside his desk and came up with a cell phone. "Take this. Always keep it on. It's a burner."

"Burner?"

"Untraceable for thirty days."

I was my turn to look dubious.

Weary cooled me out. "Nothing's perfect. One incoming call and you dump it."

I nodded and took the phone.

"They can trace you through your cell phone now. But with all this happening..." He paused and looked at me face haggard with emotion. "I had friends who went down with the towers. Firefighters, cops, lawyers..." Again he trailed off.

I started thinking about his cell phone remark I had one back at the hotel. I made a mental note to lose it.

"They're going to use this," Weary said abruptly, "the bastards *will* use this against us."

I drank my scotch. I knew what he meant but I wasn't surprised. Not after seven years with the DEA.

Weary finished his drink and set the glass down. "Where is the president?" he asked sadly.

"They've got the president at some undisclosed location," I said, wondering if Weary was drunk. "For his own safety."

"Giuliani is in the streets, taking credit for everything that happens."

I nodded, brooding over how this catastrophe would roll across America like a tsunami. I had no illusions. Every political hack in the country would drape himself in the flag and carve out a piece of the corpse. At least Rudy was out there in the front line.

"So, any other business?" Weary said, getting to his feet. "My guests are high maintenance tonight."

I slipped the phone into my breast pocket. "I'll be waiting on your call."

"Oh, I won't be the voice on the other end."

As we left the office I noticed the two hitters lounging casually on either side of the door. Well-trained and unobtrusive.

It would have been bad for to leave abruptly so I hung around, nursed another scotch and watched Weary work the room. Then I felt someone watching me. I turned and saw Terry smiling in my direction. I knew what the smile meant. Drugs, sex, and severe tire damage. Wrong night, wrong guy. Anyway, I had sworn off coke.

Then again, I conjectured, as I drifted closer, turning Terry down would send up a red flag. Rationalizing? Maybe. But I needed to maintain my cover as a fallen angel.

Terry was still smiling as I neared. It was a charming smile, warm with a hint of sly humor. With her aqua eyes, honey skin and body by Ferrari she could have been a top model. Instead she was a high-end dealer. Not that she was Ms. Big. No, Terry was boutique; small, select clientele, always welcome in high places.

As I eased beside her on the couch her smile tilted. "Angel, darlin' where have you been?" she said, voice smooth as rose petals.

I gave her the combat pilot grin. "In trouble mostly."

"We're all in trouble tonight, baby. Want a bump?"

"Just what I need."

I glanced across the room and saw Weary watching us over someone's shoulder. I nodded and he turned back to his guest.

"Try this, Angel.'

Terry was holding a mirror with two thick white lines running through the center like railroad tracks. I took the short silver straw she offered and snorted one line in each nostril.

Cat Pee has a distinctive taste, at once cold, sharp, medicinal and funky, something like powdered scotch. The effect is more like white lightning.

First reaction; a numbing of the upper front teeth followed by a rush of exhilaration.

Then the drop as the coke slides down the back of your throat, lighting up the brain area behind the eyes like a pinball machine.

Terry's blow was top shelf and as it slowly dropped it energized the thyroid glands at the back of my neck. I immediately felt both confident and optimistic which, considering my circumstances, was definitely unreal. But I did manage to have a rare moment of clarity, something most coke addicts spend their nights and their cash trying to achieve. Suddenly I knew what I could do about Delaney. I had resources he hadn't factored into his master plan.

"Refreshing isn't it?"

I leaned closer. "Just like you."

"Don't flirt unless you mean it."

"Good intentions, bad timing."

"Good intentions?" Terry arched her brows and laughed. It was a pretty laugh that evaporated into a throaty whisper. "Check your good intentions at the bedroom door."

I struggled to keep my face blank. "Profound regrets but there's some..."

."..*business* you need to take care of." Terry said. "Don't we all. Here, darlin,' call me when you're ready to kick back."

I took her card. Deep black phone number embossed on textured red paper. Tasteful and mysterious just like Terry.

"Leaving so soon," Weary said as I approached.

I checked my watch. Twenty minutes short of seven a.m.. Five hours to my meet with Delaney. "Might be hard to find a cab."

"Of course, let me arrange for a car." Weary turned and gestured to one of the sentries guarding the door of his sanctum. A hefty bald man came to the Deacon's side, received his instructions and moved to the elevator.

"Go with Dari," Weary said over his shoulder as he turned to chat up some willowy redhead. "He'll handle transport."

Dari looked as if he was born with a cell phone attached to his bullet skull. He did not acknowledge my presence during our brief descent to the street but standing at the curb was a sleek blue Caddy.

Dari opened the rear door, phone still imbedded in his ear.

As I slid inside I was met by a grim, Afro-Asian driver with a neck tattoo and attitude by Riker's Island. I got the feeling I had offended him by entering his car.

"Eighty-Second and West End."

The driver took the park. Still quite high I looked at the dark southern sky. The morning light was tinting the rolling clouds with a pastel brush. Like a cosmetician at a funeral parlor I thought, trying to out-grim the driver.

He didn't care.

When we arrived at my corner I leaned forward. "What's your name?"

He didn't bother to turn around. "Andre."

"Fine, Andre, meet me at the Plaza Hotel at twelve thirty this afternoon."

That turned him around. "Yo... I don't know if Dari..."

"You got a question call, Deacon Weary." I pulled out my burner. "Maybe we should call him right now."

Andre's expression suggested he was being forced to eat worms. "Forget it. Plaza Hotel. Twelve-thirty."

To seal it I slipped him three Franklins. No use letting Delaney's money go to waste. Andre's grimace softened and he actually nodded.

As the Caddy moved away I saw that people were out and about, moving aimlessly downtown. Nobody was going up-town, except me. I took a circuitous route using one way street to thwart mobile surveillance.

When I reached my hotel room I went to work on my cell phone. I removed the chip and destroyed it.

At nine or so I went out and started downtown. Everyone I passed looked stunned, slow, fearful. Every lamppost and signal pole was plastered with photos, messages, prayers, entreaties. The scent of burnt electrical wire hung over the city along with a grey haze. It was sobering.

At midtown I found a Greek coffee shop that was serv-ing and had a big breakfast. I lingered over coffee knowing the stores would open late, if at all. Leaving the shop I circled the area carefully until I found an electronics store with its lights on.

Inside a swarm of customers were shopping for cell phones, police scanners and a range of security devices from alarms to stun guns. I waited, browsing for items I needed. Finally a clerk with an Indian accent noticed me. I bought a portable GPS unit, an Apple laptop with all the trimmings, a mini tool kit, a few connector jacks, a pre-paid cell phone, a charger, and a small suitcase.

I was ready.

All the way back to the hotel making sure to take the wrong way on one way streets. Of course I was kidding myself. My brush with Brett convinced me they had me locked. But it was important they thought I didn't know.

Back in my room I made my adjustments. I used my new phone to call the business number on my new credit card and put the phone aside. The recorded message was on a loop which suited me fine. It would take my GPS at least twenty minutes to lock on my new phone. As Weary reminded me virtually all cell phones contain a chip that enables a GPS receiver to zero in on its location, even if the phone is off.

At noon I began gathering my things.

I put my meager possessions into my new suitcase. Before I left, I called the Plaza and made a reservation under my new name, using the credit card Delaney had given me.

I headed for the rendezvous on foot stopping at the Plaza along the way.

I explained to Sheila, the desk clerk, I was due at a meeting and would like to leave my suitcase until I returned. Sheila was only too happy to comply.

Delaney was prompt. His black town car sharked into view and stopped in front of me. I got in and it pulled away. Delaney inspected me with an expression of terminal disgust as if confronted by a child-molesting bed-wetter.

No wonder. I had been up all night, neglected to brush my hair and had scotch breath. I deliberately hadn't spruced up for the meet. It was important Delaney believe I was an alcoholic coke-head.

He believed it. "I'm giving you two items," he said, eyes raking my puffy face, "one is the key to your new apartment. The address is attached. The other is a card with the combination of your new wall safe. Everything you requested is inside the safe." He paused and squinted at me with disdain. "You get that, Sam?"

"Philip," I corrected. "Yeah, I got it."

I had been slumped against the door. I sat up, took the card and keys and secured them in my inside pocket. "Anything else?"

"You check in with me in exactly thirty days. No call and I send the terminator."

"Thanks for the support."

He leaned close, jaw clenched like an albino bulldog. "You got your support. Get me some bodies."

At my request the car dropped me in front of Tiffany's, catty-corner to the Plaza Hotel.

I didn't bother watching my back as I crossed Fifth Avenue. Delaney knew exactly where I'd be that night. What he didn't know is that I had shoved my new cell phone with its locked-on chip deep behind his car's rear seat.

Now I could track Delaney's moves. At least until the battery died. It wasn't much but it felt good.

I was starting to fight back.

I retrieved my bag from the hotel clerk, signed for my room and told her I would return later that day. When I stepped outside my Caddy was waiting.

Andre nodded when I entered, a marked improvement from our last encounter. To make sure he stayed happy I gave him another three hundred. "Just drive around midtown until I get set up."

."..Set up?"

He half turned to look at my suitcase, probably wondering what kind of weapon I was hauling.

It was my turn to look surly. "Move out."

For the next ten minutes I fiddled with my newly scored GPS receiver. Everything worked but my hidden cell phone was giving off a fuzzy signal. I didn't know if Delaney was uptown, midtown or the park.

Andre broke the silence. "What's that, GPS?"

"Yeah, why?"

"I got one here in the car."

Granted, I had done a bit of coke, had some drinks and hadn't slept but my brain was clear. I had an idea. I unzipped my tool kit, selected one of the jacks, leaned over the front seat and went to work. Minutes later Andre's GPS unit and mine were one.

There was a sharp beep and a bright red dot marked the screen grid. "Seventieth, between First and Second," I announced.

"On my way," Andre said with a trace of admiration.

As the car swung east, I kept staring at the screen wondering why the location seemed so familiar. The electronic blip remained stationary as we cruised uptown leading me to believe Delaney was parked and having lunch somewhere expensive. At the same time, the sense that I had forgotten something kept scratching at my thoughts.

When we arrived it hit me. Hard.

For a moment I was disoriented, confused. Then it all came into focus.

Delaney's car was parked in front of my ex-wife's apartment building.

Chapter 3

How did it feel? Like a serrated knife twisting into my gut. Deep and nasty.

"You okay, man?"

Andre was staring at me, face impassive as if looking at a corpse.

Actually, I was dead.

"Yeah, dandy. Just park where I can keep an eye on the car."

Andre shrugged and pulled across the street next to a fire hydrant. I hunkered down in the back seat, eyes on the side mirror. I could see part of Delaney's car and the entrance to the apartment building. Just enough to break my heart.

Within twenty minutes Delaney came strutting into view with a tall blonde woman on his arm—my grieving widow, Grace.

Sure we had been living apart for a couple of years and I owed her some support money, but Delaney? No wonder the bastard offered me a sweetheart escape hatch, all amenities included. It crossed my mind that Grace was in on the deal.

No, I decided. Delaney wouldn't risk going into business with a civilian. Grace was just another asset to him. And with me gone, Grace was finally well off. There was the insurance, death benefits and probably a pension from the Agency.

What really hurt was that she looked happy. Not that I begrudged her. Life with me deteriorated fast when I went undercover and the drugs kicked in.

But Delaney?

Andre was looking at me again, expression screwed up in a combination of curiosity and concern. "You want me to tail them?"

I shook my head.

"I could work the dude over, know what I'm sayin'?

I was touched. "It's alright," I said as Delaney's town car drove away with Grace inside.

Andre extended a silver flask. "Have a hit."

I took a healthy slug for medicinal purposes. Cognac, just what I needed to burn off my despair.

I passed the flask back and Andre took a swig.

"Fucking pussy," he said, wiping his mouth.

Suddenly I liked the kid. However I knew better than to go off on a binge with my new pal at this critical juncture.

Instead I asked, "You have a number?"

He took a card from his shirt pocket and snapped it into my hand. "Anytime, bro. What now?"

I had Andre take me a few blocks from my new, unseen apartment and walked slowly home

The good news was that the flat was a minor showplace with a dropped living room, upstairs bedroom and a view of the Hudson River.

Still reeling from the bad news I hit the bed and crashed hard.

+   +   +

For the next two days I waited for my call.

Depressed, angry and helpless, I focused on getting clean. Kept mainly indoors, worked out twice a day, lived on a diet of juices, salads and protein powder. I also organized my inventory. In the safe behind the poster in the kitchen was Lady Luger with her custom suppressor along with my Beretta Tomcat and the drugs.

I divided the heroin into sixteen uncut ounces. I left the kilo of cocaine intact. Delaney had provided everything, including a trip beam scale. The cut I'd have to purchase on my own. It was easily available at any number of neighborhood smoke shops.

Of course my apartment was bugged to the bedsprings but I had to stay close to home.

Movement in or out of the city was limited. It was still difficult to go below Fourteenth Street without a passport. In the meantime I stayed sober, avoided drinking in bars, especially J.G. Melon.

On the afternoon of the third day, the phone rang.

"Who is this?"

The voice was rough, tinged with an accent.

"Angel."

"Good. Let's meet."

"When?"

"Now."

Made sense, less chance of a set-up. For him anyway, my ass was still exposed.

"I pick the venue."

"Pick, pick..." the voice sounded exasperated.

I thought. "P.J. Clarke's, back room. I'll be wearing a blazer."

"I'll be wearing black."

"So will everyone else in the room."

"I have a prominent scar."

"Twenty minutes."

I decided to bring Mr. Tomcat along. I had lost weight and the weapon fit nicely in the waistband at the small of my back. I also carried a small shopping bag that held two ounces of pure boy and an eight-ball of pure girl. The coke was a good will gesture.

He was right. The scar was prominent.

When I entered the hallowed back room I saw a tanned, sleek man in a black pin-stripe suit with white, well-cut hair and a scar that ran from blue eye to cheekbone like a crooked red tear. He was seated at a rear table beneath the clock.

Crossing the room, I scanned the other tables. Except for the rent-a-muscle twins seated along the wall it seemed calm. Actually since the tragedy on 9/11 the entire city seemed subdued. We were all mourners at a communal wake for the fallen.

I smiled.

He didn't.

I sat down.

"Please introduce yourself."

"Angel."

His scowl eased a notch.

"So we meet."

"And exactly who am I meeting?"

"Call me Byron, like the poet."

Or Ivan, like the Terrible. But I humored him.

"Well, Mr. Byron, have you ordered?"

"I'm not here to eat."

"Better if we're the only ones who know that. Why attract attention?"

His expression relaxed. "They say the cheeseburgers here are very good."

"Excellent choice, Mr. Byron. So you were referred by...?"

He sat back, blue eyes respectful now. "The Reverend."

I nodded, equally respectful. He never mentioned Weary by name.

"Did he explain my needs?"

"Our needs co-exist, Mr. Angel."

The waiter arrived. We both ordered draft beer and cheeseburgers.

Watching him leave, I said, "My product is priced at forty thousand."

Byron studied me, eyes distant blue suns, bright but blank. "Pricey. How do we know it's worth it?"

"Nothing has come into the island for nearly a week. Besides I need more than money from you."

"Yes. The Reverend mentioned something."

"Something heavy."

The blank stare clouded. "Let's keep it at money for now. That seems heavy enough for a first date."

"Seems fair."

When the beers came Byron offered a sardonic toast.

"I like you, Mr. Angel, you have..." he searched for the word, *"..gravitas."*

"I've had a bad week." After days of austerity the beer tasted damned good.

Something like a smile crossed his smooth features. "So, when can you deliver?"

"The first installment is at my feet."

Again the eyes studied me.

"You're a trusting man."

"Do you think your steroid squad over there could take me?"

"My compliments, Mr. Angel. Again, your price?"

"Forty K or a Stinger, your choice. But next time there is no choice."

"How so?"

"No cash. Hardware only."

"You must be a very rich man."

"Money can't buy me love."

"Sadly, so true. I suggest we eat our meal and walk to my car. We can make the transfer there."

"Let's leave guns 'r' us behind."

"As you wish."

He turned his attention to the cheeseburgers being placed before us. "Bon appétit, Mr. Angel."

Clarke's rep proved to be well deserved. When we finished, Byron dropped a hundred on the table and patted his lips with a napkin. "Shall we go?"

I didn't catch the sign Byron gave his 'roid boys but they stayed put as we strolled out of the back room and through the bar. Once outside we walked around the block to a black BMW. He popped the trunk and I tossed the bag inside.

"No quality control?" I said.

"I can afford the forty. You can't afford me as an enemy."

"Nicely put. I included a sample of our uptown product."

He shut the trunk and pointed his remote. The door locks jumped open.

I got in. The leather seats had that smell.

Byron started the motor. "Open the glove compartment."

The inside was stuffed with stacks of bills. I carefully counted off four hundred Franklins and put the rest back. I had no doubt Byron knew the exact amount.

"Where can I drop you?"

"Fifty-seventh is good."

"I contact you."

"I'm sure you will."

I don't advise walking around New York with too much cash. It attracts a bad crowd. So I cabbed it cross-town and considered my next move. By now Delaney had discovered my GPS ploy and would be waiting for me to take my revenge.

Big mistake.

I had determined to move on. My sobriety had taken an interesting turn. I discovered I could have a beer, a line, whatever, without making it a career. My real problem was getting free of Delaney. Free of myself.

At Fifth Avenue I switched cabs and headed down to the Chelsea Hotel on Twenty-Third. Perhaps it was time for a pied à terre.

Just past Times Square I spotted my tail. A plain black Toyota.

Delaney was burning precious emergency resources to resolve his petty dalliance. I decided to go one better. I called him.

"What?"

"I made contact."

"Fuck contact. Get me blood."

The phone went dead but I felt better. I wanted him to think I was trying to brown nose my way out.

At the Chelsea I passed through the time capsule lobby and rented a suite for the week using Byron's money. At least Delaney's hounds would get an art lesson.

Outside I headed downtown on foot. Nothing frustrates a tail like a walker. Suddenly he's a prisoner of his vehicle. I might take a subway, a bus, or simply walk the wrong way down a one-way street—the latter being the story of my life.

It worked temporarily. But they had the tech. By the time I reached Seventeenth and Broadway I could feel the heat. Professional instinct.

There were lots of people on the streets and I figured at least two were mine.

I remembered an old client and walked downtown to Union Square. My client had been part of the Warhol scene and acquired real estate during the stone age, pun intended. Now he was lord of the novelty district.

Between Twentieth and Fourteenth Streets, on the west side of Manhattan one can find anything from a gross of pink feather boas to a dozen water pipes in the shape of Louie Armstrong's head. In between, there's faux jewelry, disco belts, fart pillows, miracle creams, switchblades, toys, cheap gadgets, knock-off watches, rolling papers, T-shirts, joy buzzers, glitter costumes; all of it jammed into the storefronts, walk-ups and workrooms crowding the cramped commercial loft buildings.

It was an ideal place to lose a tail.

I zigzagged, taking abrupt turns, blind corners, converging streets until... it became uncomfortably crowded. Slow moving pedestrians, much slower than the usual rush hour congestion.

I was near Union Square and the closer I got, the denser the humanity.

At first I saw the mass of people as ideal cover, like diving underwater. Then I took a good look.

Thousands of people were milling back and forth inside Union Square held back by the police barriers that walled Fourteenth Street. Every lamppost, bench, garbage can, statue and subway entrance was papered with photographs of lost loved ones. The faces around me were drawn, exhausted, scratched by ferocious anxiety and pain. The scent of fear mingled with the electric stench wafting over the city. It was grief central.

Suddenly a fierce weight began pressing the air from my lungs. Nausea burned my throat and for a second I thought *heart attack*. Stumbling my way through the throng of mourners I spotted something familiar, a gesture by a bag lady standing near the subway entrance. She was dressed in rags and her face was smudged but I recognized the angular, long-limbed stance.

Lady Brett in company drag.

Lady Brett. Here.

How the hell did she do that? I ranted silently. For all my highly-skilled evasive action she was right on my ass. Still talking to myself, I made a wide circle west. I could have been babbling out loud and no one would have noticed despite the odd hush. Still straining for breath I slipped into the warehouse canyons and kept circling the grimy streets until satisfied I had shaken whatever tails were on me.

Satisfied but far from certain, I strolled past St. Jack's Novelty Emporium, paused to browse the window then stepped inside like any other customer. The interior was crammed with useless junk that ranged from foam tribal wood carvings, to funny hats, glitter panties, bongs, magic playing cards, light-up bulbs, and rubber masks of prominent politicians. Maybe that was the answer, I mused, a Nixon mask might throw off the hounds.

A turbaned clerk stood behind a long glass case displaying cheap jewelry. He looked worried when I walked in. If I was wearing a turban so close to Ground Zero I'd be worried too.

I tried to smile. "Jack in?"

He sneered. "No."

"Tell him Sam Devine is here."

The clerk shrugged, turned his back and consulted his cell phone. Seconds later he gestured toward a door at the end of the long, littered room.

The moment I entered buzzers screeched. I tried to step back out but a mesh metal wall was sliding shut behind me.

"A unique transmutation of lead, copper and crystal. Jams the fucking signal."

I peered into the gloomy stacks of boxes and saw Saint Jack. He was grinning like a kid. Not unusual for Jack. The buzzers were still whining so I had to strain to hear him.

"I just had the system installed. First time its been tested under actual battle conditions. So what happened Sam? Busted again?"

As he neared I saw the .38 in his hand.

"Can you turn off the sirens?"

"Turn around and empty your pockets."

Now, Jack Strom is a large man with red hair and the face of an altar boy. His wide blue eyes are reminiscent of innocent cherubs hence the show name Saint Jack. Among other things he's a well-known performer in various clubs around the city, including his own.

By day, Jack Strom is a business and real-estate mogul. By night, Saint Jack is a drag queen and drug dealer. At the moment his gun hand was quite steady and his baby blue eyes were cold.

I put my wallet, Beretta, and 40 K on the floor.

With one foot Jack carefully swept them aside. The annoying whine continued.

"Take off the blazer."

I tossed the jacket aside. Nothing changed.

"The pants too."

"Is this a gay thing?"

"Always."

"Exactly what's happening here, Jack?"

"You're bugged, Sam, to the gills."

When I tossed the pants, the electronic whine stopped.

"Bugged how?"

Jack didn't answer, preoccupied with my blazer and trousers.

"Well, you're not wearing a wire. But you are *wired*, darling. And since you already know where to find me we must assume some trusted friend, probably a lover, planted tracking filaments all over you like mistletoe."

I got it.

"Yeah, a career slut."

I stood there in my skivvies stewing in anger, resentment, self pity, remorse and any two from column B. Burned again.

"I'm sure deep down she's good," Jack clucked as he rummaged through my blazer. "Well now, Sam, you are doing nicely."

He displayed a stack of cash from my inner pocket that I'd overlooked. The bundle Lady Brett had lifted.

"Looks like close to fifteen grand. But this batch is too hot to carry. Filaments."

"Filaments." I repeated.

"Hair thin with specific electronic signals."

"You clean the cash, you keep it. Call it a good will gesture."

The offer softened Jack's mood and he lowered the .38.

"There's also a needle trace in the cuff of your trousers."

"Needle trace. For drugs?

"No, silly, look." He lifted my discarded trousers and extracted a silver needle from my right cuff. "Tracks every step you take, baby."

"You know all this from a buzzer?"

Jack smiled indulgently and led me behind a stack of crates. Behind them were two computers with two large screens. Both were attached to double keyboards. The still image on one screen showed the outline of my body. It also displayed my Beretta, cash, keys, everything. Blinking yellow streaks revealed the tainted money in my jacket and the needle.

"State of the art. Seven steps up from airport security."

I was aching to get my hands on the advanced equipment but it would ruin my image.

Instead I said, "The sliding wall is a nice touch. I expected the ceiling to close in."

"I entertained the notion, but it's too expensive. You look very sexy in your underwear darling but we'd better find you a proper wardrobe. Then we'll talk."

I followed him past the stacks of boxes and crates to a steel door which Jack unlocked with two old-fashioned keys the size of forks. We entered yet another room piled with boxes, except these boxes were filled with designer clothes.

It was the rear of a discount men's clothing outlet, one of Jack's many enterprises in the neighborhood. He outfitted me with a black cashmere jacket, grey flannel trousers, blue shirt and black FBI raincoat. Then he broke out a bottle of Glenmorangie and two glasses.

Between sips I told him about my little flurry with Brett. I left out significant details. So far as Jack was concerned I was a mid-level dealer with a drug problem. And he was a top source.

I lit a cigarette. "At least I know how she happened to be in Union Square."

Jack's choirboy face got old and sad. "All those lost people. I feel their pain from here. No security wall can block it out."

I knew what he meant. Actually, that's why I looked him up. I needed some refuge from the reality of human suffering. Time to catch my breath, to talk to an old associate and reassure myself it wasn't all heartbreak. Even though I knew it mostly was.

In the process of taking refuge I uncovered Lady Brett's treachery. A necessary thing, granted, but bruising nonetheless. And my ego had taken some major contusions.

Whatever. Compared to the anguish out there I was just a self-indulgent beetle in a pile of dung.

"I'm sorry," I said.

"About what?"

I pulled myself together. "Sorry I came here bugged. I didn't mean to bring heat..."

"Forget it darling. My little wall scrambled the signal. When you leave you take this along." He held up the needle. "As soon as you hit the sidewalk the signal will clear. Your tail will think it was a temporary glitch. Once you're a few blocks away—lose it."

"Thanks, Jack."

"Not every day I get a fifteen grand tip."

"There is something worrying me."

"Which is?"

"What if the stash in my crib is bugged?"

Jack's face brightened. "What are you holding dear?"

"Kilo of girl, kilo of boy."

"If the girl is clean I'll take it."

"How would I know it's clean?"

"Wait here." Jack disappeared into the other room and came back holding a device that resembled a boomerang.

"Hand sweeper, weak but efficient. User simple, power on, power off. Run it over your stuff like a dustbuster. If it whines and lights up, get another apartment."

"How do I reach you?"

Jack wrote down a number. "Use this."

"That reminds me, I need a burner."

He went to a metal file cabinet and opened the middle drawer. Inside were six or seven cell phones. He picked one and gave it to me.

"Again thanks. I owe you."

"The blow will even us out. Nothing for days. FBI, CIA, ATF, DEA, CAP, FFA and whatever initials you can think of are crawling all over the island. But Sam..."

I heard the disclaimer coming.

."..my other place, my other phone, they're protected. If you or your product emits the teeniest beep—I'm going to kill you."

Pink-skinned, chubby and somewhat awkward, Jack seems like a mild gay boy from the old neighborhood who's good to his mother and goes to church on Sunday. But his face was as blank as a marble angel on a tombstone.

Brimming with optimism I walked out of the clothing store onto the street. The knowledge that Brett's needle was tracking me amplified my depression, paranoia and anxiety as I walked quickly uptown. It wasn't until I ducked into the subway maze at thirty-fourth street that I was able to breathe comfortably. By then I was sweating.

I planted the needle in a subway car headed for Brooklyn, hopped the A-train to eighty-sixth street and walked back to my flat. I knew the apartment was dirty. What remained in question were the cash and drugs,

As soon as I entered I began sweeping the place. As expected two lamps and the phone were bugged but the coke, heroin and cash were silent. This suggested Brett wasn't working for Delaney.

Which meant I had yet another agency on my ass.

It also meant I wasn't dead anymore

Thinking about it now, my decision was the only route I could take. That detour through Union Square showed me the way.

1) I didn't need to trade heroin to Byron to know he dealt arms.

2) Outsmarting Delaney only kept me dancing on his strings.

The whole thing had the stench of a decomposing corpse. Mine. In a moment of clarity I knew I had no choice.

I left the apartment carrying a kilo of blow, nearly fifty grand in cash, and Jack's sweeper in a shopping bag. I needed the device as evidence in case Jack's system picked up something strange. The Luger I left behind. I walked against traffic, changed directions then took a subway to Times Square. There I used the burner to call Jack.

He gave me an address on the East Side which turned out to be a drag bar called The Convent. I recalled being drunk there in the bad old days.

The door was locked. I knocked. No one answered. I used the burner.

"Yes, Sam," Jack barked. I could tell he was primed.

The door opened and I entered a semi-dark room. Same deal. A metal mesh wall closed behind me. For a long moment it was quiet. Finally Jack stepped into view.

"You're clean, Sam."

"Wish that were true."

Jack was wearing his work clothes. His face was heavily made up with bat-wing mascara and big red lips framed by a green feather wig. Your basic Vegas chorus girl. His plump body was encased in fishnet stockings, red panties, pearls and little else. But hell, he did own the place.

He also held a short-nosed .38 in his black velvet glove. A real lady.

"So what does this tell us, Sam?"

"Tells me it's time for a vacation. Maybe Jamaica."

It wasn't a spontaneous answer. I'd been thinking about it since my passage through the nine circles of Union Square. I was nothing more than a disposable cog in a grotesquely cruel machine. I was using my existence to destroy the souls of my fellow man.

Fuck that, I wanted out.

"Smart boy," Jack said thoughtfully, "but Manhattan is under lockdown. You practically need a passport to go to Hoboken."

Bingo.

It all came together. The big flaw in my getaway was transport. Rent a car, take a bus, a plane to anywhere and it would be scrutinized. Enlisting help would only risk betrayal. I had to vanish fast and alone. Poof, like Kaiser Sose.

First Commandment; assume everyone is working
for Delaney.

There are no other commandments.

It was about ten thirty at night, I didn't plan to return to my
new flat, I had to assume my new room at the Chelsea had been
compromised. And I had to lull Big Brother into thinking it was
business as usual.

"I need cash now."

"I need to check the merch."

"Like you said, the island is under lockdown."

"Don't bust my chops, honey, after all we've been through."

"You would have shot me if that thing beeped."

"That's beside the point. By the way do you have my sweeper? I need it."

He turned and led me to his dressing room. He flounced
over to his vanity, lay the .38 aside and began primping in
the mirror.

I knew the routine. I'd been scoring coke from Jack for
two years. He would fuss and moan, holding out for as long as
possible. When I was an addict it was annoying.

At the moment, as a seller in a seller's market I was amused.

"Do you have a taste for me?"

"For you the entire restaurant."

I reached into my bag and took out the kilo.

"Jesus."

Jack left his vanity and wobbled across the room on his
extra-high heels to make sure the door was secure.

"Jesus," he repeated.

"You do have the cash?"

"This isn't like you Sam. Usually you're more discreet."

"The less ceremony, the less attention.'

I made that up but it sounded good. Jack bought it. He had
no choice. Seller's market.

He took the kilo to his vanity and sat down. It was a nice
photo op. Saint Jack in his green wig and fishnets seated at a

mirror with a kilo of coke on one side and a .38 on the other. Miss America.

I watched him slit the duct tape with a switch blade that he took from his make-up case. He examined the sample, chopped it into lines and took a hit with a silver straw. Always elegant, our Jack.

I knew the coke was pure because I tapped the kilo for Byron's sample.

"Shit!" Jack gargled, holding his nose.

There's a reason they cut drugs. Pure heroin will kill you and pure cocaine is like snorting fire.

"It's an ounce short." I said.

Still clutching his nose Jack shrugged. "I expected no less from you."

"Even short, it's pricey."

"Pricey how?"

"Fifty grand and a safe house for forty-eight hours."

"Nothing's safe for forty-eight hours, twenty-four max."

"Good."

"Safe house won't be available until seven a.m. And my offer is thirty-five large."

"Can't do it."

"I've got the thirty-five here. Forty if you care to wait until tomorrow. Fifty is out.'

"Then I'm out."

"Be reasonable, Sam."

Jack was starting to whine. A good sign.

"How's this for reasonable. The shit is pure which means you can cut it once and come up with two kilos of excellent product. And considering my little fifteen grand donation, you're really paying thirty five anyway."

"I knew it was too good to be true," Jack sniffed.

I waited.

"Forty-five thousand. That's my best and final offer."

"Show me the money."

Grousing, he tossed me four thick stacks and one thin. I put them in my shopping bag along with the other forty or so.

"I hope you're staying for my show."

"Wouldn't miss it."

"In that case have a line."

I didn't refuse. The idea was to have everyone believe I was the same weak-willed, moral wreck I'd become in the past few years. However, the coke took me from purgatory to Hollywood. Suddenly everything was possible. I would be redeemed, transformed and assumed into heaven.

Aware it was the blow talking I just rode along, not looking to raise the ante.

After giving me an address and a key, Jack ushered me through the littered backstage area and signaled a waiter to seat me.

I gave the waiter a ten to put me at a table near the exit and ordered a scotch. The room was half full but Jack's crowd came out after midnight.

It was the usual drag show with three or four middle-aged queens lip synching to retro disco. The best was a Donna Summers look-alike. When Jack came out and went into *I Will Survive* I slipped away.

I walked for a few blocks then stopped in an empty doorway and made a call.

Weary answered.

"The offering was compromised," I said. "Please advise Andre."

"Yes. It's been straightened out." There was a long pause. "I'm glad you called, Sam. We were disappointed."

"So was I."

"Take care of yourself."

I took that to mean don't call me for two years. At least we were clear. Weary would make a deadlier enemy than the mob.

That done I found the tasteful red card and called Terry. Luckily she was in.

"It's the guy who flirted with you at Deacon's church."

"Lots of guys flirt with me."

"They call me Angel."

"Oh yes, he spoke highly of your good work."

The lady was well schooled.

"I'd like to discuss a new project."

"It's a bit late."

Two drinks and two lines later we were in her bedroom. At dawn I eased out and took a circuitous route to Jack's safe house. Along the way I picked up breakfast.

The apartment Jack provided was a basement walk-down but it had the basics: bed, bathroom, kitchen, TV. The lipstick smear on the pillow, rumpled sheets and a cloying trail of cheap perfume suggested the previous occupants had vacated recently.

I fell asleep immediately and woke up in the afternoon. I took a long shower and a short time organizing my belongings which consisted of the clothes on my back, my weapons and a bundle of cash in a shopping bag.

I had a little time to kill so I purchased a proper briefcase to hold the money and at precisely five-forty p.m. walked across Ninth Street in the Village and joined the flow of people entering the Hudson Tube.

My logic was clear. What terrorist wants to go to Hoboken?

I blended nicely with the crush of commuters despite the added security on both sides of the river. Once safely in New Jersey I took a cab to Newark Airport then hopped a junket bus to a place where an armed fugitive with a briefcase stuffed with Franklins wouldn't raise an eyebrow.

Atlantic City.

I found a seedy motel that accepted cash and a phony name and slept in for a few days. I shopped for new clothes and carefully avoided the casino cameras. I tried jogging on the boardwalk but it would take more than good intentions to reclaim my body.

From there I took a bus to Philadelphia then another to Chicago. In the Windy City I stopped long enough to find a hooker at a blues bar and let her steer me to a seedy flophouse where no names were required. Pretending to be drunk I gave my date a parting tip, threw some money at the clerk and stayed the night, one hand on my Beretta.

In the morning I had a hearty breakfast then went to a store that sold camping equipment: backpack, bedroll, canteen, flashlight, Swiss Army knife, baseball hat—the whole urban hillbilly kit, including a GPS unit.

Twelve hours later I hiked across the border into Canada and was officially in the wind.

Chapter 4

"God made the country, man made the city,
and the devil made the small town."

Ivan Doig, The Eleventh Man

The two girls waited impatiently for Carla to get off work.

Since neither of them had ever held a job, or even applied for one, the concept of finishing a shift was foreign to them. Annoyed, they watched Carla move across the room, carefully placing forks, knives and napkins at each table.

Robin sighed and leaner closer to Tami.

"Baw-rring."

Tami didn't react. She continued watching Carla with intense fascination and more than a hint of jealousy. The dark-haired girl carried herself with a woman's grace far beyond her sixteen years. All the boys noticed, the girls too. For that reason Tami and Robin were willing to sit around waiting for her. Wherever Carla went the guys came running.

And Petaluma was a dating wasteland. Nothing but mindless mall lizards. Most of their conversations included either a sports score or a drug score or both.

However Carla attracted a much higher quality. Hot rich boys, college jocks, intense young artists; they all buzzed around. She was brainy as well as beautiful, first in her class and on a fast track for a scholarship to Stanford.

Tami and Robin on the other hand, had little use for scholarly pursuits. Like most girls in their social circle all they cared about was attracting men and talking about themselves.

Then again, Carla wasn't really in their social circle.

For one thing, she was Latino. For another, her parents didn't have much money. In fact she didn't even have a father. And, of course, there was her older brother Jordan who had already acquired a rap sheet for auto theft.

But Tami and Robin overlooked Carla's social liabilities for the chance to bask in the reflected glow of her popularity.

Robin was blonde with pert features and plump thighs partially concealed by loose blue jeans. Tami was more dramatic with her spiky red hair, blue eye shadow and pierced lower lip. She was very thin and wore tight black jeans and a short shirt that showed the ring in her belly button.

Neither of them got a second glance in the usual haunts around town. But with Carla they were on the red carpet.

Carla Fuente took her time.

She knew her friends were getting restless but it didn't matter. Those girls got impatient at stop signs, she reflected, as she placed silverware on the tables. She didn't kid herself about her newly acquired status. Tami and Robin were okay pals and she enjoyed the attention even if it was just a façade.

She liked that word, façade.

Carla made it a point to learn a new word every day, especially its pronunciation. She wanted to have perfect diction, unlike most of the girls in her school who mispronounced half the few words they knew.

Lighten up, she told herself, they were no different than most of the young people out here. Soon she'd be in Cambridge, Massachusetts or Palo Alto where she'd meet people with real brains. Then she remembered her mother and a pang of guilt clouded her daydreams. No matter where she went she would have to find a way to take mama with her.

"I can't stay out too late," Carla said, hanging up her apron. "My mom is sick."

Robin and Tami exchanged glances. The show wouldn't even begin until ten.

"Can't you just like, call her?" Robin said.

"Depends," Carla said, coming out from behind the counter. "Let's have a drink and talk about it."

The drinks were also part of her newly-acquired charm, Carla thought. After closing they could always enjoy an illegal wine or beer. She locked the door and pulled the shade.

Carla had a Chardonnay, Tami and Robin chose Corona which they chugged from the bottle.

As they drank and gossiped Carla thought about the boy she was hoping to see that night. Her new pals could spoil everything.

"Who's up for Rinner's?" Robin said.

Carla shook her head. "Too far."

"No it isn't. Anyway, I have the Beamer."

That settled it. They finished their drinks.

Carla hated Rinner's, an all-night diner at the edge of town. It was a haven for bikers, truckers and losers. She knew Robin was obsessed with a good-looking jerk named Shane who rode a Harley and was reputed to be a gang-banger. Normally she would have passed but it was Friday and she'd worked hard all week. Plus, hard as it was to admit, she might need the moral support later tonight.

She would roll with it, Carla decided. There was plenty of time before the show and after a nice glass of wine she felt good.

+   +   +

"I don't see his bike." Tami said from the back seat as they neared the diner.

"Whose bike?" Robin said, parking the car.

Tami groaned. "Like we are stupid."

She leaned between Carla and Robin. "Admit it. You are so hot for Shane."

"You could do a lot better," Carla said.

Robin gave her a sly smirk. "I'm not gonna marry him."

"You're not even gonna fuck him," Tami said, "because he's not here."

"Oh wow, Miss Sherlock."

"Let's go back to town," Carla said.

"One minute, I have to pee."

Rinner's was a traditional truck stop diner perched between a bank of gasoline pumps and little else. There was plenty of space for truckers and the road cred they generated drew bikers like moths.

Carla could see a few motorcycles parked outside the diner, their owners lounging nearby. Talk about boring. The same bone stupid, turbo-macho bullshit she'd been running from since her father abandoned them for that blonde slut.

"Come with me, okay?"

Carla sighed. "Okay, but I need to get back to the Buckhorn."

"What's up at the Buckhorn?"

Tami's question caught Carla unprepared.

"Omigod, he's coming!" Robin squealed, saving her.

Carla opened the door and got out. The three of them walked slowly to the entrance, aware of the coughing motorcycles behind them.

Robin and Tami immediately went to the ladies.' Carla waited at the counter. She checked her watch. It was only seven-fifteen. Her plan was to be at the Buckhorn Café by eight or so. That would be when Todd and his band would meet for a pre-gig drink.

Todd Fletcher was a local boy who had gone to New York to be a rock star. Now, only two years later, he had returned as front man for Nose Job, the band opening for Los Lobos at the Mystic Theatre.

Earlier that day he had dropped by the restaurant and recognized Carla from high school. He was three years ahead and Carla always had harbored a crush on the lanky, blue-eyed youth with the shy smile.

Only now he was much thinner and not so shy.

"Look at you," he said grinning, "fresh as a room full of flowers."

He had her at fresh.

"Thank you, kind sir. Did you stop eating in New York?"

Todd scratched his newly tattooed forearm.

"I've been on the road for three months. Every bumfuck town in America. Tonight we end our run. After the party I'm going to stick around and veg out for a while."

Carla perked up at the news. Todd looked extremely cool in his black jeans and black shirt open to reveal a Sacred Heart tattoo. The dark circles shadowing his smoky blue eyes only heightened his decadent, rock-royalty aura.

Todd had invited her to come backstage after his set and given her a laminated all-access pass. She still hadn't told Tami and Robin for a couple of reasons.

One: They would embarrass her

Two: They would demand to go backstage with her.

Robin would get drunk, take pills and pass out as usual and Tami would get high and do god knows what in the bathroom with some roadie. Even so, Carla knew it was a lost battle. Todd had put her on the VIP list plus two for the concert and afterwards it would be impossible to shake them. The only quality time with him she could steal would be before the show at the Buckhorn.

She checked her reflection in the speckled mirror behind the counter. Not bad. She had the whole package, lustrous black hair, smoldering eyes, long legs, sensual hips, but she played it down. Not much makeup, sexy but conservative baby doll blouse over crisp black jeans.

Tami and Robin came back whispering and giggling.

"What's up, ladies?"

Robin glanced at the mirror. "Can you see him?"

Tami moved closer to the window. "He's still there talking to his dudes. Let's play pinball. I have quarters."

Repressing an exasperated sigh Carla followed them. She took a stool at the counter and ordered a Coke. A short time later Shane and his two pals ambled inside like it was a saloon in a western movie.

Carla had to admit they were good looking, especially Shane. They were even kind of nice and polite in a corny way.

Sweet but not swift, she thought. Not her type. She sipped her Coke and tried to ignore the banter across the pinball table.

"Flip it... Oh, no it's in the hole!"

Tami giggled. "That's a good thing."

"Always," said Shane's friend Gary, looking over at Carla.

Although she wished he wouldn't, she was aware of him moving closer.

"Hi, I'm Gary. You're a friend of Robin's right?"

Gary was quite handsome in a rugged sort of way, with warm brown eyes His long brown hair was pulled back in a pony tail and a red ruby dotted one ear lobe. His quick, flashy smile revealed even white teeth. Then Carla noticed his hands, blunt thick fingers bearing scars and tiny tattoos. Not a great sign.

However she knew better than to diss a biker. They were more sensitive than Latinos. So she gave him a polite smile. "Hi, I'm Carla."

"You go to school around here?"

She nodded, unwilling to reveal she was younger than her girlfriends.

"What about you?" she asked.

The idea of attending school seemed to amuse Gary. He grinned mischievously and his eyes narrowed into an expression part dismissive and part aggressive.

Carla knew that expression. She recognized it from Latino gang-bangers who resented anyone who broke out of the constrictions of the ghetto. And she had learned to deal with it.

"So do you ride a Harley?"

Gary's mood lifted and he grinned. "What else? I've had a bike since I was fifteen. My old man gave it to me."

He squinted at her curiously. "You ever ride a bike?"

"Twice was enough. My brother had one."

"Twice was enough? What's that mean?"

"I'm afraid of motorcycles. I fell the second time."

Gary looked disappointed. Carla was relieved. She knew bikers preferred girls who liked to live dangerously. Like her rich but clueless friends.

"Game over," Shane said from the pinball machine. There were four of them, Robin, Tami and another biker called Spider.

There was a pause. "Hey, maybe you girls want to cruise over to the harbor."

Another pause. Carla felt the girls looking at her.

"We can't right now," Robin said, in a show of support.

"Won't take more'n five, ten minutes," Gary said, smiling at Carla, "way we ride."

Pause.

"Okay, ten minutes," Tami said. "Okay, Carla?"

Carla turned, careful to look like she didn't care.

"No problem, just don't be too long."

"You can come, too," Gary said. He extended his hand. There were a spade, diamond, club and heart inked, one on each finger.

"Thanks, but six is a crowd."

Nobody got the joke.

" 'Kay. See you back here." Robin said quickly as if afraid she'd change her mind.

Carla checked her watch as the bikes rumbled out of the lot.

Twenty minutes later she pulled out her cell and after two unanswered text messages she called a taxi.

Actually this works, she reflected. Now she was free to meet Todd without baggage. No excuses necessary.

Unfortunately there were no cabs available for at least a half hour.

"That's too late," she said, knowing the dispatcher didn't care if she missed Todd.

"Where are you headed?"

Carla turned. The question came from a man wearing a black biker's jacket that looked brand new and seated a few stools away. He was older, with ruddy skin and short dark hair graying at the temples. His eyes, too, were pale gray and crinkled at the edges as if he'd taken too much sun.

He smiled. "If it's not too far I can run you over. I'm going past Walnut Park."

Almost too perfect, Carla thought. Walnut Park was a block from the Buckhorn Café.

However she was wary. Weirdos were everywhere and this guy definitely could qualify. Something about those eyes, like gray mirrors.

"I'm Dave,' he said, still smiling, "that's my bike out there."

He pointed to a black Honda parked near the entrance.

Carla still wasn't sure. "That's very nice of you, Dave, but..."

He dropped some money on the counter and stood up.

"Look, if you're worried, call your friends and tell them where you're going."

Fair enough, Carla thought. She looked at his hands. They were soft and white with manicured nails.

Carla opened her cell phone.

"Okay," she said, "thanks."

Chapter 5

"We came from nowhere and found we belonged nowhere else."
Dermot Bolger

San Francisco is a toy city.

Big enough to qualify as a city but really a small town grown up. One can walk from Bernal Heights to the Pacific Ocean in a few hours and after a couple of years people get to know you.

I spread my living time between Corte Madera in Marin County and North Beach under the theory I can float beneath the social radar. It had worked for a while but lately the theory has been showing cracks.

After jumping the border I spent a good two years in Canada cooling off. I also acquired yet another identity. Employing my computer skills I hacked into various databases and re-entered the USA as Max LeBlue from Vancouver.

With those same cyber skills I managed to finagle a green card before Bush & Co. dropped the steel curtain on immigration. Not that I mind being Canadian these days considering the travesties unleashed by the U.S.A. in the name of 9/11.

My name doesn't appear on any lease, phone or electric bill. In return for almost constant computer maintenance I occupy a room in a North Beach walk-up owned by Dr. Eli Safelli, a bohemian physicist I met in Café Trieste.

In Corte Madera I rent an in-law cottage behind a house belonging to another character, known as Organic Phil, a nutrition guru and psychotherapist. Only in Marin.

I pay everyone in cash and yet my set-up has a deep flaw.

I had to open a bank account. Through the wonders of the internet I established myself as a computer doctor which generates a decent income and allows me to be flexible in my schedule and available in person. Call your tech support and you'll probably end up talking to someone in India. I'm right here.

The bank account and credit card are necessary evils. You can't rent a car or a hotel room without one. And I need to process my clients' checks.

Sooner or later they'll do away with cash and we'll all be fucked. Every penny we spend or save will be noted, weighed and held against us.

The system does force me to pay taxes. So Max LeBlue is on the books even if he is off the grid.

I also have a driver's license but both my license and bank account are registered to a dummy address in Chinatown: an herb shop owned by Dr. Jimmy Shu, who holds my mail in return for my setting up and maintaining a web site and database for his business.

Not a perfect firewall but it gives me a week's cushion if they ever come looking. And eventually they will.

Secrets have a habit of clawing their way out of their graves.

For the moment however, I am cool.

Business is chugging along nicely, I have free time and I have managed to work myself back to good health. My landlord Phil extols the virtues of the vegan life and installed a vegetable juicer in my kitchen. Good nutrition, long runs, light lifting... I'm in decent shape.

Do I still drink? Once or twice a week.

Coke? Never.

Weed? Of course. Northern California is home to the best bud in America.

These days I catch up on my reading and see a lot of movies.

It's still difficult for me to sleep before two a.m. but these days San Francisco shuts down early. Ever since all those yups with high mortgages, new babies and demanding wives moved in. The old guard bohemians are not dead but they are on life support. However, I have a nose for bars that cater to insomniacs, artists and psychopaths of all stripes. Sort of a hobby of mine.

I've tried to avoid making new friends but, like I said. it's a small city.

My favorite bartender, Nina, who works at a place in the Mission District gets her coffee at Café Roma in North Beach so I bump into her at least once a week. And there's the young Italian lady, Sofia, who stands in front of the Ristorante Volare with a tray of appetizers. She knows me by name and we exchange pleasantries every time I pass.

Don't get me wrong. I realize North Beach is probably one of the last great, authentic neighborhoods in America but I have become too visible there.

By contrast, my spot in Corte Madera is comfortably anonymous, or in the words of Pink Floyd, comfortably numb. The whole area is a suburban zombie zone. People go to bed about nine and spend their days working on themselves. Personal trainers, yoga instructors, massage specialists, hypnotherapists, marriage counselors, acupuncturists, Ayurvedic doctors, herbalists, nutritionists, Rolfers, rebirth gurus, spiritual healers, life coaches, stylists, plastic surgeons, colon consultants; Marin county is the world's most beautiful convalescent home.

And all its patients are intensely self involved. The only thing that distracts their attention is a display of wealth. So I keep it low-key, except for my state-of-the-art cyber studio which no one sees.

I manage to stay anonymous in Marin, shuffling between Mill Valley and San Rafael for coffee breaks and supplies.

When you're alone, the world looks like it's behind a plate glass window. As I sat outside at the depot Café in Mill Valley watching people arrive, meet other people, talk, laugh, it occurred to me I hadn't had a real conversation in four days. I also hadn't had a drink in that time, being absorbed in a project for a top client.

It was settled then.

I would drive to San Francisco and remedy the situation. The drink part anyway.

I never did like to drink in Marin. The police hang outside the bars and pounce as soon as you slip behind the wheel. One wine and its advanced traffic school, face and prints all over the computer. Like Amy Winehouse says: No, no, no.

+   +   +

That afternoon, listening to the news while crossing the Golden Gate I realized it would be getting harder to stay out of sight. In the aftermath of the attack on the World Trade Center the administration had started to transform America into a new age Gulag.

Lockdown began with the whimsically named Patriot Act which effectively stripped us of civil rights. Anchormen and politicians were suddenly sporting flag pins and baseball fans were treated to both the National Anthem before the first pitch and God Bless America during the seventh inning stretch.

The BBC radio newscaster was telling me how people are being kidnapped off the street in various European countries and taken to secret locations to be interrogated. Something they call "rendition." I'm an ex-Marine who saw combat in the Persian Gulf and I almost spit up my Starbucks at the news.

The thing about San Francisco is its beauty. Halfway across the bridge my disgust was diluted by the magnificent view. The Palace of Fine Arts glowed in the sun like a golden turtle while behind it the eccentric dwellings of Telegraph Hill cascaded down from Coit Tower to the water. All around them, designer buildings, glass towers, and metallic spires bristled like hordes of armored invaders, laying siege to the huddled vestiges of a more gracious era.

And there in the center of the wind-flecked bay, Alcatraz Island emerged like a misty ghost. No wonder the legendary columnist Herb Caen dubbed the city Baghdad by the Bay. Would that the real Baghdad be so blessed.

My health regime notwithstanding, I hadn't fully recovered from the events in New York. I was resigned to taking the hit from my ex-wife (Delaney?) but the crushing avalanche of grief in Union Square had suffocated what was left of my lighter side.

A bumper sticker on the Volvo in front of me read 'Justice Not Vengeance.' Obviously an optimist.

I always feel better when I roll into North Beach. With its small shops, Italian cafes and family restaurants the hood has a timeless quality. On a clear day it's like stepping into a Sunday afternoon by Seurat.

I got lucky, found a parking space, which meant I could enjoy a coffee at Mario's Bohemian Cigar Store.

Mario's sits on the corner across from Washington Square Park and the corner window table affords a wide view of the bustling activity. The gothic towers of St. Peter and Paul's church watch over the park's lawns while the busy intersection of Columbus Avenue and Union Street funnels a steady stream of colorful traffic.

It was just five-thirty and the evening regulars lounged on park benches as others, mainly women, arrived to walk their dogs. On the sidewalks, people coming home from work mingled with tourists, artists and various local characters passing by. I sipped my double espresso, drinking in the scene.

At the moment I might have been in Paris or Rome. And as it turned out I probably should have been.

After coffee I left my car in its precious legal spot and strolled through the park.

Eli Sarfelli's apartment is a third floor walk-up on Chestnut Street. He was home when I entered. Eli is Central Casting for a college professor; paunchy, owlish and perpetually curious. His gray eyes are youthful under a full head of long white hair. He had transformed his living room into a command center dominated by three Macs and stacks of books and papers. He didn't look up from his computer screen as I came in.

"Oh, Max. I'm glad you're here. Listen, my laptop is on the fritz again."

I shrugged. That was how I came to board at Eli's in the first place. I was sitting at the next table in Café Trieste one morning when his laptop seized up. This threw Eli into a panic. Among other things he maintains a vigorous email correspondence which is most dear to his heart. I find this difficult to fathom because his pen pals spend all of their time insulting each other. In the old days you fought a duel. E-sulting is safer. Forget honor.

Anyway I offered to fix his problem and, during the relatively simple procedure, mentioned I was looking for a studio in the neighborhood.

"Well, that's amazing," Eli said, "one of my room mates just moved out. It's just a single with kitchen privileges but you can take a look at it. Umm... what's your name?'

That's Eli, innocently spontaneous.

Turned out his room had a nice view of the back yard and the kitchen was sunny and comfortable. The third roommate was a mathematician from India named Sanjin who had a five-year teaching fellowship at Berkeley. Like me, Sanjin wasn't there all the time.

"Umm, can you pay three months in advance?" Eli said, obviously having second thoughts.

I could and over time the arrangement has suited everyone. I pay my rent promptly and fix Eli's computers when they crash, which is often. Besides his untidy cyber habits Eli's mad scientist e-mails attract a fair quantity of virus attacks. My room is comparable to Eli's office except for the double bed I installed in a flush of optimism. I have a dresser and a large desk that holds a PC and a laptop. There's also a full-sized bookcase but my books share space with DVDs, CDs and various pieces of electronic equipment.

I began working on Eli's laptop then caught a whiff of curry. Sanjin was in the house.

Soon there came a delicate knock on the half-closed door.

"I've made some vegetables and rice if you'd like some," Sanjin said.

Sanjin is a shy, Indian scholar whose room features two white wall boards covered with complicated formulas. Sanjin has a habit of highlighting disparate elements or numbers in various colors making it easier to follow the mathematical map.

For Sanjin and Eli maybe it was easier but I still needed a GPS.

We ate in the kitchen, Sanjin pausing between bites to yell down the hall, "Eli, it's getting cold!"

"Be right there." Eli assured him.

A mutual glance said we both knew better. Sanjin was a fine cook and I was grateful for a food base before venturing out.

"Really good curry," I said.

Sanjin nodded modestly. "Did you have a chance to look at my new formulas, Max?"

"Been occupied with Eli's Mac," I said, by way of apology. "What's the theme?"

"How do you mean that 'theme'?" he challenged.

"Musically."

He grinned. "Good answer. I have a new theory concerning dark matter."

"Which is?"

"That this so-called dark matter is an extremely dense vacuum which *slows* light rather than bend it. You see?"

I was starting to. I helped myself to more rice. "Makes sense. Can you prove it?"

Eli came into the kitchen, hair and beard neatly combed, fresh black shirt, black leather vest, flannel trousers, Gucci loafers.

"I have a date with Wendy," he announced.

Wendy was a fifty-five year old divorcee Eli had been seeing for years but he made it sound like a prom date. I envied him.

Lately, I envied almost everybody.

Later, walking outside I wished my life could be that simple. Even though I'd put my house in some semblance of order, the attic was crawling with vengeful ghosts.

I parked at 22nd and Valencia. I walked down the block and gratefully entered the black-lacquered sanctuary of The Lone Palm bar and took a stool at the far end. Nina was on shift and brought me a Patron without my asking, I knocked it back and motioned for another.

Nina arched an eyebrow. "Slow down, the night is young."

"But I'm not."

"Hey, you look great." She moved off to get my drink.

The three ages of man: Youth, middle age and you look great.

Nina on the other hand was young, maybe thirty, I speculated. There were other speculations as I watched her smoothly dip a glass in ice, shake it dry and pour a generous ration of Patron.

One of the pleasures of drinking is watching a good bartender work.

In Nina's case it took on another dimension. She had youth and grace, a dark jaguar with a Madonna's face. One night she had mentioned she was a dancer and I believed her.

"Drive carefully," she said, setting my glass on a napkin.

The second Patron did its job and I relaxed a bit. Tequila is festive, scotch is more contemplative. Still part of my brain warned me not to get too festive. If Delaney got a hint I was still around I'd have to keep running for the rest of my short, unhappy life.

I had two reasons for not cashing in the rest of the heroin in my safe in New York.

1: There is already too much of that shit on the streets.

2: It would lead Delaney to conclude I had met with foul play. Not totally of course but enough to insert a doubt in his fossil brain. That, and leaving the Luger behind.

Maybe.

"You're very pensive tonight."

Nina was looking at me with concern.

"Business."

She turned and slid a CD in the slot.

"Oh, what do you do?"

"Computers."

"Sometimes you disappoint me."

"Alright if I smoke?"

Her smile could light up Christmas.

"Then you go and redeem yourself."

She checked the room. It was still early. There were a scattering of regulars I half-recognized. One sulking figure in the corner I didn't.

"Okay. You can smoke as long as you give me one."

"You?"

"Didn't you know? Dancers are mad nicotine addicts."

We lit up and listened to Nina's compilation. There is a rather cool custom at the Lone Palm whereby the bartenders provide their own music. At the moment Steely Dan was asking the musical question, is there gas in the car? Appropriate.

When she stubbed out her Camel I requested another drink. She gave me a look that was supposed to chasten me. Little did she know. Yet I was touched by Nina's concern. Not to mention flattered.

It had been months since my last visit to Vancouver where I had a sometime lady friend. And Nina was special. Bright, beautiful and caring. Why she cared for me was her problem.

Maybe it was mine too, I thought. Nina could have a weakness for lost causes.

"Dude, you are such a grouch," she said when she returned. "Did you even notice my new skirt?"

I looked. She was wearing a camouflage fabric mini skirt that framed long thighs in black leotards as well as her world-class ass.

"Some new commando uniform?"

"Bastard."

Nina flounced off to the end of the bar where the sullen figure had lifted a hand to summon her.

For some reason it annoyed me. I put it off to petty, schoolboy jealousy and tried to rise above it.

Half a drink later, I saw the man stand and make threatening gestures in Nina's direction. Festive gave way to primitive and I was off the stool with alacrity, if not agility. All things considered I reached the end of the bar in surprisingly fast time.

Nina whirled and gave me a "Why the hell are you here?" look that stopped me cold.

I quietly returned to my stool.

I was getting used to being dismissed. Sooner or later most of my lady friends have lost patience with me. But in Nina's case it was awfully soon. I listened to Mick trying to get a little drink from that loving cup. Good luck.

"Sorry, Max, it was a personal thing."

Nina was standing in front of me. Her rueful pout lightened my disposition.

"Boyfriend?"

She rolled her eyes. "My cousin Jordan. Max—you're not jealous?"

I rolled back. "Me? The situation looked volatile."

"Jordan wants me to go up north with him tomorrow. He says my cousin Carla, that's his sister, hasn't been home for almost a week."

She rested her elbows on the bar, neatly framing her breasts. "You ever been to Petaluma?"

"Once, on my way to wine country."

"Why don't you ride up with me? I'll show you the town. It's got beautiful farmland. We could have a picnic."

A picnic.

I started to beg off but something underneath Nina's light tone prodded me. I prodded back.

"Never bullshit a bullshitter. What's the agenda behind this gracious invitation?"

"You are mean. You know that, Max?"

"So I've heard." I finished my drink.

"Okay, first of all I don't like driving back alone."

"Second of all?"

She absently wiped off a spot on the bar. "I have to visit the police station."

"Jordan didn't do that already? It's been over five days."

Nina leaned closer, expression serious. She smelled of soap and apple.

"My cousin doesn't relate well to the police. He says he tried but they laughed him off. I'm afraid he's going to do something dumb."

Police. Missing girl. Angry cousin. I did something dumb. "What time are you leaving?"

Her smile broke like dawn. "Ten too early?"

"Yes, but I'll sleep in the car."

"Maybe you should switch to water."

"Do you serve overproof water?"

A customer waved frantically and she moved off.

Look at me, I brooded, getting involved, cracking jokes, one more knight flying past forty on a quest for a fair young maiden

Don't get dramatic, I countered, it's just a day in the country. Still I felt a tad foolish. I didn't even know Nina that well. She wiggled the bait and I snapped.

Truth?

I figured we'd go back to her place and drive north after breakfast. That fantasy collapsed when Nina returned.

"So, where do I pick you up?"

She must have seen my wan reaction and leaned closer.

"Jordan is crashing at my place tonight. Anyway, I don't know you that well."

I shrank back in disbelief. "Did somebody hit on you? You invited me, remember?"

She leaned very close. "I remember. And maybe you're not the only one who's disappointed."

It was more information than I could handle. . I managed to stay on point.

"Café Roma, ten o'clock."

She cocked her head as if to say, this guy needs work.

To piss her off I ordered another tequila.

+   +   +

I left the Lone Palm feeling pathetic.

I drove carefully back to North Beach, circled for over forty minutes before finding a parking spot and hiked to my bachelor pad, such as it was.

For some reason I had committed to go on a doomed quest to the Petaluma Police Station and file a formal report on a missing person I didn't know. I felt like a rookie.

Rule One: Avoid the authorities.

So why did I agree to tag along on this lost cause?

Chemistry.

Nina had my quantum number and apparently I had hers. Yet again Captain Johnson was leading the charge.

In the morning I was ready to ditch the whole project.

I woke up with a hangover and a stomach that clenched at the thought of car travel. A few tokes of herb cooled the spasms but the headache required an aspirin.

It sort of worked. I arrived late at Café Roma and found Nina waiting, my coffee in hand.

I blinked when I saw her. In contrast to her usual punk/ballet persona she looked almost demure. Pale blue silk blouse, designer jeans, red heels, black hair pulled back to reveal understated gold earrings—an upwardly mobile California girl by Frida Kahlo.

"Another minute and I would have called you," she scolded, handing me the coffee.

"You don't have my number."

"This is a dysfunctional relationship. Get in the car."

A dark male was glaring at me from the front seat. I reached for the rear handle but Nina stopped me.

"Jordan, this is Max. Let him sit up front with me."

All the way to Petaluma I could feel Jordan's glare heating the back of my neck. However, as promised it was a lovely drive on a sunny morning and the coffee revived my senses.

Traffic was light and we cruised easily past the horse ranches, farms and dairies between Marin and Sonoma County. We didn't talk much, listening to KFOG until we neared our destination.

"Jordan, please tell Max what happened."

"Nothing happened. Carla went out Friday night with her girlfriends and she didn't come home."

"Did you go to the police?" I ventured.

He looked as if I'd called him a name. "Yeah, of course. I called them Sunday afternoon and they told me to call on Monday if she was still missing. I called again and they ran me around."

"Called? You didn't go in, give them a photograph..."

"We're going to take care of that today," Nina said quickly. "Jordan doesn't relate well to cops."

"She's trying to say I have a record. Car theft. I'm on probation."

"First offense?"

"Jordan is at Sonoma State studying computer science."

I empathized recalling my own college bust. "Missing persons reports are pretty much routine," I said.

Jordan snorted. "Not for us."

I heard. He didn't mean people on probation

"There's still a lot of resistance up here," Nina said diplomatically.

I got back on point. "Okay, first thing you need to do is get a photo of Carla. Bring it down to the station, file a report. Then make up flyers with Carla's picture and post them around town."

Nina glanced at Jordan in the rear view.

"We'll have to stop at your Mom's house." She didn't seem happy about it.

Carla had been missing since Friday night. This was Wednesday. As we veered off 101 onto Petaluma Boulevard I wondered what I was doing there.

Chapter 6

Carla had lost all track of time.

The windowless room was always dark. Unless her keeper was there.

Then he would blindfold her and turn on the single electric light in the ceiling. She could tell from the glow seeping through the cloth over her eyes.

Her keeper came often. To give her food and drink...or for other reasons. Sometimes he would make her do things; sometimes he would do things to her. If she resisted, as she had at first, he would slap her face so hard that her burning ear would ring in the silence long after he was gone.

If he was displeased with her performance he would deny her water. Soon, she learned it was useless to resist and did whatever he asked.

He smelled bad. The stench preceded his frequent visits. She had learned to anticipate them but the rest of her had shut down. In the beginning she had thought about her family, her friends, school but now she knew all that was an illusion.

The Tasks.

She had named them that in a desperate effort to distance herself from the obscene attacks on her body and soul.

The Tasks were vile but methodical. As if her keeper had set out to give her a crash course in sexual perversion. Carla complied but she had cut the tie between herself and her hellish reality.

She was nothing more than a breathing Task machine. No longer human.

No past, no future.

Once in a while, huddled in a fetal position on her filthy mattress, arms wrapped tight around her knees, she thought she could hear someone screaming.

Chapter 7

"There are more haunted hearts than haunted houses."

Jennifer Boyle

Petaluma is the egg capitol, duck capitol and wrist-wrestling capitol of America, if not the world. To prove it Nina showed me the local statue of two male torsos, faces strained, forearms locked in combat, on our way to visit Jordan's mother.

I got the sense Nina and Jordan were reluctant to see the woman, especially when they detoured again for coffee and donuts.

When we finally got there, I understood why.

The house was nice enough, a neat two-bedroom on a tree-lined street. But inside it was as somber as a mausoleum. Interspersed between the votive candles, pictures of Catholic saints, and vials of holy water on top of the piano were ponies of tequila and cigars for the Santeria gods. An equal opportunity shrine,

Even in grief Jordan's mother was a handsome woman. Cloaked in a black shawl that framed high cheekbones and shadowed dark eyes, she seemed an older, sadder version of Nina. The deep sorrow etched in her face set off an emotional reaction inside me.

But when Nina introduced me, Maria Fuente stood and drew her shawl around herself defensively.

"It's okay, mama," Jordan said gently, "Max is here to help us find Carla."

Jordan was a different person near his mother. The sullen gangster glare was replaced by a sensitive concern verging on the noble. I saw what Nina liked about him.

"Hello, Mrs. Fuente," I said, "I'm sorry for your trouble. I'm here to help if I can."

Her expression cleared and she took my hand. Her skin was cold.

"Forgive me, please. I'm so... I haven't slept. Can I get you anything, some coffee?"

"All we need is a picture of Carla," Nina said, "then we can go to the police."

At the word "police" Mrs. Fuente began to weep.

Nina comforted her while Jordan went to get a photo of his sister.

Mrs. Fuente wiped her tears and tried to smile. "Dear, would you make me a cup of tea?"

"Of course, mama." Nina glanced at me on her way to the kitchen.

When she was gone Mrs. Fuente examined me as if weighing my fate. She nodded as if satisfied with what she saw.

"Thank you for coming, Max," she said softly, "I think you understand suffering."

I half-nodded, uncertain of where this was going.

"Only someone who has suffered in their life can understand what it means."

She took my hand. "Was your mother good to you?"

The question came from left field, whipping me back to a forgotten place. My mother, Vita, was a native-born Italian imported to Brooklyn by my American father, Antonio, a musician—saxophone and piano to be specific—who met Vita in Naples while on tour and the rest is history. Not.

Their first child, the sister I never met, died shortly after birth, of what I don't know, because Italian families never talk about anything. I only know my father left a year after I was

born and by then my mother had used up all her love. There
was none left for me. Strict business only.

Like Mick says, you get what you need. It wasn't enough.

My mom drank but, to her credit, she kept things together.
Problem was she got mean when she felt like it and she always
felt like it. By the time I entered high school I had developed
survival skills. One was the computer which offered sanctuary
from reality. The other was basketball which, along with my
grades, earned me a scholarship to Columbia.

My father never showed up for even one game in high
school. For that matter neither did my mother.

The scholarship took care of basics but I started dealing
weed to augment my allowance. Senior year I got busted, facing
five years until the judge gave me an escape clause. Join the
military or go to jail.

During my sixth week of basic training at Quantico my
mother died of cirrhosis.

There weren't many people at the funeral, certainly not my
father. When I got back to the Marines, they informed me I
would have to start basic training all over again.

That made fourteen weeks. By the time basic 2 was finished
I was a hard case.

Shortly thereafter they provided the Persian Gulf War. Six
bloody months and back to real life.

Sure.

Oddly, I thought of my mother often while I was in combat. Mostly it was about her anger but I kept recalling one
afternoon when I was six or so. We took the subway and got
off next to a Nedick's where we both ate hot dogs washed
down with orange juice. From there she took me to Macy's and
deposited me in the toy department. I was in kid heaven since
there were few toys under my bed and they were well used. I
played with everything available on the shelves, already smart
enough to make myself invisible.

Then mom collected me and we went home. That was it, my number one memory.

All that and less flashed by at Mrs. Fuente's question. Her next statement startled me.

"You can't keep running always," she said gravely, "sometime you have to trust somebody."

Mama Fuente leaned closer. I caught the scent of fear and rosewater. The light touch of her fingers on my hand compelled my full attention...

"My little girl is my life, she's life itself," she whispered, as if sharing a secret. "You and I have lost so many things. Carla doesn't deserve to be lost, I swear to you, Max."

The sound of my name, a hoarse syllable, triggered a struggle of emotions. Choking for breath I nodded.

"I'll do all I can, Mama. I promise."

Nina came in holding a tray.

"I made tea for everybody," she announced cheerfully.

Then she picked up the vibe and glanced from me to Mama Fuente.

"You guys okay?"

Mama reached out and touched my shoulder. "Of course, dear. Max and I were getting to know each other a little bit."

Our eyes met briefly, memory and tragedy igniting another silent outburst.

I felt Nina watching me and tersely requested directions to the restroom. In this case the facility was aptly termed. Safe behind the locked door, I took a few deep breaths and doused cold water over my face.

Taking another long breath, I looked at my reflection in the mirror. Teary green eyes belied the stone cut features.

Jesus, what just happened?

I couldn't say.

+   +   +

Back in the car, on our way to the local police station, I could still feel the connection to Mama Fuente's pain.

Nina sensed it too. She gave me a smile both apologetic and grim.

"Thanks, Max, this means a lot. You don't know Carla. This isn't like her, not at all. She's not like most of the girls around here. She's smart, works hard..."

We had made color enlargements of a recent snapshot. Studying the laughing girl's face I saw the family resemblance; strong cheekbones, sensuous mouth, dark, intelligent eyes. Carla was more than just pretty.

She was stunning.

Her sharply defined features photographed extremely well. She could have been a model.

"Carla's been accepted to Stanford," Nina said, "she's a family girl, not hard like..."

"Like who?"

"...like me."

I suppressed a smile. "You think you're hard?"

"Harder than I want to be."

I looked away. Nina might be a tough cookie but not hard. She hadn't encountered real evil. Not yet.

The Petaluma Police Station was located at the edge of town. It was a low, flat-faced modern building, white and beige tile brick over concrete that bore a passing resemblance to a mausoleum. Which made sense since directly behind the station was a large cemetery.

The desk sergeant behind the bullet-proof glass barrier examined us like a Southern sheriff eyeballing Snoop Dogg. He was hefty, with blotchy white skin and a thick neck that rolled over his blue collar. His small, blue eyes peered at us from deep inside his puffy face and his expression said this was a bad time.

"We're here to report a missing girl," I said, trying to sound official.

"Sure, sure, just a minute while I find the form."

We stood patiently while he patted his pockets, extracted his bifocals, picked out the correct form and located a pen. He glanced up at us, pen poised.

"Name?"

"Carla Fuente," Nina said. She spelled it out for him.

He laboriously wrote it down. I looked at his nametag, Sergeant Verona. He looked at me like I had stolen his donut.

"Relation?"

"What?" Nina asked.

"Your relationship to the alleged missing person."

"I'm her cousin and there is no *alleged.* Carla wouldn't go off..."

"I got it, lady," Verona snapped, "how long has she been missing?"

"Six days. Since Saturday night."

"That qualifies," he said with a hint of disappointment, "over seventy-two hours."

"We brought a photograph," I said, trying to be helpful.

His eyes flicked at me like a lizard picks off a fly.

"Not yet."

I started to flick back but Nina gave me a warning look.

It took a while. Finally Verona accepted the photo and without looking at it, stapled it to the form Nina had just signed.

"What happens now?"

My question seemed to rankle the sergeant. He stood up slowly. I realized he wasn't fat, he was big. Maybe six-four, two-ninety, none of it flab except around the neck and face— sure sign of a heavy drinker.

"Now I put it in the Missing Person in-box. The information and image gets entered in a nation-wide data base along with the other seven reports we received today."

He looked at Nina. "You might want to inquire if she has a boyfriend. Lots of these cases are runaway lovers..."

Verona turned to me as if exchanging a confidence. "...you know, young girls, hot-blooded." He all but winked. "And, oh, you might check for any gang ties. Lots of that out here."

This time I had to give Nina the look.

Over lunch at a local Mexican taqueria, she was still fuming.

"Hot blooded, can you imagine? Racist bastard."

I didn't comment, preoccupied with the finest beef burrito I had ever come across.

"Now you see why Jordan couldn't make a report," she added, eyes shooting black sparks. She rolled them in his direction. "Of course he has gang ties. Mama has gang ties. I had gang ties until I moved out."

"He'd probably revoke my probation and book me," Jordan said, "suspicion of being Latino."

"You mentioned Carla has girlfriends," I said, trying to get back on point.

He nodded. "Yeah, couple of rich bitches..."

"Jordan!"

He backed off gracefully with a boyish smile. "Sorry, cuz. But everybody knows they're like country club bimbos."

Nina didn't let him off the hook.

"Yeah, well maybe everybody knows where we can find Carla."

+   +   +

Sections of Petaluma resemble New England.

Robin Falker's home had a stone fence been-here-two-hundred-years façade belied by its Hollywood interior.

Nina and I were met at the door by an affable, plump man in lime-green pants and a yellow, checked shirt, holding a drink in a plastic glass. Golfer chic.

"Sorry to intrude, Mr. Falker," I said. As an ex-cop I knew dropping his name sent a signal. He got it.

"We'd like to speak to Robin about Carla Fuente."

"She's my cousin," Nina added giving him a neon smile I'd never seen before.

It worked. Mr. Falker lit up.

"I'm Robin's dad, Ed Falker," he said. "She's out by the pool. Why don't you step inside?"

A stairway divided the large open space on the first floor. Obviously Ed had knocked down the walls. My question was why.

On the right of the stairway was a den area, rooms beyond, possibly a bath. On the left was a set for a Fred Astaire movie. The entire space had been converted to a lounge furnished in white Deco including a pearl-white bar complemented by lacquered, red stools.

Sliding glass doors looked out at the pool and patio.

Robin was reclined beneath a striped umbrella, head plugged into an iPod. When herb father roused her, Robin looked annoyed then slowly rolled off the recliner. She removed her earphones, snatched up a towel and slowly walked toward us.

She was young, blonde and plump which only amplified her blatant sexuality. Hard to believe she was only seventeen. Her blue bikini was stretched tight across ample hips and perky breasts.

The towel was an afterthought. She let it trail as she entered the room, sized us up and gave me a sly smirk.

"You know Carla?"

"I'm her cousin."

For the first time she seemed aware of Nina's presence.

Robin arranged her towel into a crude sarong.

"Oh yeah, Nina. You're a dancer right?"

"Carla hasn't been home since Saturday night."

"Oh wow, that's weird."

"Did you see her on Saturday?" I pressed.

"Uh, yeah, well, early but then we split up."

"Can you be more explicit?"

She looked blank.

"You know, like details," I said. "Did you meet someplace that night?"

"Uh, we met Carla where she works. Then we drove out to Rinner's. We were all supposed to go to this concert at the Mystic."

"But you didn't?"

Robin twisted her blonde forelock. "Well, um, these guys at Rinner's took us for a ride on their bikes. But Carla didn't want to go. We were gone longer than we thought."

"So Carla stayed behind?"

"Yeah, right. But then I got a text from her saying she got a ride with some guy called Dave Honda and she'd meet us at the show."

"You didn't think that was strange?" Nina asked sharply.

Robin instantly retreated behind a sullen wall. Pure teenage bitch.

"No, why? We thought she was with this guy, Dave."

I knew she wouldn't be giving us much more and daddy Ed had returned to monitor the proceedings.

"You said 'we.' Who else was with you?" I asked.

She shrugged and glanced at her father. "Just Tami."

"I don't think you should say any more until we know what this is all about," Ed said.

I kept my tone casual and respectful. "I understand. Think you could give us Tami's number?"

Robin grudgingly complied and we left before Ed threw us out. He smelled a potential lawsuit. I smelled bullshit.

"If we call ahead Tami will be prepared," Nina said as we drove back to the town center.

"Robin's talking to her right now."

"You're so smart."

"You're so hot blooded."

"You don't know."

True, but I hoped to learn.

+   +   +

It took three calls and two wines before Tami Kratchett responded. She agreed to meet us at a Starbucks in a mini-mall known as The Promenade.

Tami was attractive in a thin, knobby kind of way with ragged red hair and dark eye shadow. Tight jeans, rings in lip and belly button, barbed attitude: Sid Vicious on hormones.

I kept it casual and as expected she repeated the same story Robin had told us.

"I saw the message," she said, "got ride Dave Honda see you at show."

I nodded. "How come you remember so well?"

She half-sneered. "I thought it was funny, the guy's name and all. Like the car."

Like the car. Funny. Neither Tami nor Robin seemed overly concerned for their missing friend.

I looked out at the idyllic little mall with its cute shops and loitering youth. The kids affected a surf/hop style that included absurd baggy jeans hung well below underwear, skull caps, unlaced sneakers, off-the-shoulder hoodies, menacing posture. Tats and piercings abounded. *Lord of the Flies* meets *A Clockwork Orange*.

When Tami left Nina slumped dejectedly in her chair. "What am I supposed to tell mama?"

"Phone Jordan. Ask him if he knows a Dave Honda."

"Good idea." She found her cell and called.

Jordan had never heard of Dave Honda or a Dave anybody. However he knew Rinner's was a biker hangout, definitely not Carla's kind of scene.

"Let's drive by," I suggested, trying to soothe Nina's anxiety. "We can show them Carla's picture, maybe somebody will remember."

Nobody remembered. And nobody wanted to talk to us save for the waitress who took the ten dollar tip, studied the photo and shook her head.

"If this girl was in here Saturday you need to talk to Regine. I was up in Eureka."

"When does Regine come in?"

She fanned herself with the photo. "Tomorrow afternoon. She works a double on Fridays."

"Shit, Max, this is more than I can handle," Nina said as we walked outside. "I'm teaching class tomorrow and then work my regular shift. I don't mind canceling the class but what do I do here? I'm no private eye.'

She distractedly ran a hand through her hair. For some reason the gesture touched me, a Kundera moment. The unbearable lightness of stupidity.

"I can drive back up tomorrow," I offered, "check in with the police. I'll copy Carla's photo, maybe hang some flyers."

Nina gave me a big kiss. Not a sexy kiss and not a friendly kiss. I was still analyzing it on the drive back to the city.

We didn't talk much but the conversation circled around Carla and Nina's family. She wasn't as detached and bohemian as she liked to let on. Guard down, Nina's distress was visible. She gripped the wheel tightly and stared straight ahead.

I knew and she knew but I wasn't in the mood for a mercy fuck and Nina didn't need another obligation.

"Drop me at Café Roma," I said as we crossed the bridge.

For the first time since leaving Petaluma, Nina smiled. "Someday you'll tell me where you live."

"I don't know where you live."

"You could..." she paused, realizing she'd said too much. "I mean it's not a state secret."

"I'll see you at the Palm tomorrow night."

She seemed relieved. "Call me before that okay? I need to know what's happening so I can tell mama. This is ripping her apart."

In North Beach she parked at a hydrant and leaned close to kiss me goodnight. It was a special kiss, at once shy and promising. No analysis required.

As I drove back across the bridge to my Marin hideaway I kept arguing with myself. Meeting face to face with a hostile police sergeant was hardly wise.

On the other hand, my name wasn't involved. And the promise in Nina's kiss trumped wisdom.

While parking in my driveway I noticed Organic Phil was still awake. Probably on his Colima board.

Back home, I hit my computer and went to work. I hacked into DMV and found nine Daves with registered Hondas in the Petaluma area. I also hacked into the Petaluma Police missing person database for Carla Fuente.

She wasn't there.

Chapter 8

Carla had never actually seen her keeper.
Whenever he opened the door he told her to put on the hood.

In the beginning when she didn't react quickly he would tighten the hood's drawstring, suffocating her. He would bring her to the brink of unconsciousness, relax the tension so she could take a few breaths, then choke her again.

Now the moment she heard the door rattle she reached for the hood, nausea bubbling in her throat.

Only his odor identified him. And his bestial, never-ending demands.

It might have been a month or a year, she couldn't tell anymore. At first she clung to her past, like a life preserver in a violent storm, only to have it wash away leaving her to drown in this eternal torment. She no longer remembered her mother or the life she once had. All she had left was empty darkness.

Her prayers too, had long been swallowed by the brutal silence. Finally she had to stop herself from cursing God.

He had abandoned her, just like her father.

Then, without warning, there came a change. A new keeper entered.

This one smelled clean and he handled her with restraint, if not care.

"Ain't too proud now, are you bitch?" he said, voice strained by the effort of thrusting into her. "Soon you're gonna be the goddamn Queen of Sheba."

His voice was vaguely familiar, a rough whisper from a dim past.

She didn't know what he meant but it didn't matter. She just wanted him to finish and leave. So she could go back to sleep in her own corner of hell.

Chapter 9

"No, that maverick shit is overrated."

Ken Bruen, Blitz

I awoke with lover's remorse.

It was barely dawn so I stretched, took a run, stretched again and went for one of those breakfasts Organic Phil deplored; short stack, bacon, eggs easy.

I checked the Petaluma Police database but Carla Fuente was still missing from Missing Persons. It was too early to call Nina and I didn't want to give her bad news anyway. So I went outside and smoked a J.

Between the morning air and the herb it came to me.

During our Rinner's drive-by we had encountered undisguised hostility from the few bikers we approached.

Because to them we were civilians.

When in Rome, my new *philosophia burrito.*

Inspired, I drove to an unobtrusive garage on the wrong side of Highway 101.

Len Zane is an expert car mechanic as well as my herb dealer. Tall, lean, cowboy lanky, Len can fix any motor engineered by man. Or build one that hasn't been invented yet. He is also a biker.

Len was there when I pulled in, working underneath a vintage Caddy.

"You're up early, problem with your ride?"

Not really. I drive a dark green 1994 Mercury Sable which had just hit the 90,000 mile mark. I don't need glamorous, I need invisible.

The Green Ghost is just that. It could be a Taurus, it could be... who cares. It's just a disposable paper cup with a four hundred horsepower motor. Len had muscled up the engine for me a few months earlier.

"Runs fine but it could use a tune," I said, "maybe you could bring it up to speed."

Len rolled out from beneath the Caddy and stood up, wiping his hands with a cloth.

"What's that mean?"

I thought, careful not to offend. Clearly Len was sensitive about things mechanical.

What I needed was for Len to work on my car so I could borrow one of his bikes.

"I've been thinking the car could be faster," I began, then had a flash, "and I could use a stash panel or two."

Len's craggy features remained impassive as he looked inside my car. "Stash panel you say."

"For my herb. Just in case."

Since Len was the man who supplied my grass it was in his best interest to make certain it remained concealed during the tricky ride home. Driving in California makes you extremely vulnerable. You can be stopped for any reason and searched. Sure you can call your lawyer but you're still fucked.

In contrast a New York cop needs a very good reason to bust a citizen strolling down Madison Avenue.

"I can do that—and more—if you like," Len said after checking the interior. "Take some time though."

"How long?"

"Today's Friday, say Monday noon. That okay?"

"I'll need wheels. Can you loan out a bike?"

Len's deadpan seemed skeptical. "You ride?"

"Some."

He nodded, wiped his hands some more. "Let's take a look."

In the rear of the garage behind the oil pit and hydraulic lift, three motorcycles leaned on their kickstands. One was a tricked out Harley, red with custom tank and fairing, chrome, big wheels. The other two were stripped-down BMWs. Both had a bad industrial look, oversized tank and racing tires, low seat, but one was 1000ccs the other 1500. I couldn't resist.

"The fifteen hundred okay?"

"Good taste. I got it primed last week. But lemme warn you buddy it is one hellacious beast."

The BMW was balanced like a Calder Mobile and just as sensitive to shifting conditions. Its raw power shot away from me as if I was riding on ice. It took three hours of practice on local roads before I dared brave the freeway. I hadn't ridden a bike since the Marines. The first part came back easily: pulling out, turning, stopping. However, when I cranked it past fifty, the bike took over.

How cautious can you be on a freeway? One tap and you're all over the asphalt at the dubious mercy of oncoming traffic. I stayed far right and kept it under sixty all the way to Petaluma.

I had brought a few items with me. Len had provided a helmet but the sleek, understated machine was low on amenities. In the metal saddlebag was a laptop, clean cell, black sweatshirt and my Beretta. The Beretta was clean as well.

I didn't trust Delaney to issue me a weapon he couldn't trace. So I had dumped the original in Canada and picked up a fresh piece at a Nevada gun show. No ID required.

The stress of navigating the freeway had me sweating when I arrived. And in town it was even worse. For some reason Petaluma has lots of bad drivers. I was nearly sideswiped twice before I found a spot and proceeded on foot.

A local copy shop made up forty fliers. They were crude; an enlargement of Carla's photo with the word MISSING on top and Nina's cell number on the bottom. I stopped for coffee and ducked into the restroom to wash the road dust from my face. Then I called Nina and asked her to have Jordan meet me at the police station. She hesitated, wanted to know why but I fended her off by saying I needed help with the fliers. No sense adding needless anguish to the mix.

I took my time getting to the station. As expected, Jordan arrived late. He was wearing an oxford blue shirt over straight black jeans and running shoes. The backpack he carried suggested it was a school day. However, his expression was far from collegiate. The sullen gangster had returned and his dark eyes flashed annoyance.

"Yo, Max, what's your problem? I had to cut class for this shit? We covered it yesterday."

"He didn't file the report."

"The fuck you sayin'?"

"Verona, the racist bastard. He didn't file the report. Carla's not in the database. I checked."

Confusion and fear skipped across his stony features. For a moment he was silent. He knew what I wanted. It was his worst nightmare. Dealing with the machine.

"You have to file again. I brought Carla's photo, the fliers."

"Why can't Nina..."

"Because you're the man of the house."

To his credit, Jordan didn't waffle. He ran a resigned hand through his hair then led the way into the station.

A different sergeant sat behind the bullet-proof glass, name tag read Lowell. He was tall with a blond buzz cut, swat team scowl. He regarded Jordan carefully.

"You've been here before."

"Yes, sir. My sister is missing. I want to make a report.'

Lowell started filling out the forms. He was much better at it then Verona.

Midway he paused. "Jordan Fuente. I remember. Didn't I bust you last year?"

Jordan kept his cool. "Yes, sir. I'm on probation. Back in school.'

"Good. Make sure you stay there."

"We brought a photograph."

Lowell gave me a hard blue stare. "And who are you?"

"Family lawyer."

I had gotten tired of his paternalistic routine. I saw Jordan restrain a grin.

Lowell took the photo and went to an inner office. He returned a short time later.

"That's it," he said with a trace of pride, "we'll have this on a national data base within the hour. It's already been relayed to officers in the field."

"What about the other cases?" I asked.

He looked at me quizzically. "What other cases? We haven't had a missing person for over a week."

So much for poor, overworked Verona.

Outside Jordan smacked a fist against his palm. "Motherfuckers never let you forget, always on you…"

"You did good in there," I said, "kept your temper, did your job, helped your sister."

He ducked his head like someone unaccustomed to praise. "Yeah, okay."

I slipped Jordan two hundred bucks and gave him half the fliers I'd run off.

"Post these where you think they'll do some good. I'll check the database and call you later."

Jordan went off and I entered phase 2. First I found a local barber shop and cut my hair radically short. I'm balding anyway so this removed the pathetic factor.

From there I searched out a thrift shop and after a bit of rummaging came up with the sleeveless remnant of a black motorcycle jacket. Classic.

In the changing room I experienced a brief twinge of anxiety when I realized I was back doing what I'd been trained to do for the DEA.

Infiltrate, move up the food chain, become one of them.

The person staring back at me in the mirror didn't look like Sam Devino or Philip Munson or even Max LeBlue. This guy was a California Cro-Magnon with a 9mm.

The short hair and weight loss accentuated my angular features. The deep-set eyes were clear green betrayed by a wild glint. Added to that were my recently buffed deltoids, nicely framed by the sleeveless motorcycle jacket. I found a pair of shades to cap the look.

I walked around town, occasionally pausing to post Carla's picture. I had about six flyers left when I reached Walnut Park. The place has a folksy, town square feel with a band box and playground so I found a bench and sat for a few minutes. I lit a cigarette and got a hostile glare from a passing matron.

I blew a smoke ring.

The sun had set and I was hungry. I posted a flyer on each side of the park then crossed the street and walked over to a place I had seen when I arrived in town, the Buckhorn Bar. I stopped to hang Carla's picture before I entered.

The Buckhorn proved to be a find, a real American drinking establishment. The walls were decorated with elk heads, moose heads, antelope heads, even a jackalope. Over the register was a portrait of the original owner and everywhere were photographs of loyal patrons. There were two pool tables in the rear and the ubiquitous pinball machine nearby.

I showed the lady tending bar the flyer but she didn't recognize Carla. However I liked the place so much I ordered an Irish coffee.

While waiting I opened my laptop and hacked through the Petaluma Police firewall like a Hanzo sword.

My initial relief at seeing her picture and vital information was dissolved by acidic outrage. The kid was barely sixteen.

The outrage continued to fume as I walked slowly back to where I'd parked the bike.

I stood for a minute breathing in the crisp night air.

Light traffic helped bolster my confidence and to my surprise the bike responded. I rolled into Rinner's vast parking area like I knew what I was doing.

It was a real truck stop replete with a weighing station, gas pumps and late night diner.

Six or seven bikers were scattered around the lot in small groups. Two semis were parked side by side near the fuel station.

I hung one flyer on a gas pump another on a lamppost then headed to the diner for more coffee. Along the way I noticed a shambling figure slumped against a dumpster drinking from a paper bag. I walked over holding the flyer in one hand a twenty in the other.

"Excuse me," I said, always polite to drunks and derelicts. "Did you ever see this girl around here? Maybe last weekend?"

The guy peered at me then at the flyer. He might have been thirty or sixty underneath the long, gray-streaked hair and beard. He was very thin from his wine and cheese diet and his watery eyes stared brightly at the twenty.

"Sorry, my dear sir," he said with real regret, "I can't recall last weekend."

I gave him the bill and went inside. There were two biker types playing pinball and in a far booth three men in down vests and baseball hats who looked like truckers.

Regine the waitress was over fifty with a brassy bee hive, pale white skin and a patient smile that won me over immediately.

"Just coffee," I said. When she came back I showed her the flyer.

"Do you recall seeing this girl in here last Friday or so?" She took the flyer and squinted at it under the light.

"Yes, I do remember. She was in here. Nice girl too. Wouldn't have any truck with those bikers hittin' on her. Not like her friends. Those young girls were flirtin' with trouble you ask me."

It occurred to me that the pinball machine was silent. I turned and saw the bikers going out the door.

"Do you remember if she left here with anyone?"

"Yes, now I recollect. She couldn't get a taxi. This guy, Dave, offered her a ride."

"Dave? You know him?"

She picked up her order pad. "Oh, sure. See him a lot in here. 'Scuse me a minute."

I watched her walk briskly to the trucker's booth. Quick and skinny, an independent woman, salt of the earth.

"What about this guy, Dave?" I asked when she returned.

"He's here a lot. Maybe three, four nights a week. Rides a blue Nighthawk."

Of course, Dave Honda was a motorcycle not a car.

"You know a lot about bikes," I said.

"Working here fifteen years I learned a lot about bikes and bikers. But you know what?"

"What?"

"You're all just little boys."

Not me. I felt like the ancient mariner. I left a twenty on the counter intending to check the DMV database for Dave. As I exited the diner I heard a low voice.

"Psst... Hey..."

I paused.

"Over here."

My friend the drunk. He was half concealed behind the dumpster. I moved closer.

"What?"

"Those guys... by the pumps. Vandals."

I turned. The two bikers who'd been playing pinball were now propped on their bikes having a smoke. Both of them were barrel-chested dudes on heavy Harleys.

"Yeah, so?"

"Took down your pictures man. Vandals took the handle..." his rough chuckle ended in a coughing fit.

I looked over at the lamppost. Carla's flyer was gone.

Perhaps it was the caffeine but my simmering anger spiked. I felt adrenaline singing behind my ears as I walked to my bike, stopped and pretended to see the lamppost for the first time.

From long distance I could sense the bikers focusing on me. I looked around as if surprised, then went to the pump where I'd posted the other flyer. It too was missing.

The bikers stared at me with a mixture of amusement and contempt.

I walked closer.

These little boys were baby bulls. One had shoulder-length hair and the other appeared bald under his leather Confederate army cap. Both had prominent neck tattoos—a flaming red skull, knife clenched in its madly grinning teeth—which pretty much made them unemployable.

I kept my tone neutral. "You happen to see the poster I hung on the pump?"

The long haired one sneered.

"You mean the spic bitch?"

Snap.

Lifting from the bottom of my pent up anger I swiveled, caught him on the ear with my right fist, drilled into his liver with the left hook as he staggered back.

Until then I was doing well.

Out of nowhere or more precisely from between the gas pumps, a dark blur emerged and my face exploded.

Brain clanging, I instinctively rolled away. Frantically I clawed for my Beretta, but one hand was pinned under my body while the other tried to ward off a second whack. I glimpsed a boot on my left and kept rolling.

Face down, I made contact with my weapon and yanked it free. One wild shot in the air and everything froze.

A nanosecond later the truce shattered.

"Shit!"

As if it was a military command the first two scattered and my unseen attacker slung an aluminum bat at me. He ducked between the pumps as the bat whanged an inch past my left eye. I fired into the shadows but he was gone. A metallic growl behind me grabbed my attention. I turned and saw the long haired biker bearing down on his Harley brandishing what looked like a hammer.

My first shot hit the front tire. The next ripped the skidding bike's tank and hot metal sparks ignited the spewed gasoline. The Harley blossomed into an orange and black bonfire. Somehow, the biker managed to get up despite one leg being on fire and he hopped back like some runaway birthday candle, swatting at the flames.

Seconds later his buddy appeared riding an almost identical Harley. He stopped and long hair clambered aboard, leg still smoking.

It occurred to me that I made an easy target against the burning motorcycle and stepped back behind the pumps as the bikers retreated noisily out of the lot.

I stood for long moments until the sound faded, peering into the surrounding darkness for my attacker. I knew he was still nearby, watching me, most likely in or around those parked trucks. I weighed going after him.

The hot pain bolting across my cheek and jaw settled the question. The entire right side of my face throbbed sheer agony. I was lucky I could walk.

But could I ride?

I considered a detour to the diner washroom but knew whoever bashed me was anxious to do it again. And he'd come back with more than a baseball bat.

Then too, there were the rising sirens in the distance.

Wisest move was a hasty flight. I clumsily mounted the bike and revved the motor.

The sirens wailed louder as I rolled into the street. I saw a few faces in the light of the burning motorcycle, gaping at me. I accelerated and headed for the freeway.

Swollen brain banging like a clapper against my damaged skull, I made a wobbly right turn and tried to read the signs directing me to 101 North. I stopped at a red light grateful for the chance to breathe and gather myself for the long, painful trip home.

Dimly I became aware of a distant rumble, like twenty hip hop Escalades pumping big bass speakers. I glanced back and got a starker picture.

Twenty or thirty motorcycles were soaring lazily around the corner like a low flying bomber squadron.

And I was ground zero.

Chapter 10

Finally, after she'd lost all hope, they came and took her away.

Even behind the hood she could see brief sunlight before being placed face down in some sort of padded vehicle. She had learned to control the nausea by relaxing her stomach. But she felt numb, hungry, thirsty and dirty.

All that changed when they arrived at their destination.

Someone carefully helped her out of the vehicle and walked her into the house. He guided her upstairs, sat her on a bed then left. Exhausted she sank down on the soft mattress and fell asleep.

The scent of food awakened her. Someone had placed a tray on the night table. On the tray was a cheeseburger, fries and a can of Coke. She quickly devoured everything on the tray and fell back on the bed.

A large man in black woke her up. A mask covered his face but the black jeans, leather vest and boots identified him as a biker.

"Bathroom's in there," he said. "Clean yourself up."

Having access to soap, hot water and towels was like finding treasure. She luxuriated in the shower for a long time then toweled herself dry. The bath was equipped with a hairdryer, toothbrush, toothpaste, hair brushes, combs, Tampax, tweezers, all the accoutrements of feminine hygiene, even lipstick.

Everything but a door lock.

After she had dried herself, scrubbed her teeth, brushed her hair, Carla discovered her clothes were gone. She went into the room and saw a red dress, black thong panties and red shoes arranged on the bed. She put them on and waited.

Again she was dozing when the masked man came in. He held out a container.

"You're a sleepy girl," he said. "You need some coffee."

It was sweet and warm but after a few gulps it had a bitter aftertaste. She started to put it aside but the masked man stopped her.

"All of it, girl."

Carla drank it. The man took the empty container and left the room.

This time Carla didn't doze. Within minutes the numbing fog over her brain burned off, leaving a cool clarity. She went into the bathroom and studied her reflection. She was a lot thinner, with gaunt cheeks. Hollow circles shadowed her wide eyes. Bright, frantic eyes like those of a trapped animal.

Impulsively she began searching for a way out. The bathroom window was barred and the outer room was windowless. She looked around for something she could use as a weapon. The heaviest object was the lamp on the night table.

Her heart began pumping faster and she went into the bathroom for a glass of water. Senses alert she heard footsteps at the door and moved back to the bedroom. She positioned herself so she could see outside when the door opened.

As the view widened she saw someone leaning against a terrace railing. Even at night the sharp body angle was familiar.

Shock, disbelief, confusion, elation, all collided in her skull.

Tami.

Tami had come to get her out, she thought wildly.

Then another familiar figure loomed in the doorway, blocking her sight. Carla nearly vomited. Even from that distance she could smell him. Acid bile seared her throat.

She reeled back, teetering between panic and revulsion. She started to scream.

The masked man lifted a warning finger.

That's all he had to do.

She dug her fist into her mouth stifling the sound. At that moment she wasn't sure what she'd seen... a shadow, someone else, no one. It could have been imagination, hallucination.

The man's stench engulfed her. Roughly he pushed her to the bed and sat her down.

"A very good friend of mine is going to visit you," he said. "You are going to do whatever he wants. You understand, bitch?"

She nodded uncertainly averting his gaze.

He cuffed her face. "If he ain't happy, you get retraining. And I won't be so easy."

His fingers left a dirty scent on her skin. She wanted desperately to wash it off.

"I don't hear you, bitch."

"Yes. He will be happy."

"If he ain't, it's your ass."

She nodded, afraid to move.

He gave a short laugh, moved his thick hands across her chest and squeezed her nipples.

"Your new boyfriend's comin' to call. Make sure you make him feel welcome."

To punctuate his statement he drew a knife from his belt and ran it down her face from eye to chin.

"Be a shame to mess up a star like you."

He turned and left the room. She heard the door lock. After a few minutes she went into the bathroom, splashed water on her face and rinsed the burning bile from her mouth.

She found scented soap and used it on her tainted skin.

Heart still racing she sat on the bed and waited.

Ten minutes passed but she remained where she was.

Finally she heard the door unlock and a man entered.

He was old, with a pinched face and narrow eyes that regarded her coldly, as if she was an item on a menu.

Slowly, Carla stood up and smiled.

Chapter 11

"Is this supposed to be a comedy? You better circle the jokes."
Tom Waits

Goddamn cell phones. The gang behind me had rallied way too quickly.

I tried to control the swerving bike as I gunned it across the intersection, narrowly missing a horrified motorist. With more muscle than skill I managed to gain some semblance of balance and opened the throttle. The machine responded like a thoroughbred but my bruised, throbbing skull limited my options to fast, faster and suicide.

Not that I would mind a quick romantic exit on 101 rather being torn apart by my rabid band of pursuers. Face it, trashing someone's ride is the worst crime one can commit in biker land.

It's a hanging matter—if you're lucky enough to make the gallows.

Over the roaring engine I heard hoots and yells behind me. The boys were enjoying this. Heavy metal shot sparks on the road ahead and bounced high. Someone had winged a hammer at me. I wondered if anyone had a gun.

A moment later a bullet spat past my ear. I lay across the tank and opened it up

I entered the freeway doing 90 and nudged it past 100 on the darkened two-lane. Traffic was sparse and I could hear the angry drums of thirty Harleys on the warpath. I also heard more shots and despite my limited skills began to weave between cars.

Minutes later, I gave it up. I had to slow down to execute these intricate maneuvers. Not good.

I hugged the center stripe and let it all out until the needle hit 107. At that speed the shooters couldn't hit a truck.

Harsh wind slapped my face and I wished I had remembered to slip on a helmet. I'd gained some distance from the pack but there was nowhere to go but fast. It was just a matter of minutes before the bullets, hammers and hogs would catch up with me.

When the road straightened I saw my chance.

Marked by a large discount gas station was an old-fashioned farm crossing right there on the freeway. An accident waiting to happen.

The oncoming lanes had scattered traffic while those ahead were empty. I veered right and made a sweeping left onto the crossing lane. It put me at excessive risk but it gave me options. Needless to say I chose the hardest.

Straight into speeding traffic.

A car swerved to avoid me and I skidded onto the shoulder against oncoming SUVs and semis, creating a barrier between me and the raging posse across the freeway.

Now I had three problems; avoiding a head-on, trying to see in the dazzling glare of headlights—and losing the rider who had made the same move. More would have followed but the second man clipped a fender. He and his Harley went airborne.

The bike crushed the hood of a truck causing a chain of noisy collisions while the rider landed on the freeway ahead. I glimpsed his surprised face before it splattered against a passing windshield.

Could easily have been me I thought, acutely aware of the looming growl behind me. Still, factors were tilting my way. The collisions had stopped traffic and there was only one mad dog to deal with. I pushed it as far as I dared until I spotted an exit.

A line of vehicles clogged the lane on my right giving me barely fifteen inches to operate. I braked, stomped one

foot into the ground and made a skin-tight left hoping for
open road.

I found it. Straight ahead were two dark lanes that ran between darker farmland. No barriers no lights. Somewhere I had
bonded with my BMW and rather than trying to stay upright I
was thinking of ways to elude the relentless predator on my ass.

Then I remembered.

I was strapped.

My Beretta had at least five rounds left. With some effort
I turned and saw him; a burly, bearded mountain man with a
shiny Nazi helmet and ape-hanger handlebars on his chopper.
His Harley sounded like 100,000cc's as we raced through the
surreal quiet, red-hot engines shrieking.

My BMW responded surging toward a blind curve far
ahead. I needed distance and the bike gave it to me. When I hit
the turn, I went neutral, shut the motor and lights and coasted
into the shadows. I cruised to a stop between a pair of trees
and yanked the piece from my belt.

Seconds later the Harley rolled cautiously around the curve.

The instant his light caught my metal fender he braked
coming to a sideways stop. I shot a round into the asphalt between us to get his attention. His hands were visible on the high
handlebars so I moved forward.

"Freeze!" I croaked.

With an air of insouciant leisure, as if emerging from his
limo at the door of a club, the huge biker swung his leg over
the tank and strolled toward me. As he neared he lifted a long
knife from the scabbard on his hip. Transfixed I watched him
break into a heavy-footed trot then glimpsed the dull gleam of
his blade waving hello.

It was a scene from Lewis and Clark. Wearing fringed chaps
and some kind of beaded suede shirt under his leather vest
he looked like an insane trapper who came down for beans,
bullets, and whiskey every autumn then retreated to his cave.
Something between mountain man and bigfoot.

I fired two rounds.

Both disappeared into his barrel chest but he kept coming, grinning like a grizzly bear at a barbecue. It was the grin that scared me. Like I was shooting blanks and he knew it. I fired again and the grin disintegrated, swallowed by a bloody sinkhole on the right side of his face. Pure savage instinct kept him charging.

Before I could fire the last round he collapsed.

Suddenly focused, I hobbled to his bike and laboriously pushed the heavy machine behind the trees. I made sure the biker was dead then hauled his body off the edge of the road.

His pockets yielded a thick wad of hundred dollar bills and a driver's license identifying him as Leroy Underwood of San Bernardino. On impulse I checked his saddle bag. Leroy was hauling two tape wrapped bricks with a familiar heft. I took the money and one of the bricks leaving the wallet and the other kilo for the police.

Cold? Perhaps.

By combat standards it was fair enough. I turned back and took the first road south.

Eventually I hooked up with 101 North. Certain my hunters were scouring the freeway. I pushed the needle past ninety, at ease now with anything below mach speed, finally at one with Len's magnificent machine.

Fortunately nobody came to test my euphoric new skills. I was high on adrenaline and violence. By the time I reached Corte Madera I was crashing.

I had killed a man.

Fuck self defense. Neither the State of California nor the Vandals M.C. nation would let this slide. If the Vandals couldn't draw and quarter me they would definitely drop a dime. It was only a matter of time before they rooted me out. My connection to Carla made the whole Fuente family vulnerable. Especially Mama.

Aware the BMW's engine would disturb my landlord I manually rolled it behind my cottage and covered it with a tarp. The first thing I did when I got inside was gulp down three aspirin and a generous measure of scotch. Then I took a long, hot shower ending with alternate blasts of scalding and freezing. My reflection in the steamy mirror wasn't pretty, even misted over. My swollen face resembled a Van Gogh sky, all purple and yellow on one side. The other side looked like Michael Corleone

I didn't like him.

I had killed a man. The realization seeped into my core like an oil spill, dirty and thick. Another scotch dulled the pain but the depression deepened.

Obviously my subconscious needed to tear apart the little safety net I had spent so much time and thought weaving together. It had always been the same, I brooded counting the ways.

High school: top student, good athlete with a penchant for the wrong crowd. College: busted for dealing pot. Marine Corps: arrested for popping a chicken shit Army captain in Kuwait, sent home and allowed early discharge in light of my combat record. Marriage: a disaster zone. DEA: a perfect storm of self-destruction.

Now, here I sat, a fugitive from my past, wanted by a major motorcycle gang, my identity compromised all because I had to get involved. Had to get that adrenaline fix. Had to play detective, bringing new meaning to the term private dick.

Infiltrate, become part of the food chain, fuck up big time.

Lifted by a wave of manic energy I went outside to retrieve my laptop from the BMW's saddle bag. I also found the taped package I'd taken from the dead biker.

A quick examination showed it wasn't coke or heroin. It was crystal meth. America's drug.

I checked the wad of money as well. Seven thousand dollars.

Without warning all my energy drained as if flushed, leaving me with a black hole depression and I nearly fell. Listing like a battered old pug on watery legs, I made it to my bed and crawled inside.

+   +   +

Morning was no bargain.

I awoke with a hangover, headache and a heavy black shroud around my soul. Simple breathing threatened to shatter my brain.

I made the mistake of hitting on my landlord Organic Phil for a few aspirin. His face registered pure horror.

"Max, what happened?"

I tried to think. "I had an accident."

"I mean your hair."

Among other things Phil is my barber. A top Roman hairdresser in a previous life he himself sports a pure white shock Mick Jagger might envy. At the moment his dramatic features were highly indignant.

"You cut it off, why?"

"I just did a movie. Bit part."

Instantly Phil's expression morphed to admiration. "Yeah? Who's in it?"

"John Travolta." I was rolling now. "That's how I got hurt. While we were shooting." Which was almost true.

"Let's see that." Phil came closer to examine my bruised cheek.

"I need a few aspirin."

"You need more than that, come inside."

Phil gave me strong herb tea, various tablets, none of which were aspirin and rubbed arnica on my wounded face. It definitely helped but Phil was right, I needed more.

"So when are they shooting again?" Phil asked, all fan.

I moved to the door. "They wrapped," I said employing the inside term, "they'll be cutting in LA."

I paused to shake his hand. "Thanks, friend. I appreciate the TLC."

He shrugged. "Just call me the next time you do a movie."

Show business. Jimmy Durante was right. Everybody wants to get into the act.

If you don't have wheels in Marin you can walk or wait for the phantom bus. Being in no condition for either I took a cab to Larkspur Landing and hopped a ferry to the city.

At first it seemed like the best decision I'd made all week. Whatever Phil had given me worked. My headache was down to a dull pulse and I actually craved solid food.

A chill, grey haze shrouded the city and the water got choppy as we passed Alcatraz. The blustery wind and rolling deck soon offset Organic Phil's good work. When we reached the ferry building my headache had escalated and my stomach was churning. An added attraction was my stiff, crooked spine. I hadn't bounced around on concrete for years.

Unable to find a cab, I walked and entered the gates of Chinatown with some relief. My spine was still bent, my head hurt and there was a pool of acid in my belly that seemed to be hatching alien life forms. But help was near.

Jackson Street will make you forget you're in America. Herb shops, fruit stands, dim sum kitchens, bakery cafes, bamboo covered newsstands, strange alleyways, the click of Mah Jong tiles beating time to atonal string music, Asian pop songs, acupuncture parlors, foot reflexology clinics, women holding pastel-colored umbrellas, people hurrying everywhere: all that's missing are rickshaws. And that's only two blocks worth.

My friend Jimmy Shu has an herb shop smack in the middle of things.

When I entered he was packaging up some stuff that resembled a pile of black thorns for an old man in a plaid suit and yellow slippers. Without changing expression Jimmy motioned me into the back room behind an antique, lacquered screen.

I gingerly settled on the edge of his padded massage table and waited. It took a while.

The first thing Jimmy did when he appeared was turn on a bright overhead light. Anyone who's spent time in Chinatown knows the residents are fond of strong fluorescent lighting. So much for Feng Shui

But this was as intense as a sun lamp.

Jimmy studied my contused face his placid, unlined features concerned as he peered into my eyeballs.

"How's your back?"

"Spine feels like it's welded to my hip"

"Not surprised. Your pupils show extreme stress, alcohol and nicotine. How did this happen... get mugged?"

I decided to stay consistent. "Accident. I was working on a movie and walked into the camera."

"You an actor now?"

"Special computer effects."

He nodded, not quite believing me but at least it made more sense than the acting routine I'd fed Phil.

Jimmy left the room and came back with a terrycloth robe.

"Strip down to your shorts and put this on. Then lie down on your stomach. I'll be a few minutes."

As I complied, Jimmy went out front and locked the door. He rummaged through his myriad herb bins and returned with a tray bearing a number of paper bundles. Ignoring me, he vanished behind a further screen. Soon, an unpleasant, bitter scent wafted into the room. Meanwhile the heat from the lamp was penetrating my locked muscles.

Twenty minutes later Jimmy emerged holding a large, steaming mug.

"Drink all, please."

The vile brew tasted like castor oil laced with ginger. Keeping it down was touch and go.

"Okay, now you lie on back, face up."

Jimmy carefully applied an aromatic compress over my wounded cheek then draped what smelled like camphorated towels over my thighs and stomach.

"Not move, okay? Sweat it all out."

Minutes later I understood what he meant. Perspiration began running from every pore from my knees to my neck. At the same time, the compress seemed to be sucking the pain from my skull. I closed my eyes.

A half hour later I woke up. Headache gone, body buzzing with energy, I tentatively tried to rise.

Some vertebrae were fused to my hip, others to my neck, still others to one shoulder. None wanted to stand erect. I managed to roll to a sitting position, feet dangling and sat hunched over, dimly aware my robe was soaked wet.

Jimmy entered with a couple of dry towels. He turned off the lamp and gave me a big smile.

"How you feel now?"

"Great, except I'll have to walk sideways."

"No problem. Don't move. Relax, deep breath."

He embraced my head and chin, twisted, and *crack* I could turn my neck and shoulders.

"Stand up. Cross both arms over chest. Relax, breathe..."

Jimmy was slender but he easily lifted me off the ground and hefted my torso like a sack of grain. I could hear things clicking into place. When he put me down again My spine was straight and limber.

"Get dressed and come outside."

I felt totally rejuvenated. Checking my reflection in a small mirror I saw the swollen bruise had receded leaving a purple blotch. Minimal change cosmetically but, internally, the cure was slightly left of miraculous. The headache was gone and my brain had regained the ability to process simple thoughts.

Jimmy had a small stack of envelopes on the counter.

"Here's your mail."

"How's the website?"

"Could use maintenance."

I nodded, grateful I could move my neck. "I'll tweak it this week. Maybe add an option or two. What do you think about mail order service?"

He thought it over. "I don't know, Max. For me healing is best one on one.'

I could not agree more.

"Stay away from movie camera," he called as I left.

I arrived at my North Beach flat feeling fresh. Luckily my roomies were elsewhere. I took care of my bills then lay back and tried to figure things out.

My biker persona had to go. I needed a new disguise for Petaluma. I also needed to zero in on Dave Honda.

I went into the living room Eli had converted to a physics lab and slipped behind his big Mac.

Bingo.

A Honda Nighthawk motorcycle was registered to one David Alan Paul who resided in Petaluma. Never trust a man with three first names.

On impulse, I hacked into police records for Leroy Underwood.

Leroy had a serious problem with authority. He had done seven years in Pelican Bay for manslaughter, been acquitted on a rape charge, and on bail for aggravated assault. He had used a combat knife during a carjack. The victim had lost an ear and part of his nose. I recalled Leroy's fondness for blades.

There were also numerous drug, burglary and home invasion raps he had managed to beat. He had once been charged with unlawful imprisonment of a fifteen-year-old girl.

I felt a notch better.

I took a cab to the Yucatan Taqueria on Mission Street and wolfed three fish tacos washed down with a Pacifico beer. Brimming with optimism I headed for the Lone Palm.

Nina was working a crowded bar. I paused at the entrance to watch her take orders, mix drinks, ring up cash, rinse glasses, replenish supplies, and charm the patrons. In between she changed CD's. I knew she'd burned it herself. James Brown was having a funky good time and the crowd responded. Nina should have her own joint, I thought. She's a natural.

When she caught sight of me her welcome smile crumbled. I eased over to the end of the bar, Nina watching me all the way.

"No biggie," I said before she could ask. "Accident. I'll explain later."

She moved off and returned with a double tequila.

"Go easy tonight, Max. I want you lucid."

It was difficult to pace myself and I made a note to go on the wagon. I went outside for a cigarette and took my time coming back. Two very carefully nursed drinks later I saw Nina start to close the register.

Shortly after midnight, Nina bought the remaining five customers a round and told them she was shutting down early so the plumbers could come in and clear the pipes. Everyone seemed to buy it and Nina locked the door after them.

She poured herself a Patron and lit a cigarette.

"What's going down, Max?"

"I have a line on this Dave Honda."

She lifted her hand. "Back up. You look like a damned gang-banger. Your head's shaved, your face has combat wounds and I didn't even recognize you at first."

I got the distinct impression Nina was pissed.

Without getting too dramatic I explained how I decided to go underground to locate Carla and incurred the wrath of the Vandals. I omitted the part about killing Leroy.

Nina listened gravely. "Some woman called earlier and left a message on my cell.

Said she had information on Carla. She saw one of the fliers you left," she added, something new in her voice. Respect.

Her voice lowered. "I'm so sorry you got hurt because of me."

I shrugged, manly to the last.

She leaned close and I caught a clean apple scent. "Wanna walk me home?"

Nina shared a large flat with two roommates. Hers was a comfortable room with high ceilings that contained a double bed, a Chinese lacquered bureau, and two art posters; one by Degas, the other by Larry Rivers. There was also a small photo of Betty Page in bondage.

We stood in awkward silence. Then she said, "I'll light some candles."

The soft flickering light accentuated Nina's shadowy grace. She sat on the bed and motioned me to join her. I held her gently when we kissed, as if holding an exquisite Faberge egg. She moaned softly and pulled me down beside her.

We were swept by a shared vision. This night was all we had and we would cherish every nanosecond. What seemed like hours passed before we eased apart and breathed separately.

It went far beyond sex. And it was the nastiest kind of sex. We made love.

In the exhausted quiet, Nina asked me, "Did anything else happen last night?"

"What gave you that idea?"

She got up on one elbow and looked at me. Deep.

"I don't know. It's not just the radical haircut. You just seem different. Sadder maybe."

How about guilty and scared. Killing someone carries its own special gravitas.

"I need to borrow your car tomorrow. Going up north again."

"I'm going with you."

Before I could argue she snuggled against my shoulder and closed her eyes.

Chapter 12

Fifteen minutes outside of town were hills crisscrossed with rich dairy farms and secluded country estates that posed as farms by housing the requisite number of cows or goats. Whatever qualified for the tax deduction.

One of these estates served as David's special hideaway. He liked to ride his motorcycle up along the narrow roads at night. The darkness was total, enabling him to see the starry ribbons overhead.

Starry ribbons, he'd have to put that in a poem David thought. He'd make a note of it when he reached the house.

David considered himself a romantic, a throwback to a more sophisticated era. Certainly he had little in common with the primitives he was forced to deal with. Even if the barbarians had satisfied his deepest needs. His groin throbbed against the growling machine when he thought of the harem that awaited him.

He enjoyed the silence, keeping his throttle down to a throaty roll as he passed a large dairy farm and approached a gate. The periodic gates couldn't really stop committed trespassers but they were a deterrent to tourists and teens looking for a place to party.

Of course, David had the code. It came with the territory. He turned his motor off and drank in the stillness. Up here he was king of all he surveyed. Complete with ladies in waiting. Amused by his little joke he punched the keys then stared at the glittering sky as the gate yawned open.

There were two more gates before he reached his turnoff. David rolled slowly up the narrow road, anticipating his arrival.

David didn't really need to work but his business offered special perks. For one, he had full use of the guest house. For another the owners were rarely there. They paid him well to oversee the estate in their absence.

And, most importantly, it enabled him to keep his dark hobby secret.

Two electric gates later David turned off the narrow two-lane onto a dirt road that seemingly led to a tangle of trees and shrubs. In fact, the road emerged onto a terraced clearing.

A low house sat at the edge of the clearing facing the thick grove. While the house seemed modest, closer inspection would reveal amenities like a pool heated by solar panels, sauna, steam, spectacular views everywhere, and an elevator to a lower-level office, guest facility and screening room.

David shut down the motor, coasting blind along the gravel path that led to the front door. He knew the way well. His crunching footsteps were comforting in the quiet as was the familiarity of the interior. The décor was rustic but every piece was first-rate.

He paused to hang up his leather jacket then veered into the small bathroom behind the kitchen to wash off the road dust. Then he went into the dining room and poured himself a large scotch. Holding his drink he went directly into the large library and moved through the darkened room to his black leather throne.

David took a long swallow.

The alcohol set fire to his empty stomach and sent the fumes rushing to his brain. He turned on the desk lamp.

There they were, as he had left them, posed just the way he liked.

The first two were bound to their chairs, the third to a hook in the ceiling beam.

However, the other three were more domesticated. One naked with a goblet of wine, the next brazen with a red vibrator and the last innocent and frightened... like the one he had to put down.

The memory amplified his urges. He had intended to savor the moment but his fingers were already fumbling with his zipper. Tongue darting snakelike through his parted lips he frantically began to masturbate.

Chapter 13

"Time, what is time? The Swiss manufacture it, the French hoard it, the Italians squander it, the Americans say it is money, the Hindus say it doesn't exist... I say time is a crook."
Peter Lorre, Beat the Devil

"Why do you like me, Max?" Nina asked on the drive north to Petaluma.

Women.

"Why do you like me?" I countered, stalling.

"Chemistry."

"With me it's physics."

"Physics?"

"Einstein's theory of inevitability."

She chuckled. "Which means?"

"When I saw you I knew something was there."

"Chemistry."

"*Ass*-trophysics."

A second later she got it. "Clever but corny Max."

"I'm all about corny."

"I noticed. What's with these clothes?"

I had made a quick shopping run at North Face: khaki cargo pants, blue down vest, trail sneakers, baseball cap, orange shades, and—this was the convincer—a fanny pack.

The Vandals were looking for a biker.

I was a hiker.

"Confucius says, 'Nail that sticks out gets hammered.'"

Nina rolled her eyes at that but she seemed relaxed, lovers on an outing, until we neared Petaluma. The weather inside the car changed from sunny to overcast with storm warnings.

"I can't face mama," she said, voice strained.

"That's not why we're here," I reminded her. "You check the woman who called and I'll have a talk with this David Paul."

"How will I find you?"

Good question. I had a pre-paid cell which I would discard in a month. I gave Nina the number and she drove me to the address on David Alan Paul's DMV records.

As I opened the door to get out Nina put a hand on my shoulder.

"Please come with me to talk to this woman."

I understood. Playing cop was a tad heavy for an already stressed psyche.

"Sure," I said, easing back inside, "let's see what she's got."

The woman's name was Helga and she was night bartender at the Buckhorn on weekends. She lived in an apartment complex not far from the bar. Helga was polite, even snatching a bunch of clothes from the couch when she showed us in.

We accepted her offer of tea and when she finally settled down Helga began telling me about the night she saw Carla.

"The girl on the poster was with this rock group," Helga said, ignoring Nina. "I'm sure that was her with those brats." She gave me an encouraging smile.

Helga was plump with ambitions. She rouged her milky cheeks and wore her jeans low, exposing a roll of baby fat. I tried my best to stay neutral but it wasn't my day.

"These young girls, 'round here, they're all trash," she said confidentially. "Prancin' around in their nose rings and butt tattoos. They wouldn't know how to be a real woman."

Helga's wink suggested she knew how, alright. She was a trucker's dream with generous breasts filling out an abbreviated pink sweatshirt, thinning peroxide hair and big red lips.

I nodded, my mind on something else. "Was Carla with any other girls?"

"Sure. Of course. They're always hangin' onto these rock groups play at the Mystic. This bunch even comes from around here."

"What bunch is that?"

"You know, those rockers. They were playin' at the Mystic that night. I'm positive 'cause I recognized one of them...Ted, or something like that."

"And he was with Carla?" Nina asked abruptly.

Helga seemed startled by the question. As if she'd forgotten Nina was in the room. Her eyes narrowed. "There was a bunch of them, like I said. These local musicians and maybe four girls."

I had an idea.

"Well, thank you Helga," I said, glancing at Nina, "you've been very helpful. If you think of anything please call."

Nina seemed confused but got up when I did.

Helga gave me a big, wet smile. "Come over for a real drink some time. I'm on Friday through Sunday."

Real woman, real drink, real pistol.

"Why the rush?" Nina said, outside.

"Hunch. Where did we meet that skinny girlfriend, Tami?"

"The Starbuck's at the Promenade. Why?"

"We're going there for coffee."

"You go, Max, I need to look in on mama. Anyway you're much better at this."

The Promenade was within walking distance. It was a nice walk.

Along the way Nina asked, "Shouldn't we go to the police with this?"

"Yes. But later. Ask for a cop named Lowell."

"Max?"

"Yeah?"

"Thanks for all this."

That's when she kissed me.

"You're just worried about Helga," I said when I finally recovered my breath.

She half-smiled. "I'm worried about Carla."

As we neared the Promenade, we parted company. Nina went off to comfort Carla's distraught mother while I entered the mini-mall and headed for my mini stake-out at Starbuck's.

Do you want room for cream? The new existential question. I found a good table with a view of both the mall and the street opposite. First thing I noticed were the three Harleys parked there.

The music was good, REM followed by Coldplay, followed by the Stones. I nursed my coffee, got a refill, read the local paper, saw nothing in the police blotter about Carla, checked the street, the mall; basic surveillance is boring.

A third coffee was out of the question but the sandwiches looked fresh. I kept watching the kids hanging about, boys with their studied street cred moves, pants dragging off their ass; hostile, heavyset girls with their lower back tramp stamps; all of them waiting for something to make them feel alive. Having met the Vandals I wondered what else was hiding in this cozy suburb.

I kept close tabs on the bikes but the owners were elsewhere. My fingers were on the cell in my pocket, ready to call Nina, when I spotted Tami. If possible she was thinner than the last time I saw her. Her body's hard angles communicated a combination of anger, sex and anger. Abandon all hope ye who enter.

The caffeine had me primed so I watched anxiously as Tami strolled in my direction. I calmed down the moment she entered. Tami was in my house now.

She ordered something complicated, one pierced ear glued to her cell while her free hand stroked her neck. I waited, listening to Clapton, one eye on the bikes parked across the street.

Tami didn't recognize my new persona.

Still on her cell when I arrived she looked up suddenly nostrils flared as if overcome by a noxious odor.

"Tami. Nice to see you again. Mind if I sit?"

She peered at me then it dawned. She folded her phone and sat back.

"What?"

I shrugged. "Still looking for your friend Carla."

"So?"

If nothing else Tami was concise. "So this person told me Carla was at the Buckhorn Bar with a rock musician called Ted. Said he lived around here."

Tami snorted derisively. "They mean Todd. Yeah, Todd. Carla had a thing for him."

"Was he playing at the Mystic?"

"Right. We were all supposed to go backstage after the band's show."

"What band is that exactly?"

"They're, uh, called Nose Job. What happened to your face?"

Tami was rapidly retreating into defensive mode. But I had an ace up my hiking shorts. Maybe. Actually I was bluffing.

"Anyway this person said you were at the Buckhorn with Carla."

The pierced lips clamped shut. Limbs tensed, she glared at me with feverish brown eyes. Then she relaxed and her familiar sneer returned.

"Well, yeah. I did drop by the Buckhorn. But only for a minute. I don't even remember if Carla was there or not."

"Do you even care she's missing?"

I couldn't help it. The words came out by themselves. Interview over.

"Fuck you!"

Tami paused to glare hate at me before she stormed out. In that moment I clearly saw her eyes were distended, overly bright. Her gaunt features looked greasy as if she'd been

up too long and a swarm of tiny red pimples decorated her
scrawny arms.

I watched her hurry away. She crossed the street and headed
directly to the shop where the Harleys were parked. Obviously
a local biker shop. Some Sherlock.

I realized I'd better vanish before Tami's biker pals came
out looking for me. I left the mall by way of the narrow street
entrance and headed for what seemed to be a main drag in
search of sanctuary. I found Graziano's restaurant and bar,
a cool, dark refuge from the heat outside. I ordered a Sierra
Nevada and gathered my thoughts.

Tami had lied about the last time she saw Carla. She also
had a drug problem. Most likely meth. And she reported to her
biker friends.

I considered calling Nina over to get us the hell out of
Dodge but I still had someone to see. The bartender informed
me that David Alan Paul's address was within walking distance.

To avoid beer breath I lit a cigarette and made my way
briskly, ever alert for any loud motors. Once or twice the sound
of a lawnmower made me twitch.

David Paul lived in a two story Queen Anne house set back
from the street. Its gloomy turrets and vaulted windows were
partially obscured by two old trees that faced each other, leafy
branches arching over the entrance.

I paused to call Nina and give her the address. I didn't
want to be out in public any more that necessary. By now,
Tami's friends would be combing the streets for me. I hoped
David Paul was at home, if only to duck out of sight until
Nina arrived.

The blue-haired lady who answered was anything but old
or fragile despite her advanced years. She stood straight as a dry
wood rail and drilled into me with diamond-sharp eyes. I felt
like a kid caught stealing cookies.

"Good afternoon, ma'am. I'm here to see David."

"About what, young man?"

I grabbed the nearest straw. "It's concerning his motorcycle. I understand it's for sale."

She studied me suspiciously. "I certainly hope so. I've been telling him to get rid of the noisy thing."

She shut the door in my face. On the off chance it might open again I rummaged through my pockets for Carla's flyer.

I had almost given up hope when the door reopened. The man standing there was a pale imitation of his mother. His grey eyes were unfocused, empty as mirrors. About forty, he was a soft-looking dude with cropped. steely hair. He looked at me then back inside as if being prompted.

"Look, my bike's not for sale. I don't know how you..."

I handed him the flyer. "Actually we were told you gave Carla Fuente a ride on your Honda last Saturday night." The "we" made it sound official.

I watched him closely as he studied the flyer. David Paul didn't blink. Calm as a clam.

Until his mother called from inside the house, "Why don't you show it to him? Out back."

The old woman's voice cracked his composure. He blinked rapidly and took a deep breath. "I'll handle this, mother."

"I'd like very much to see your motorcycle," I said loud enough for her to hear. "Honda Nighthawk isn't it?"

He shot me a glance of pure malice. "Yes. Alright. But I told you, it's not for sale."

He led me around the side to the house then turned and stared me down, grey eyes glinting like a harried fox. "What do you want?"

"I want to find Carla Fuente. You were one of the last to see her."

He heaved a long sigh. "Okay, I gave her a lift from Rinner's. She couldn't get a cab."

"Where did you take her?"

He shrugged as if it was obvious. "I dropped her near Walnut Park close to the Buckhorn."

"Then what?"

"Then nothing. She walked over to the Buckhorn and I rolled home."

"Can you prove that?"

He stiffened and I saw reflections of his mother.

"Can you prove I didn't?"

Had me there. But my gut told me David Paul was wrong.

I backed out gracefully before he asked for my ID. When I reached the sidewalk Nina was waiting.

"Tell you on the way. Can we go by way of Walnut Park?"

As Nina drove past the placid square I saw the Buckhorn Bar up ahead and the tumblers suddenly clicked into place

"Max, if you don't tell me what's up I'm going to stop right here."

"No. Not here. Tami set the dogs on me."

"What dogs, Max?" Nina sounded impatient.

"Okay, let's say hogs. Of the biker variety. Tami ran to see them right after I busted her telling a big lie."

"She lied?"

"Tami was with Carla at the Buckhorn."

"What about this Ted?"

"His name is Todd. He was there as well. I also spoke to David Paul."

"And?"

"He confirms Carla went to the Buckhorn from Rinner's."

"You believe him?"

"Story checks so far."

As we entered the freeway south to San Francisco, I started to relax. We had come away unscathed with some answers. Next on my hit list would be this Todd.

"Shit."

Bright head beams flooded the car. In the rear view I saw revolving red and blue lights accompanied by the low whine of a siren.

"Shit," Nina said again, "this isn't right."

I agreed. Nina was a cautious driver.

Then I looked back. "Oh shit, it's him?"

"Who?"

A bull-necked police officer was coming up slowly on the driver's side, hand on his weapon. He looked serious.

He also looked familiar.

As he drew the Glock from his holster I remembered. It was our friendly desk sergeant, Verona.

Chapter 14

David was a good actor. He had to be to live with his bitch of a mother.

But the guy who showed up at his door caught him completely unaware with his bullshit about buying the Nighthawk.

Didn't get a name, check his ID, David thought, belly churning.

"David."

Her voice triggered a spasm of nausea as always.

"Yes, mother?"

"I want you to sell that dreadful machine as soon as possible."

"Not yet, mother. I need it for business."

"Yes, business," she sniffed, appearing in the doorway like a wraith, "a business with only one client."

"I'm leaving now, mother, can I get you anything?"

"Cigarettes."

"You know what Dr. Burnett said."

"I've outlived two doctors. Now will you do as I ask?"

"Of course, mother."

Anything to hasten your fucking demise.

It was a short, refreshing ride to Rinner's. By the time he arrived the nausea had subsided but the fear lingered. How in hell had this guy connected him to the girl? Who was he?"

Lowering the kickstand he looked across the lot and saw the others. Immediately his fears ebbed. The guy was fishing. How could he possibly know? He felt stronger in the company of his comrades, his fellow bikers.

Confidence restored he went into the diner for his usual BLT, apple pie, and coffee.

Nothing to be afraid of, he reminded himself. There was no way anyone could find out. He was protected. Big time.

Over his second cup he made plans. He would ride up to his hideaway in the hills and have a long visit with his harem.

Chapter 15

"I don't have a drug problem, I have a police problem."

Keith Richards

A hostile cop with a drawn gun is a California motorist's worst nightmare.

There are no misdemeanors in California. We are all moving violations, felons, no vote, no rights, three strikes, it's over. Add the fact that West Coast cops have a tendency to shoot unarmed citizens with amazing regularity and you have real cause for alarm.

And we knew Verona had a hard-on for us. At least I knew. Nina was dutifully fumbling for her license.

"Hands where I can see 'em.'

Jesus, a routine traffic stop and here was Verona in full SWAT mode.

We both surrendered.

Verona made a rolling gesture with his free hand.

"Window," I prompted.

"Damnit, Max, I know."

Now everybody hated me. Especially Sergeant Verona. Ignoring Nina he sighted on me across the wheel.

"Step out of the car."

I started for the handle until,

"Right there, fella! Hands where I can see 'em."

I froze, slowly lifted my hands.

"Okay, get out slow, put both hands on top of the car."

When I was settled he gestured at Nina with the gun.

"You, outside."

"Shit," Nina muttered. It was redundant.

"Hands on the roof," Verona said in a practiced drawl.

I knew what was coming. I had seen it in the NYPD and the DEA. Sergeant Verona was about to frame us or kill us. I guessed the former considering the public venue. But even if I was wrong Verona would slide scot free and I'd be another dead dealer. Max LeBlue never existed.

"Come around this way," Verona coaxed.

"What's wrong officer?" I said calmly. "We spoke to you the other..."

"Quiet! Come around slowly..."

"Do you want to see my license?" I persisted. Which was absurd since I hadn't been driving.

Then I caught it. Verona was pulling something out of his pocket. It looked like a baggie full of white powder. Classic plant. Now I would be in the system and fucked.

"Hands on the roof of the car."

As I moved closer a surprised look flashed across his face followed by rage. I thought he was about to gun me down right there.

A second later another set of revolving lights eased behind the car and I saw Verona shove the baggie back into his pocket. We all watched a tall police officer cautiously exit his vehicle and walk toward Verona.

"Need some assistance there, Walter?"

"Under control, Bob." His raspy snarl was almost civil. "Just about to toss the vehicle."

The tall man moved into the light. It was Lowell. The officer who posted the report Verona had lost.

"Well, since you got it secured out here I'll check the car."

Verona was having trouble faking gratitude. "Yeah, sure, do it," he said.

Lowell took his time, like he really wanted to find something. He even looked underneath the chassis. But to his credit he played by the rules.

"Nothing, Walter," he said finally. "Who's the driver?"

Verona jerked his head at Nina, his Glock down an inch. "Run her ticket?" Lowell asked.

"Just about to."

After you planted the dope, I thought. In the real world, you run the ID *then* search the vehicle if necessary.

"May we see your license, ma'am?" Lowell said affably. He had the easy authority of a quarterback. Charming, humble, rugged.

At this point Verona's raised Glock seemed ridiculous, even to him. Neck swelling like a pink bullfrog he lowered his weapon. We waited, hands on the car, while Lowell put Nina's ID through the computer.

"No priors," he reported, handing Nina her license.

"She's got one now," Verona said, voice flat. "She ran a stop sign back there."

I heard Nina's sharp intake of breath and braced for the worst. To my complete relief, she cooled it. My hero. A ticket was the least of all possible evils.

Lowell waited, rugged features impassive while Verona wrote us up.

"Want to meet me for beer at Graziano's?" he asked as we got back inside the car. He wasn't talking to us.

Verona shook his head. "I'm on my way home."

But he took time out to hold us hostage as part of his civic duty. Admirable.

"What's happening, Max?" Nina said when we reached the wide, well-lit lanes of Novato. Until then we'd both been quiet, listening to jazz and nursing our little trauma.

"We are in deep shit. Verona never filed your report, Tami lied about Carla and now we have the thugs *and* the cops on our ass."

"What about the second cop, Lowell?"

"He seems honest. But what about Carla?"

"I don't follow."

"She's been missing over a week. Not only did Verona lose Carla's report, he was about to plant drugs in the car."

"No, really? I didn't see..."

"Trust me, I did. Then there's the biker gang that attacked me." I left out the part about the killing.

"So what's your point, Max?"

"I believe Carla's been kidnapped."

"That's crazy. Her family can't afford ransom."

"The good news... I'm sure she's still alive."

"Bad news?"

"Some dangerous people seem to have a strong interest in Carla's staying disappeared."

I thought about Verona's attempted bust... Lowell showing up at the right time. As William Burroughs liked to say, there's no such thing as coincidence.

Then, too, there was David Paul and Todd the rocker. Not to mention Tami's connection to the Vandals. All those loose ends sizzling like snapped power lines.

Touch the wrong one, you're fried, Max.

+   +   +

The Golden Gate was fogged over that night, its rust-red pylons floating over billowy grey mist. Nina drove slowly, KPOO had switched to blues and Big Mama Thornton was doing the dirty version of *Hound Dog*.

Jimmy Shu's healing power had worn off, leaving me with a dull ache on one side of my skull. I was stiff, hungry and badly in need of sleep. For all those reasons I asked Nina to drop me in North Beach.

At Yuet Lee's restaurant I ate salt and pepper shrimp washed down with Heineken beer under bilious fluorescent lights that turned everyone's skin sickly green. For some reason the place reminded me of Kerouac and his Chinatown dove poems. The fog, the light, the third beer.

My alarm sounded at five-thirty a.m. and I jumped onto the computer. An hour later I had good intel on David and Todd. David Paul ran a property management firm which at the moment managed one property—a small goat farm outside Petaluma.

Todd Fletcher, lead singer of Nose Job, had been raised in Petaluma. The photo showed a sullen young man with big hair sitting in a barber chair holding a straight razor in one hand and the barber's neck in the other. The album was titled *Just A Trim*.

Checking MySpace, I learned the barber was actually the drummer who was named Shank. Nose Job had just signed with a major label and their new album was due to drop in November. I also learned Todd had 9,737 friends.

I was hoping for one.

Further inquiry led me to Todd's home, or more accurately, his parent's house. For all I knew Todd was on a bus somewhere in Georgia.

I rolled onto the floor and stretched out my significant kinks, aches and bruises. Then in a burst of inspiration put on my shorts and Sauconys and jogged over to the Ferry Building. It was still early and with light traffic it took less than forty minutes.

The clock tower overlooking the Embarcadero housed an array of gourmet shops that sold everything from farm fresh fruit and vegetables to cheese, wine, organic meats, fish, Asian treats, oysters, pastries and hand made chocolate. At that hour everyone was opening for business and there was a certain concentration of purpose.

I picked up a quart of freshly squeezed orange juice, two newly-baked breakfast buns and blissfully sailed through the morning mist to Larkspur Landing.

Ferry boats are as Zen as arrows.

A cab deposited me a block away from my Marin hideaway. There was a paper bag on my doorstep. Inside was a tube of arnica and a note that said, "come over for lunch."

Organic Phil was an early riser.

A nap, a long shower and I felt ready for lunch.

"You look better," Phil said, ushering me inside the house. The front area was an immense kitchen where Organic Phil ruled. I sat at the counter and watched him slice and dice tomatoes, kale, carrots, onions, mangoes, papaya, romaine, and various herbs—building one of his hundred dollar salads.

"So what's going on in your life. Still acting?"

"That's over. But I met a lady. No big thing... few days a week." Nothing like romance to account for erratic behavior.

"That's fantastic." He set a heaping plate of salad in front of me. "When do I get to meet her?"

It was a trick question.

"You? Not a chance," Phil wouldn't reveal his age but he was a superbly conditioned geezer.

He gave me a hound dog grin. "Of course. Once I cook my pasta for them it's all over."

I had no doubt. Phil was the poster boy for eternal life in Marin County.

He turned to a waiting blender packed with nuts, berries, and flax seed. He added soy milk and turned it on full blast.

"I went for a total check up and medical scan the other day," he said, above the mechanical whine.

"Yeah, and?"

With a flourish he turned off the blender and poured me a large glass of beige liquid.

"And the doctor said I have the cleanest colon he's ever seen."

Much more information than I needed. But Phil is a rare human on this violent planet so I looked impressed and drank up.

"Look, Phil, I hate to eat and run but I could use a ride to Book Passage."

"Fine. Just give me six minutes."

Exactly six minutes later Phil had cleaned up and was ready to go.

"So, tell me more about this girl," he said as we drove to the small mall that housed one of my favorite haunts.

"She's a dancer, she tends bar at a place in the city."

He shook his head. "Bars are toxic environments."

Two miles from the pristine environs of Ross, Kentfield, and Mill Valley—just over the Richmond Bridge—was a complex of oil refineries pumping god-knows-what into the bay. The area has the highest incidence of breast cancer in the country. Talk about toxic.

"It's a short life, Phil, even if you live to be a hundred."

"Where's your car?"

"Being repaired. I'll call the garage after I buy some magazines."

"Get me a copy of Auto Trends."

Book Passage was a cover. I didn't want Phil to know where Len's shop was located. Old habits. On the other hand all bookstores are an oasis, especially those with a café.

I bought a copy of Hunter S. Thompson's book on the Hell's Angels and ordered a coffee.

For a peaceful half hour I immersed myself in gonzo biker culture. Then I got back on the clock. Before I left the store, I called Len.

Even so, he seemed surprised to see me arrive on foot. His usually impassive features swung from amused to suspicious. After all I had his custom BMW. And quite a prize it was.

He folded his arms as I neared.

I gave him a double thumbs-up. "Bike's okay. No worries."

Despite my enthusiasm the suspicion remained etched in Len's furrowed brow.

"Where's it at?"

"Back at my place. Man, it is a beast."

He softened a bit. "Your ride is ready."

We went into the garage to take a look. On the outside my invisible Mercury was the same. Inside things had changed. The leather dash had been remolded so the bulge beneath the wheel was undetectable.

"Put a radar scanner down there, along with the stash box," Len said. He reached under the dash and pressed a button. A panel slid open revealing a small screen that lit up automatically.

"The detectors are actually under the headlights. When a radar beam hits, the screen flashes red and you'll hear a high beep. That's your sign to slow down or take the nearest exit."

I nodded admiringly.

Then Len showed me how to pull out the volume control on the radio and turn it like a light switch. When I did a drawer the size of a book slid open. A baggie of thick green buds was inside.

"Compliments of the house," Len said.

I smiled, he didn't. Clearly Len wasn't sure about me or his bike.

"I also put in a new radio. FM4 here gets you the police scanner."

He handed me the keys and moved around to the passenger side.

The engine throbbed like big cats growl, low and ominous. Pulling out I felt a slight tug at the wheel but the car stuck tight to the road through three snug turns.

"Feels good but different," I said. "Balance maybe, or suspension."

"Little of both. I put a little extra weight underneath to compensate for your added power."

Radar, police scanner, stash panel, maxed out motor; I felt like Robert Mitchum in *Thunder Road*.

"You ever see *Thunder Road*?"

Len's stony expression relaxed a notch. "Only about a dozen times."

"This is an outlaw's dream."

He tapped the stash box "That fresh Humboldt bud in there makes you an outlaw."

True enough. Smoke a little weed and you're a criminal. Drink a pint of bourbon and you're a good old boy.

"Pull over, Max."

He sounded serious. I parked at the curb.

"Overhead light switch on the right—turn it on and off."

I did as instructed.

"Now the middle switch—turn it on and off."

When I did a square container the size of a dictionary dropped from the ceiling.

"That's brilliant," was all I could say.

It was enough for Len. "They might find the first stash," he said with a dash of pride, "but the main box takes figurin.'"

I had to agree. Mathematically the code was tougher than it seemed. Like everything it would buy me a little time, which is all we can ask on this planet.

Len looked at me. "I heard some dude on a custom BMW locked horns with some Vandals, blew up one of their bikes."

I nodded, didn't answer.

"You were wise to leave the bike. They're lookin' for anybody with a BMW. Lucky I had the other one behind closed doors."

"They came here, to your shop?"

Len game me a regretful smile. "Vandals rule out here. Every mechanic within two hundred miles is on their radar."

I didn't even try to deny it. "Sorry for putting you on the spot."

He leaned closer. "I hate those bastards, Max. I got respect for what you did."

"I'm just trying to find a missing girl."

That got his attention. Len sat up, eyes narrowed. "There's been talk that the Vandals are runnin' hookers."

"This girl isn't a hooker. She's not even a senior in high school."

"It's a brave new world, Max."

I couldn't answer. I just drove back to the shop.

"By the way, Max?"

"Yeah?"

"The ceiling stash only works if the motor's on."

"How much do I owe you?"

"Five grand."

I gave Len six . "The extra grand is for bike rental.'

Len nodded. "Long as you need it, bro."

I drove off with new purpose. The Vandals were actively on my case. I had to find out who took Carla and why. I needed to talk to Todd Fletcher and check out David Alan Paul's client.

I also needed a new pistol. My Beretta was hot, having been involved in a homicide.

One thing at a time.

I fetched the Beretta and stashed it in the ceiling compartment. I left the bud at home minus a joint which I secured in the dashboard panel. Then I headed for Petaluma and Todd.

Todd Fletcher's parents owned a rustic two-story house with a nice lawn and a picket fence that needed a whitewash. But the young man who came to the door was no Tom Sawyer.

He was tall, London thin, with long, straggly hair and red-rimmed purple eyes deep inside dark sockets. There was a newly-inked Sacred Heart tattoo on his chest and the ace of spades on his left wrist. He looked as if he'd just got out of bed.

"Todd Fletcher?"

He scratched his neck. "Yeah?"

"I'd like to ask you a few questions about Carla Fuente."

"What about her?"

"She's been missing since last Saturday."

He pouted as if this was the first time he had heard. "No shit."

Yeah, right. Small towns transmit gossip faster that the internet. I was developing an odd reaction or, more precisely, an aversion to Todd. It was more than his punk attitude.

In that respect he was just another mall rat. No, it went far deeper. Those youthful good looks concealed a long-festering evil. Something old and decadent moldered inside that photogenic skull.

"I saw Carla last Saturday," Todd said, "I went to the place where she works and invited her to the show."

He paused, expecting me to ask what show.

"Tami Kratchett said you were with Carla at the Buckhorn Bar that night."

That woke him up. The word *bitch* formed on his pouty lips but never came. He caught himself, gave me an exasperated smile and said, "Yesh, we were all there. Tami included."

"Where did you all go from the Buckhorn?"

Wrong question. I should have known better.

"I went to do my show at the Mystic." He paused and squinted at me playfully. "You a cop?"

"Just a family friend trying to find Carla."

"Well, look, family friend, I don't know where Carla went. Like I said, I was performing at the Mystic in front of a thousand witnesses."

Witnesses. Interesting choice of words. I wanted to push a few more of his buttons but Todd was revving into his aggressive mode; eyes hard, thin frame tensed, chin lifted. As in the martial arts. I backed off, leaving him off balance.

"Well, thanks for your time. Sorry I missed your show. Will your band be playing again soon?"

The question confused him. "Uh no, not until the album drops."

One or two steps down the path I turned. "Do you know anything about a gang called the Vandals?"

That caught him unaware and his reaction was classic. "What? No! Hey, look, you better leave or I'll call the cops."

Call the cops. Not bloody likely. I lifted my hands in mock surrender and walked to my car feeling I had come in contact with something unclean. Another pal of Carla's who didn't seem to care she was gone.

The drive did much to scale off the toxic residue of the encounter. In fact the next few hours were exhilarating. I drove south to the Richmond Bridge and slipped onto 80 for Sacramento, my old Sable purring all the way. The added center weight altered the steering, giving me more of a sense of control. Or out of control since there was a slight slide factor at speeds above ninety-eight.

It was early enough to beat the commuter traffic and once past Sacramento and into the mountain curves leading to Lake Tahoe I put the car through its paces. I wanted to learn how far I could push it—and how fast. The green ghost darted nicely at high speeds but it had a heavy skid on tight curves that took getting used to. I still didn't have the hang of it when I pulled into the parking lot of the Cal-Neva Casino.

One side of the casino is in California, the other side in Nevada. Frank Sinatra was married there. So was Dan Hicks. You could look it up, as Casey Stengel used to say.

I ordered a turkey club at the bar and checked my laptop while I ate, ignoring the constant babble of electronic sounds emitted by the slots.

There were any number of shops licensed to sell firearms on the Nevada side but—even better—there was a gun show nearby. When I arrived at the building that housed the event I saw a few motorcycles parked outside. I pulled down my baseball cap, doffed my shades and entered cautiously.

I looked like half the customers there. Americans are natural-born criminals. After a minimum of shopping around I made a deal for a fully loaded Sig Sauer 228 and two spare clips of hollow points. Which gave me forty rounds, you do the math. I also picked up a Colt .45 Defender which was selling as a collectible. Compact, reliable, accurate. All I needed was cash and a phony ID I had purchased at a Haight Ashbury head shop. The kind high school kids use to buy cigarettes and beer. Nobody checks IDs at a gun show—especially in Nevada.

On my way back I stopped at a Camping Emporium and General Store outside Truckee and bought extra rounds for the Colt, a Kevlar vest and a shoulder holster for the Sig. Shades of DeNiro in *Taxi Driver*. I also took the time to break down my hot Beretta and dump the parts separately.

Thanks to Len's expertise, my old Mercury zipped back to the Bay in about three hours and change. I kept the scanner and radar detector on, mindful of the hardware in the car. Never commit a misdemeanor on your way to committing a felony.

On impulse, I detoured over the Richmond Bridge and curled north to Petaluma. That's the problem with being armed. You start thinking with your gun. And go where angels fear to tread.

The town seemed shut down as I cruised the darkened streets. All the flyers I had posted around town were gone. The Vandals were efficient if nothing else. The Buckhorn Bar was open as was Rinner's. I made a reconnaissance pass around the diner and its huge parking lot but oddly enough there were no motorcycles or Vandals in sight. Or anyone else for that matter.

I took the Colt from the stash box and tucked it into my belt before going inside. Regine, my favorite, was off that night which was just as well since the place was empty.

The burger I ordered proved to be delicious, down home American diner cuisine with fries as crisp as Tommy Lee's cymbals. No wonder the Vandals liked the place. It was the biker version of The French Laundry.

After dinner I stepped outside to smoke the J I'd taken with me and after lighting up noticed an oddly familiar figure behind the dumpster. I took a twenty from my pocket and held it out. He hesitated, glassy blue eyes peering at me through a tangle of hair like a curious porcupine.

"You're the guy," he said breathlessly.

"What guy?"

"The guy they're looking for."

I wiggled the twenty. "Who's looking for me?"

"Vandals."

"Where is everybody?"

He snatched the bill from my fingers. "Molly's."

"What's Molly's?"

"Bar where they hang out. They're getting ready for the funeral tomorrow."

"Funeral?"

"Yes. One of them was shot. By chance would you have a drink or some other libation on your person, sir?"

I relit my joint, took two deep hits and passed, just as Snoop suggests.

My new pal took it eagerly and when it was gone he gave me a flawed smile.

"Excellent."

"Where's the funeral?"

He giggled. "Be here tomorrow at sunset and you can't miss it."

"Why sunset?"

"That's when the deceased liked to wake up."

I gave him another twenty and left him still giggling behind the dumpster. Good boo.

Driving back to my Corte Madera hideaway, I realized it was Leroy Underwood's funeral. The man I killed. My sobered thoughts circled back to Carla. Her disappearance went deeper than a kidnapping-slash-serial killer case. Too many people from Sergeant Walter Verona to Tami Kratchett were involved.

The more I thought the clearer it became that David Paul and Tami were the weakest links. Certainly I wouldn't get squat from Verona. And Todd was too wise to talk to me again. From what I'd observed, David Paul's vulnerable spot was his mother. As for Tami she didn't seem to care about anything but her own bony ass.

When I reached home I doused my headlights and drove past the house, checking the area for stalkers. Then I doubled back and parked behind Phil's garage.

Once inside my flat I poured myself a Laphroaig, which is one of the last of the 86 proof scotches. Some global conspiracy has lowered formerly revered spirits such as Glenlivet, Jack Daniels, Jameson, Chivas and many others to a pale 80 proof. So these days I found myself scouring labels to make sure my booze is uncut.

Reasonably relaxed, listening to Tupac's *All Eyes On Me* on FM I knew how he felt. I also knew I had to attend Leroy's funeral, like it or not. But if the guy behind the dumpster could recognize me I would need a better disguise than a baseball hat.

Chapter 16

"What is good? To crush your enemies, to see them driven before you, to hear the cries and lamentations of the women."
Arnold Schwarzenegger, Conan

It began as a typical Marin day: bright sunny morning, gas up the car, gym, jog, steam, lunch at Il Fornaio, nap. Civilized.

When I awoke an hour later I went into barbarian mode. I oiled my new Sig Sauer, reassembled it, slipped a 9mm in the spout and snapped the thirteen-round clip in place. I did the same for the Colt .45; oiled it, one in the chamber, seven in the clip. Then I drove to San Rafael for supplies.

There's a costume store on Fourth Street that caters to the little theater groups and independent filmmakers who abound in the area. There I picked up a black wig with matching Fu Manchu moustache. The saleslady assured me the moustache would stay fixed. I bought the glue, remover and a large red-striped sweatshirt straight out of Dr. Seuss. As I paid I spotted a black leather vest hanging nearby and added it to my new wardrobe.

Sunset came at six-fifty-three that evening. I fell out of my house at four-thirty wearing the red-striped sweatshirt over my Kevlar girdle, topped off by the black leather vest. Black jeans, black boots, long black hair, moustache, shades; I would blend in.

Sure I would.

The Sig Sauer and spare clips were tucked in the ceiling stash, the Colt along with a bag of Leroy's meth was under the dash. I was good to go.

K-Fog's commuter radio was heavy with classics including David Byrne assuring me this ain't no foolin' around. I was fully aware I was driving into something I couldn't handle with a howitzer, much less a Colt. I assured myself it was just recon, get a line on the players before it's too dark to tell.

My scalp was moist under the wig and began to itch. I checked the mirror to make sure my moustache was on tight as I hit the Petaluma Boulevard exit.

Rinner's truck stop was conveniently located right off the freeway. Passing slowly by I saw at least forty Harleys bunched near the diner. No sense going inside, I'd never get any service. Instead I parked about a hundred yards beyond the area at a main traffic light. The road from Rinner's ran one-way so any procession would have to pass by me. I regretted not bringing a camera. However, from long stake-out experience I had brought along water, energy drink, protein bar, trail mix and Krispy Kreme. Guess which went first.

While flicking the remnants of sugar glaze from my moustache became aware of a low electric rumble behind me. My first thought was an oncoming thunderstorm but I was mistaken.

The rumble escalated to a ground trembling roar and at precisely six-fifty-three my windows began to vibrate. The funeral procession was rolling my way. Instinctively I started the car and put it in gear as the roar swelled to tornado proportions.

Forget cameras. I gripped the wheel tight as a phalanx of bikers rode past like heavy metal centurions, jackets blazoned with their colors. They kept coming and coming and coming. Two bikers on either side halted cross traffic enabling the hordes to pass undisturbed. Nobody seemed to complain about the delay.

Eleven minutes later the last row of Vandals was joined by the road guards. I tried to slip out after them but the light turned red. An impatient driver blocked the intersection delaying me further.

It wasn't difficult to catch up. Keeping a prudent distance I followed them to a small gated cemetery a few miles outside of town. It seemed like a nice peaceful place. Even the booming engines were muted by its thick trees and newly-mowed grass lawns.

Cemeteries are easy to enter but hard to leave. I left the car parked outside the gates, grill pointed toward the main road, and hoofed it to the ceremony. Along the way I noticed a similarity of theme on the headstones and monuments. Lots of wheels, winged Harleys even one of those skulls biting a dagger. The whole damned bone yard was reserved for bikers.

Just as well I left the car.

The narrow roads, grassy hillside and all available spaces between graves were clogged with Harley Davidsons. I climbed the low hill and paused at the crest.

It could have been a Sicilian Mafia funeral with horse-drawn glass carriage, priest, ornate wreaths and professional mourners. Except in this parallel universe the ceremony was being conducted by a tall, bearded minister with flowing brown hair not unlike depictions of JC, backed by four female gospel singers. Dressed in a white cassock with a large glitter-trim gold cross embroidered on the front, the minister delivered an energetic eulogy

The excessive flower arrangements ranged from red rose Harleys with blue and white wheels to a floral portrait of the deceased. There was even one in the shape of an AK-47. A pair of white rose skulls with flaming orange hair and blue knives in teeth bookended the large grave. Later, I saw why it was so large.

The minister was quite good, extolling Leroy as a free-souled adventurer in America's pioneer tradition, loyal friend, great husband to four wives and a knight of the open road.

With that the gospel singers broke out with Sweet Chariot while Leroy's Harley was lowered into the grave.

Leroy's coffin followed accompanied by the strains of *Amazing Grace* followed by *Midnight Train To Georgia* which I learned later was Leroy's favorite.

There was a multitude of mourners, three, maybe four hundred. Most of them seem to come from the same parents. Burly and barrel-chested like offensive linemen or WWF bad boys, three-quarters sported facial hair, half wore shades and one hundred percent were heavily tattooed. But, what the hell, so were most cheerleaders these days.

Many in the ranks had brought their own sacraments and were passing pints and beer cans during the proceeding. I edged closer trying to get a fix on who was who.

The minister had taken a seat beside a bereaved widow dressed in black spike heels, long black leather coat and dark glasses. On the other flank sat a tall, lean man with long white hair and silver-blue eyes like a wolf. Dressed in black leather pants, engineer boots and black jacket he had an aura of lethal authority.

He sat back, emotionally removed, those predator eyes constantly scanning. Even from where I stood I could see them flash on me as if taking a photograph, Yes, he was alpha wolf and behind him were three very big, very stoic betas.

Okay fine, now you know, I told myself, so what? The only crime I could charge them with was tearing down my flyers. And even if I had smoking gun evidence the Vandals kidnapped Carla, I couldn't take on four hundred maniac barbarians. Not to mention the fact that I was the reason they were gathered there.

Even with all this, I wasn't smart enough to call it a funeral. Oh no, I needed that adrenaline rush that comes from doing something stupid and dangerous. That was my real addiction. But I kept trying to convince myself that I needed more if I hoped to find Carla.

My contact behind Rinner's dumpster had mentioned a place called Molly's where the pre-event rituals had been observed. It took a bit of searching but I finally arrived at a rickety roadhouse with a large parking lot and a single spotlight illuminating the name *Molly* in red gothic above the entrance.

Inside it looked hastily reconstructed after a hurricane. Stacks of dirty glasses occupied one end of the bar and two hefty bartenders were working their way down the other, marrying bottles, hefting beer barrels, that kind of thing. Two equally hefty waitresses distributed pitchers of beer onto the stained tables that filled the surprisingly large room. A circular clearing at one side of the room probably served as a dance floor.

I went to the bar, put down a twenty and ordered a double Herradura.

The bartender shook his head. "Private party."

"I'm a friend of Leroy's." I said.

He pushed the twenty back. "Leroy is buyin.'"

I nodded solemnly and carried my drink to a far table next to the pool room. Settling down, I waited for the mourners to arrive. I left the tequila untouched but poured a short beer after carefully wiping my glass. A half-hour later I learned that glasses are for effete sissies. Real men drink straight from the pitcher.

The place filled rapidly after my arrival and within twenty minutes it was a scene from The Vikings where drunken brutes hurl axes at fair maidens to chop off their braids. Loud chaos accompanied by Motorhead, Metallica, and who could hear in that instant mosh pit writhing with wide, hairy bodies in leather. There were babes on hand, mostly with big boobs and pastel halters, more raucous than the men if possible. Dante would have drawn a new circle.

I managed to stay anonymous in my corner table, the tequila untouched in front of me, sipping my beer glass when no one was looking. But it couldn't last. Three good old boys plunked themselves down. One of them smiled, two did not. One of the non-smilers grabbed the beer pitcher and began

chugging it down, the other glowered at me. He was bald
with a thick black swastika inked on his right arm and Conan
on the left.

"Fuck you doin' here?" He said.

"I'm a friend of Leroy's up from San Bernardino."

My response seemed to hit a clinker. Now none of them
were smiling.

Then I remembered Hunter Thompson's treatise on the
Hell's Angels. It wasn't pronounced San Bernardino dummy.

"Say what?" Conan said, a mean edge to his tone.

"San Berdoo—me and Leroy are homeboys."

"How'd you hear?" The other non-smiler asked. His
Van Dyke and slick black hair gave him a gothic Dracula
kind of look.

"I was in Cisco getting my bike fixed. Guy comes in tells
my mechanic Leroy Underwood's dead. I know the name, asked
the guy what happened. He says he don't know. I say I want to
pay my respects and here I am. Somethin' wrong with that?"

It could have tipped either way. I had the Sig in my belt
and the Colt in my boot but righteous indignation was my
best weapon.

It worked. The boys lightened up and backed off.

"Let's get some tequila over here," Dracula said, waving at
a waitress.

When she came over I handed her a Franklin. "Bottle of
Herradura."

"Leroy's..."

"I know Leroy's buyin' and I know he would want you to
have this."

She accepted gracefully and my new compatriots grunted
approval. One foot in the door.

Conan gestured at the untouched glass. "You're
not drinkin?"

I lifted my double. "To Leroy, One tough mother."

It seemed to hit the right note. Of course I was speaking from experience.

The problem with drinking with macho psychos is that you're on a moment-to-moment basis. Everything is great, best of buddies, then one bad joke, one misspeak and you're drinking a bullet. So I sat back quiet behind my moustache and shades.

The Smiler was young, maybe twenty-five, with cherubic features and blond curly hair adorning an oversized head set on a neck that began at his ears and ended at his shoulders. His arms were covered by a black sweatshirt, thick wrist circled by a silver chain.

"Let's do some lines for Leroy," he suggested.

I was in for a dicey time. From painful experience working undercover I knew better than to dance around. Any sign of reluctance and I'd be dead meat. The only way out was to shut up and do the damn line.

Smiley dumped a paltry mound of white powder on the table and cut four thin lines with his switchblade.

"There's been a fuckin' drought," he said.

"Dry two days," Conan testified.

Interesting. I might have interrupted some local supply route.

Dracula handed me a short straw. I didn't hesitate, snorting the nearest line with gusto. Big mistake.

It wasn't blow but some variation of scouring powder. It burned my nose severely, coating my membranes with a sulphuric, sandy substance.

Smiler nodded apologetically. "It's shit but that's all there is."

He wasn't talking about cocaine. He was talking about speed, low grade meth to be specific. Up all night followed by a hellish crash I thought, belly churning at the prospect.

My nose was seared and my sinuses pounded at my brain. In desperation I grabbed the tequila bottle and took a long swig. My compatriots nodded approval. I was in.

Surprisingly the tequila offset the pain and kick-started whatever meth was in the mix. Within minutes I was confident, fearless, up for any challenge. I scanned the noisy room and spotted the alpha wolf holding court at a large table surrounded by big glaring betas.

Then I looked closer.

Seated beside Alpha Wolf was his bull-necked counterpart—Sergeant Verona of the Petaluma P.D.

Chapter 17

"Don't look back, somethin' may be gainin' on you."
Satchel Paige

Talk about a smoking gun. Top cop huddles with gang leader. Front page, maybe even CNN. And there I sat with no way to verify. Until my revved up brain reminded me.

Camera phone, stupid.

It would take some doing. The room seethed like a Bruegel canvas, everybody loud and sweaty and drunk and drugged, bumping into everybody else, lurching in time to the taunting screech of Axl Rose against Slash's lunatic guitar. Welcome to the jungle, baby.

"Big Bug would've liked this," Smiley said.

My attention was on the royal table so I didn't ask who Big Bug was, which is just as well.

"Leroy liked to party hard," Dracula agreed, clearing things up.

Leroy's widow was seated at the royal table staring straight ahead while Verona kept jawing at Alpha Wolf. But even through the rough confusion of bodies staggering around the table Alpha Wolf's eyes were alert, clocking anything that came too close and everything on the way. It would be difficult to get past those silver lasers for a photo op. I'd have to be standing about two feet away to get any kind of shot. What could I say? I needed a picture for my memory book? Right, feed his body parts to the pigs.

But the speed convinced me it could be done.

"Drink up, bud," Conan said, extending the bottle.

I drank. The tequila fired up the meth like nitrous. I was a road runner on a stealth mission. Get close to the big table, take some pictures and split before they realize what happened.

First Problem: considering the noise level, cell phone use would arouse suspicion.

I zoomed past that obstacle with one word: text.

Second Problem: my camera phone skills were minimal.

Easy solution, I broke out my cell and started practicing right there at the table. My new pals got into it, mugging for the tiny screen.

I glanced back in time to see the widow slowly slide down and disappear beneath the royal table. Seconds later Alpha Wolf's predator alertness dimmed to that of a sleepy puppy. My window had opened. I had maybe three to seven minutes depending on the widow's skills.

To create a diversion I took the baggie from my vest and dumped a small heap of powder on the table. Three pairs of eyes bulged at the sight.

Smiler snapped his switchblade and immediately set to work. I tapped Conan lightly.

"Ain't that Tiny Bob over there by the big table?" I said, tilting my head at a lumbering grizzly of a man, obviously stoned, trying to dance and not succeeding.

"Shit, that's Old Crow. Fucked up for years."

Armed and cranked I deftly tapped a text message on my screen: *Crow call me Babe.*

Then while the boys were busy inhaling the meth I began threading my way through the raging herd, aware of the hell primed to detonate at the slightest provocation. I felt like a match dancing on a striker, floating on a sea of gasoline.

Old Crow hadn't moved far when I arrived, bobbing and weaving right in front of the royal table. Alpha Wolf sat slumped back, eyes half closed. Undeterred, Sergeant Verona was still talking in his ear.

Abruptly a bullet-headed, steroid fed beta stepped in front of me. The taut veins roping his neck and biceps made him look like a human erection. He gave me a hard, contemptuous glare and without speaking conveyed his message: Where the fuck you going, bitch?

I showed him the phone text then pointed at Crow.

He leaned close to my ear. "Good luck."

With an amused snort he moved aside. I edged over to Crow, put the phone up to his face and pointed at the screen.

"Crow, you got mail."

He peered at the screen, then at me and continued dancing.

Perfect. I set the camera and pretended to show Crow the phone. He paid no attention. Blindly I took three over the shoulder shots of the royal table. I would have taken four but as I snapped the third, the music paused. The tiny click seemed to resound in the relative quiet.

Crow paid no notice. For him the music never stopped. He continued shuffling in time to some inner Stravinsky.

I shrugged and slowly moved back to my table. When I arrived half the meth was gone and the rest distributed into thick white lines. My new buddies welcomed me enthusiastically. A fresh bottle of Herradura was on hand and I took a good swallow. I glanced back in Crow's direction and saw the widow had emerged from beneath the table.

Alpha Wolf whispered in her ear and she left the table and began walking slowly through the crowd, unsteady on her high spike heels.

"Yo buddy, boss shit," Smiley said offering me the straw.

I had already done more speed than I needed. I passed the straw to Conan who shook me off.

"For Big Bug, man."

Since I had shot him, I couldn't refuse. Mindful of my sore membranes I inhaled half a line. Light, absorbent, very clean, high grade product. I finished the line.

If you've been clean for years the first hit of anything reminds you of why you started in the first place. Lifting my head I felt a rush of exhilarating clarity. I saw, I understood, I knew every fucking thing on the planet, give or take a few billion facts.

I felt capital.

Equipped with Leica lenses for eyes I watched the widow come in my direction, narrowly avoiding being bumped to the wet floor. She took a woozy right turn and walked into the pool room.

The other boys at my table watched her too. Conan half-crouched, straw frozen over a line as the pool players made way for her entrance.

Without preamble the widow opened her long, black leather coat.

She was naked underneath.

I saw one pool player lift her up and lay her on the green felt table before someone shut the door.

We all looked at each other.

"Big Bug's gone," Smiler said, not smiling. "His bitch is a momma now. Belongs to everybody."

I nodded solemnly.

"Primo crank, baby," Dracula said, "where'd you score?"

"Dago," I told him. "Come through Tijuana."

Smiler nodded absently. They all looked at the closed door.

"Maybe we should get a taste," Dracula suggested.

"Go on ahead," Conan said.

I took a long pull of tequila. "I gotta piss."

Not too fast not too slow, I walked to the front entrance like a man with a purpose. And believe me I had one. Get out as fast as possible.

My enhanced senses were screaming like a chorus of smoke alarms. However I maintained a calm, even pace. I was out the door, breathing fresh air, the cacophony behind me, a few bikers in the lot, smoking, talking. I kept moving until I was past the circle of light. Just to cap my cover I actually unzipped my jeans and took a whiz.

"Yo!"

I glanced back and saw Smiley and Conan. I assumed Dracula was comforting the widow.

"What's up?"

"We gotta talk." Conan said.

Smiley wasn't smiling and Conan was edging sideways.

"What's up?" I repeated figuring it was wise to act stupid. "Your crank, it's blue flake. Big Bug always cooked it special. Nobody else but Big Bug."

"The fuck is blue flake?"

"The shit you dumped on the table."

Short and to the point.

"The fuck you sayin?"

Blunt but not brilliant

"That crank belongs to Big Bug," Smiler said, "only he's dead and you're holdin' his product."

Conan was quick. Before I could answer he had me in a choke hold. Smiley kicked me in the balls ending any resistance. As I started to collapse, Conan frisked me and pulled the pistol from my belt.

"Looky here, brand new Siggy."

Smiler didn't bother with the niceties. With a fierce lunge he slashed my kidney with his switchblade.

Thank God for Kevlar. The vest deflected the blade, throwing Smiley off balance. I groaned and dropped to the ground as if stabbed, rolled, jammed a hand in my boot and came up holding the Colt.

My first shot grazed Conan's shoulder. The impact spun him around. He dropped the gun and ran. I swung my weapon but Smiley was scrambling after him.

The bikers loitering outside jerked to attention. They saw Smiley and Conan running at them but weren't sure what was happening. I fired two bullets over their heads, snatched my Sig and sprinted to the car.

I had left the door unlocked and the key in the ignition. Wise. I dove inside and started the engine in one wheezing move. I pulled out fast, lights out. Foot squeezing the racing pedal, I activated my radar detector and police scanner.

The meth gave me incredible facility. Supremely confident and lightning sharp I pushed the green ghost past a hundred but I knew it was a lost cause. The motorcycles were faster and there were more of them. By now the call to arms had put a small army on my ass.

I considered going north but there were fewer options, long stretches with no exits. I ran south coming off the side road with a messy skid. I righted the car and leapt south to 101. A rising boom informed me the Vandals were minutes behind.

I hit the entrance at 115 mph and pushed it. The scattered traffic ahead posed a problem. I was forced to weave in and out which slowed me down. I drove with reckless abandon but I could still see single headlights in my mirror. Although the meth amplified my reflexes most of my pursuers were equally charged so it was a push.

A crackling drone broke the intense silence. "All Marin units Code Red. Suspect fleeing south on 101. Armed and dangerous. Set roadblocks at Novato. Code Red."

Verona. He'd made an emergency call.

Now I had the law up ahead, the Vandals behind.

Beneath my wig, Kevlar vest and striped shirt I was sweating bullets. Surprisingly calm, I perused my options. There were none.

I nudged the needle past 120 but the motorcycle beams dotted my rearview.

Novato's wide, well-lit stretch of freeway was coming fast. The radar detector beeped furiously and I could see red and blue flickers on the horizon. I switched off the lights as I approached the San Marin exit, swung left and sent the car into a skidding right turn off the freeway. I wrestled the wheel but at one point I had to slow hard, flashing my red brake lights.

I heard most of the pack roar past the exit but to my dismay two headlights at the rear peeled off after me. That made twice in one week. My odds were sure to turn bad. The Merc handled well on the narrow, tightly curved road but the bikers stayed in my mirror.

Suddenly the rear window shattered. A steel fist whacked my left shoulder hard enough to drive it against the wheel. For a second I lost control and that's all it took. The car skidded into a 180 and left me facing the wrong side of life.

Left shoulder drooping helplessly I peeked over the dash.

Bearing down on me like some Apache warrior on horseback was a long-haired figure with a studded headband laying flat on his bike blasting wildly with two guns.

Reluctant to lift my head I switched on the brights, blinding him long enough to grab my Sig and fire through the side window as he boomed past.

I straightened up intending to flee until I spotted the second biker fifty yards ahead. He was rolling slowly to the side rather than attacking like his buddy.

I looked back. The other Vandal had paused to reload.

I was caught in a neat crossfire.

Gathering myself I prepared to crash past the biker waiting in front of me. Problem was I couldn't drive and shoot at the same time. My right arm hung uselessly.

Stay or go I was fucked. I decided to stay and shoot. Trying to zoom past the man ahead would expose my entire right side. Even if I ran that gauntlet they'd be hot on my trail and eventually another bullet would find me.

My numbed arm had trouble with the door. I used the Sig to help me get out. The open door afforded another option. In the dark a target on the ground is difficult to hit. Especially from a moving vehicle

I turned off the headlights, crawled out and lay beside my front left tire.

The momentary standoff confused them. A coughing growl to my left signaled another attack. The man on my right revved up as well.

I glimpsed a flash as a slug ripped through my door. I fired back, aiming for the front man's headlamp. I missed.

The front biker charged. I swung the pistol around expecting the man behind to swoop down. Instead he pulled up and blinked his light. His buddy slowed and looked back.

So did I.

Red and blue flashes rotated in the darkness like a lighthouse.

The front biker opened the throttle and blew by me. firing as he followed his retreating buddy. Then the only thing I could hear was my ragged breathing.

It was a mixed blessing. I was holding drugs and two guns. My wig felt like a volcano. Sweat streaming down my face and neck I got back inside the car. With one hand I opened the overhead box, slipped the Sig and meth inside and dropped the Colt in the dashboard stash just before the police car rolled to a stop about twenty feet ahead.

An armed cop got out and approached cautiously.

Only it wasn't officially a police car.

The rotating flasher was slightly askew and the cop wasn't in uniform.

"Hands where I can see them."

Calm, professional.

I stepped out, right hand high.

"My left arm got hit."

"Step away from the car—now."

I did as he asked until I was in full view.

"Thank God. Those bikers tried to hijack me. I was driving along and..."

He came closer, silhouetted against the headlights.

"Turn around."

That voice.

It belonged to Sergeant Lowell.

Chapter 18

"..the world is run by men who don't listen to music anyway."
Bob Dylan

My scalp felt like a bee hive under the hot wig and perspiration oozed from every pore on my face.
"You're sweating. You sick?"
I pointed to my head.
"Can I remove my wig?"
Lowell lifted his weapon.
"Go ahead, but slow."
With immense relief I got rid of the damned horse blanket. I pulled at my moustache but only half came off.   .
Lowell squinted.
"You're the one looking for the Fuente girl."
"Yes."
"What's the wig all about?"
"I dressed up to crash the funeral."
He shook his head wearily as if to say another joker thinks he's James Bond.
"Okay, let's see your license."
I took a deep breath, speed throbbing at my temples.
"I have a valid license."
"Let's see it."
"There's a problem."
He gave me a disappointed smile. "You don't have it on you."
"Oh, I have it. I just don't want you to run me through the computer."

That seemed to take him aback. But he kept his voice, and gun, steady.

"Now, why exactly is that?"

"I'm on the job," I said, inspired by the stimulants I'd imbibed.

For a moment Lowell was silent. "What job?"

"I'm undercover."

Lowell's square-jawed features tensed. "The license— let's have it."

I slowly fished out my wallet and handed it over.

As he studied my likeness I remembered.

"I have something here that should prove it."

"Yeah?" He said in a bored tone, still inspecting my ID. "You've got something?"

"Camera phone. I think I got a picture of Sergeant Verona socializing with a top Vandal."

He looked up, blue eyes alert.

"Show me."

His gun didn't waver from my chest as I reached across with my good arm and produced the phone. It occurred to me I might have nothing, considering I took the photos over my shoulder.

Lowell waited while I flipped it open and punched up the pictures.

First was a blur.

Second a shot of some scowling biker eyeing me suspiciously.

I began sweating again. No photo and my ass would be in the system. Worst case scenario? Lowell hauls me in and I'm dead by sunup. Another jailhouse suicide.

The third picture came up like an ace on the river card, a medium shot of Verona in close conversation with Alpha Wolf's ear.

Lowell studied it with a mixture of anger and regret, like a kid who just found out wrestling is fixed.

"Can I ask you something?" I ventured.

He glanced up from the small screen, rugged features clouded.

"Why aren't you in uniform?"

Lowell didn't lie well. He set himself before answering.

"I heard the Code Red on my car radio."

"You have a scanner in your Toyota?"

He lowered his weapon.

"Okay, I was staking out the funeral. Truth is I've been on to Verona for some time. Who you with?"

"DEA."

Easy enough to convince a small town cop with authentic details from my checkered past. Fortunately, he bought it.

Absently he passed me the phone, weapon at half mast. "What's up with Verona?"

"The Vandals are running large amounts of meth, possibly girls. I wasn't sure about Verona until I saw him at Molly's with the big dog.

Lowell nodded. "Walter just bought a vacation house in Clear Lake and a boat. The guy he's talking with is Shane Hazer, president of the Vandal Nation which includes international chapters. We're talking global conspiracy."

"So, may I have my wallet?"

"We need to talk but not here. You sneeze in Petaluma and ten people catch a cold. Anyplace in the city. I've been trying to get you people on this case for months."

"How do you mean?"

"Memos. I've been sending memos to the FBI, DEA, everybody."

"What about specifically?"

"Murders, home invasions, drugs. Didn't have hard evidence until now."

"Nailing Verona is one thing. Nailing the Vandals might be easier if we can get him to flip. Give me your email. I'll send you a copy of the picture."

"Thanks." He groped his pockets, came up with a card.

I put it away with my cell. "What about my ID?"

"We need to talk," he repeated.

I heard police sirens wailing in the distance.

"Tony Nik's in North Beach, eight o'clock."

"I know the place."

"Good. How about my wallet?"

His rugged features regarded me with a cop's cynicism. "I'll give you the wallet at Tony Nik's. In the meantime drive carefully."

Lowell had a great future in law enforcement.

Chapter 19

Shane Hazer had very big plans.

He looked almost scholarly, hunched over the Apple, sculpted features lit by the computer screen. Until he lifted his head and one could see the lethal intensity in his silver eyes. He stood up, long limbs charged with animal grace that belied his age as he moved to the kitchen area.

In profile, he resembled some ancient Roman general. Actually, his people had come from Oklahoma, more or less. His father had left home early for a career as a carney daredevil. Roy Hazer would ride his bike around a metal cage while sideways, then execute a full 360 turn upside down. Later on he added flaming wheels, setting his tires on fire for the big finale. He did pretty well for a few years until the traveling shows gave way to TV.

Shane's mother left carnival life—and him—before he was five. To his credit Roy did not abandon his son, taking him along as the carnival drifted from one small town to another in rural America. The ladies in the show took care of young Shane who already showed signs of having exceptional talent. A natural athlete, he could ride a motorcycle by the time he was seven. At nine he debuted as a daredevil cage rider with his father. That night one of the dancers taught him how to make love to a woman. And, as with everything else, Shane exhibited unusual skill for a beginner.

The nature of carnival life precluded formal schooling but Shane had a number of mentors. One was an alcoholic roustabout, known as Professor, who was rumored to have actually taught in college until drink and scandal forced him to find a new and anonymous life.

The Professor supplied Shane with a steady flow of well-used books, starting him off slow with fairytales, then on to boy's adventure like the Hardy Boys before exposing him to Rudyard Kipling and Charles Dickens.

The professor knew what he was doing and Shane was hungry for diversion. Carnival life had a numbing sameness and because it was a traveling show he rarely got to watch movies or TV.

In 1968, a year after Shane's debut as a daredevil rider, the carnival finally stopped. They played their last show in El Paso, Texas. That very night Roy Hazer packed his son, their motorcycles and meager possessions into a U-Haul and headed straight for Hollywood.

As a parting gift the Professor gave Shane a copy of *Oliver Twist*.

For a while Roy actually found steady work in movies as a stuntman. It was the first time Shane had lived anywhere longer than two weeks and the first time he was enrolled in school.

It wasn't a good experience. In the carnival, outsiders were known contemptuously as rubes but here, Shane was the outsider, even worse, a freak. To compound his problems his hair had turned prematurely gray.

All of this made him a target. However, he wasn't like most kids his age. Shane made short, brutal work of the first two boys to taunt him, a lesson he'd learned early. After that, many of the students stayed clear of him, but almost as many became followers. Instinctively, Shane knew how to keep them in line. His confidence was building.

Unfortunately, two years later his father got hurt performing a cliff jump for a B movie. As his brief stuntman career plummeted, Roy Hazer's dependence on painkillers and booze escalated until everything collapsed. To keep them from being evicted, Shane, already tall for his age, found work as a motorcycle messenger. Then one day, Wes Hart, a noted stuntman, came by for a visit and invited them to watch him perform a major gag in a movie starring Steve McQueen.

Roy stayed reasonably sober for a change and Shane could hardly suppress his excitement. Energized by the air of intensity and glamour on the location set he stayed back watching intently as Wes prepared for the stunt. His motorcycle had to clear a burning car, land upright and catch up to a runaway truck. From there Wes would snatch the rungs of a metal ladder and swing aboard the truck's cab.

Roy confided that Wes was getting twenty grand for the stunt.

It all went like clockwork until Wes hit the road wobbling. Still unsteady as he reached for the ladder his hand slipped. He bounced off the concrete and tumbled thirty yards. When it was over he had three cracked ribs a fractured arm and a broken hip.

As they took Wes off to the waiting ambulance, the director began ranting helplessly.

"I'm fucked! This is our money shot! The whole fucking production is fucked!"

Then he saw Roy standing nearby. "You—you're a stuntman right? Fifteen grand to do the gag."

Roy shrugged. "Wish I could. Busted pelvis, bum knee."

"I can do it."

The director glared at Shane. "Who the fuck are you, kid?"

"He's my son," Roy said, "and he can ride with the best."

"I can do it," Shane repeated. "But my fee is twenty thousand."

The director weighed his options. He had none.

"Okay, you say you can do it, let's do it. Get wardrobe and make up, we roll in thirty."

Shane nailed it on the first take and became an instant star. Steve McQueen took him under his wing, introducing him to celebrities, helping him get work. Shane, barely high school age drank it all in. His stunt work brought him good money and a small measure of celebrity among working filmmakers. There was even talk of a small speaking part.

Certainly the ladies found him attractive. From script girl to actress they all had a yen for the young stuntman. Unfortunately, so did a male assistant director.

He came on to Shane behind the trailer on a location shoot. A black rage dropped over Shane like a hood. He drew the knife he carried in his boot and drove it into the man's throat. What's more, standing there, nostrils filled with the smell of blood and body flush with conquest, Shane found he exulted in it.

To his surprise no one in Hollywood took his calls while he awaited trial or came to visit during his five-year stretch for manslaughter.

Shane killed two men while in prison. He was suspected but never charged. By his third year inside he was running his own crew. During that time his father died. When he was released, Shane found the world had changed—and it didn't want violent ex-cons. He hooked up with a couple of pals he'd met in the slam and they began running cocaine on their motorcycles.

Suddenly, Hollywood was taking his calls again but not for stunt work. Shane was no longer the fresh new face and despite his striking good looks there was something scary about him that discouraged his drug clients from getting too close. It made no difference to Shane, he liked being an outlaw. He was good at it.

Shane's ferocious skills handling a bike and his bloody temper made him an underground legend. In a short time his gang grew to over fifty members and they incorporated, just like the Angels. It took Shane two more decades to take his organization global. Coke, meth, ludes, ecstasy, smack, whatever, they supplied it. As their ranks grew and Vandal chapters spread as far as Montreal and Norway, they began running guns and prostitutes through their international network.

Shane had charted it all. Now it was time to step up to the major league.

Engrossed in his thoughts, Shane opened his refrigerator and selected a bottle of green wheat grass. He also picked out a bottle of carrot juice. He drained the bitter wheatgrass first, closely followed by the sweet carrot. Shane was a big believer in discipline. He rarely drank, practiced martial arts rigorously and avoided drugs. For that reason he looked more like thirty-five than fifty. He had only one addiction and it was incurable: Power.

The hunger reached far beyond the provincial empire he now ruled. He needed to go to the next level. It had taken him thirty years to get here and the best he could summon was one, maybe two, thousand soldiers and twenty million in cash. Chump change. These days a million wouldn't pay their lawyer fees.

Methamphetamine had become more profitable than coke and with him controlling production there was no middleman. He had the labs, he had the chefs. Big Bug's unfortunate passing was a temporary glitch. But dealing drugs was an extremely unstable business. This new enterprise would give him maximum juice with a minimum of heat.

Like Suge Knight, like Diddy, Shane was going into the music business. Nose Job's album would be their first release and Vandal Records had the muscle to ensure the album would get heard and distributed. Big rewards, low risk.

Or so he thought, until this cowboy blundered in looking for the girl. The asshole doesn't know who he's dealing with, Shane fumed. He had this whole thing organized right down to the last gram: Three sex units for four hundred thousand cash and fifty kilos of meth in trade for a truckload of weapons—from Stingers and grenades to .50 caliber armor-piercing machine guns.

Guns, money and lawyers, everything he needed to move up in the world.

A light knock interrupted his calculations.

Slow Pain opened the door slightly. "He's here."

Shane moved back behind his desk. He centered himself, prepared for the coming tantrum.

Verona started complaining before he was inside. "This is some bad shit. We got serious problems. First one guy starts asking around and now this dude."

Shane stared at him. "I know you can handle the traffic arrests."

"Best I can," Verona said, clearly uncomfortable. "We've got eleven citations to deal with."

"No. *You* have eleven citations," Shane snapped. He was annoyed and with good reason. Eleven of his soldiers had been snared by a road block called in by Verona himself. Meanwhile the goddamned rabbit escaped.

"This is serious," Verona said, voice subdued, "two guys now."

"It's all serious. Use your head. Most likely it's the same guy that's been looking for the girl. Big Bug went after him and got shot. This motherfucker shows up at his funeral holding Bug's product. What do you think?"

"I think we are exposed here. Maybe we should abort the transfer."

"Not an option," Shane said. "The man's due and everything's ready to move. Your end is fifty grand," he reminded Verona.

As expected the figure calmed Verona down but not completely. "It's just that we've got too many loose ends."

Shane had to agree. There were a number of weak links—especially Verona. In time they would all be severed. But not until business with the big man had been consummated.

"I'll handle the loose ends,' he said. "You take care of the damn citations."

When Verona left, he thought it over. As much as he hated to lose a hundred and fifty grand, Carla Fuente had to be eliminated. It was cheaper than the possible alternatives.

He sent for Slow Pain.

The hulking psycho was his most trusted bodyguard but Shane had never gotten used to his acidic body odor. Of course, he never mentioned it. Men like Slow Pain had intense sensitivities.

"That bitch you like," Shane said, "you know, the young one?"

Slow nodded, simian brow knotted in concentration.

"She's trouble. We have to get rid of her."

The biker's thick features became childlike. "Aw... really?"

Shane knew how he felt. The girl was one of the jewels of his collection. His client would be disappointed.

"Do whatever you want," Shane said slowly, making sure he understood, "but it's very important nobody finds her... ever."

"But you said..."

"What I'm saying now is you can take care of her anyway you want. Understand?"

For a moment the biker was silent. Then a shadow fell over the childlike expression and his lips curled in a sadistic smile.

Shane knew what the smile meant. They didn't call him Slow Pain for nothing.

"...today?"

"Not today. I need you for the loading. You know that. I'll tell you when."

Slow left pouting and shuffling but he'd get over it after they finished packaging the new product.

Later, Shane called Todd in for a meeting.

The young singer arrived late, having taken time to shower and change his clothes following an all-night binge. However, Todd made damn sure to be alert and his usual arrogant manner was carefully subservient. He was well aware of Shane's quick temper.

"This man who came to see you about the Fuente girl," Shane began, "can you tell me anything about him?"

"Well, he was dressed like a nerd on a nature hike but up close he looked like a hard dude."

"Anything else? Think, it's important."

"Uh..." Todd rummaged through his tattered memory. "Oh wait... Tami said the guy has a girlfriend. Carla's cousin, I think she said. Yeah, that's it. She works in some bar in San Francisco."

Shane showed no emotion but he felt a rush of triumph. Checkmate.

He reached into his desk drawer and put a small stack of cash and a bag of white powder on the desk. "This is for you. A bonus for having a good memory."

He noticed that Todd reached for the drugs first.

"I want you to do me a favor," Shane said.

"Sure, like what?"

"I need you to go to the city and convince that cousin to come see me."

Todd looked slightly panicked. "How am I supposed to do that?"

"You're creative. You'll think of something, right?"

"Right," Todd said, voice trailing off.

Leaving the office, Todd felt a mixture of apprehension and anticipation. Like before a big show. He was already going over how he'd do it. He'd give her some bullshit about her cousin. And if that didn't work he'd bring the bitch at gunpoint. He fingered the baggy in his pocket. Anything to be a rock star.

Chapter 20

Driving home one-handed, wind whipping through my shattered windows I realized I needed Sergeant Lowell. Lots of men were brave, few were honest. Most cops in his position wouldn't risk their careers. They'd keep their sheep heads down and give the Veronas of this world a pass.

As soon as I arrived, I emailed the photo to Lowell. I also printed two hard copies and put one on CD. Another I uploaded to a private cybervault I maintain.

I hate speed, the grinding inevitability of it. All I had was valium and scotch which blunted but failed to stop the adrenaline enhanced charge to nowhere.

I showered and took another valium to put me down. But not out. I slept fitfully until nine then drove over to Len's shop.

He cast the same disappointed eye on me as he did the Mercury.

"That didn't take you long."

"I had help, believe me. Can you fix it today?"

"Door too?"

"Just the windows."

"No problem. You look like shit."

I couldn't argue. I was suffering from classic crank comedown: toxic depression, fatigue, and self-loathing.

"Anyplace I can crash while you fix the damage?"

He led me to a small room behind the office. Slanted sunlight, fresh flowers, floor mat and futon gave it a Zen tranquility. No doubt it was intentional.

Len left me on the futon and returned with a cup of tea and a J.

"This boo is for terminal patients," he said. "Drink the tea first."

I soon came to understand why he specified the order. My first puff nearly put me in a catatonic state. I took another. Now, mind you, I endorse cannabis in the spirit of healing and expanded consciousness but Len's herb cut through the speed, wrapped my synapses in a cozy blanket and laid me out on the futon.

When Len woke me the J was still clutched between my thumb and index finger.

I gingerly gave it back.

"Definitely medicinal."

"That's what it's for. You okay?"

I checked my body parts. Except for my numbed left shoulder I was operational.

Outside my battered Mercury sported new tinted windows.

"Figured we'd make it harder to sight you," Len said modestly.

I was touched.

Feeling almost human I drove to North Beach, found a spot and walked to Chinatown. An hour with Jimmy Shu put life back in my arm. I returned to the flat on Chestnut carrying a bag full of take-out.

I immediately sat at my computer and started hacking with a vengeance, eating as I went. My target: David Alan Paul. I had already gone into his PC but I had a hunch.

David Paul's company managed a small goat farm outside Petaluma. The farm was owned by Mr. Milton Pechman who also resided in Manhattan. He had two email addresses, one for his law firm in New York, the other a private address, registered in Petaluma.

Privacy? Gone with the Walkman.

Everything you send, receive or browse using your computer or phone is scrutinized and recorded: time, date, subject, proclivities. Your credit card purchases, bank account, driving record, travel arrangements, even your damn toll fees for bridges and tunnels. It's all there somewhere in the great digital book of judgment.

Conversations can be recorded from across the street, your phone doesn't have to be turned on to eavesdrop, cameras can be concealed in flag pins. Anybody who wants privacy needs to find an island with no electricity or Visa. And even then a Google satellite will pinpoint your location within twenty feet.

Before I finished my pot stickers, I found it.

In a way, I wished I hadn't.

Once polluted, you really can't delete things entirely. Which meant I'd have to replace my Mac.

Buried deep in Mr. Pechman's hard drive was an album of fifty-nine photos. Since the latest had been entered only a few days earlier I surmised it belonged to David Paul. I could see why he wouldn't want it on his own computer.

The first was a photo of a nine-year old girl wearing lipstick and provocative lingerie. Other photos were more graphic, showing girls from six to twelve in various stages of sex with older males and females, their faces out of frame. One series featured girls from fourteen to sixteen in bondage. Carla was not among those.

I had a flash. If David Paul was using his client's computer he might be using the premises to house the odd slave.

It was worth a shot.

+   +   +

Tony Nik's is the real thing. An old school bar with a bottle glass front and edgy music. I arrived early but Lowell was already at a rear table. One point for professionalism, get there first, scope out the arena.

He was drinking a screwdriver, I ordered tequila.

"Your ID," he said, pushing my wallet across the table. "I wanted to make sure you'd show."

"Nothing else?"

"Routine check. You're too clean, always a red flag."

I smiled. "What about Walter? Anybody else in the department dirty?"

He shook his head. "I first knew something was wrong when Verona lost the evidence in a Vandal homicide case. Gang member shot a drug witness in broad daylight. French tourist caught it on video. Next thing you know the camera disappears from the evidence room. Last guy in was Verona."

I nodded.

"Half the kids up there are on meth. The Vandals have labs all over, Marin, Reno, Tahoe..."

He took a long swig. "I can't do much alone."

"Missing girls?"

"A few, but no link to the Vandals."

"Tell me about Shane Hazer."

He straightened up, competitive streak awakened. "Smart son of a bitch. Did a nickel in Pelican Bay for manslaughter when he was seventeen. Inside he was prime suspect in two killings. Never proven. Became a leader in the Aryan Nation. Since his release he's stayed squeaky clean. Got legitimate buffers and lawyers. After he was elected president the Vandals incorporated and acquired a web site."

Lowell drained his glass and signaled for another. He looked battle weary.

"Anything on Carla Fuente?"

He shook his head. "Checked local hospitals, nothing there."

When the waitress came I ordered another Patron.

"Do you know a local named David Alan Paul?"

His brows lifted. "Sure. He's a local joke. Thinks he's a motorcycle hood. Hangs around Rinner's trying to impress the big boys."

"Take a look at this."

I opened my laptop and brought up the pictures.

Lowell tried to keep his expression hard but wavered, innocence, disbelief, disgust and outrage all registering on his clean-cut features. It was like showing child porn to Tom Brady. I felt vaguely ashamed, as if I was responsible. Kill the messenger.

"You think he may have taken the Fuente girl?"

"He's admitted giving her a lift to Walnut Park. He's using his client's computer to store this shit. He has access to a remote house. Let's go up to this goat farm and check it out."

"When?"

"Tonight."

He looked at me, weighing my motives. A moment later he shrugged, a real pioneer.

"I'm in."

+   +   +

We took separate cars north. On the way I called Nina.

"Max, the place is jammed I can't talk but there's a guy here who knows about Carla."

"What guy?"

"Just a sec, be right there," I heard her say from a distance. Then closer. "Max, I can't talk. Call me later." Out.

I hate that.

In Petaluma I parked the Merc and rode shotgun in Lowell's Toyota. I had GPSed the location of Milton Pechman's farm and Lowell knew the access codes to the various electric fences along the way.

The hills above Petaluma abound with dairy farms and the tax loopholes afforded gentleman farmers. Lowell's four wheel drive easily handled the narrow dirt road leading to the Pechman place. We passed three fences before we reached a two-rut trail exiting the road. Lowell parked fifty yards in and we went on foot. I had left my hardware concealed in the Mercury. And with each step I was acutely aware of being unarmed.

"How do we proceed?" Lowell asked.

I suddenly realized he was deferring to me, the man from the DEA.

"You have a weapon?"

"Yes."

"Deploy and follow me." What a dick.

My eyes slowly adjusted to the darkness as we followed the crude trail to the main house. We came around a curve and I stopped short.

There were lights on inside the house.

Chapter 21

Carla hummed softly as she dusted the table beside her bed.

It was a song her mother used to sing to her.

She liked the new place. It had a bathroom, a real bed, lights—a great improvement from the windowless cell where she'd first been held. So she kept it clean and neat.

Two or three men came to visit but Carla had learned how to handle them. Twenty minutes and they were out the door leaving her in blessed solitude. Alone, locked inside the walls of this dwelling, she felt a sliver of hope. She felt almost safe.

Carla had begun a strict routine, daily shower, personal grooming... keeping the tiny apartment spotless. It was her way of marking time.

Tami had seen her. Carla was certain. Very soon they would come for her. Until then it was important that she kept the apartment clean.

Suddenly tired, Carla lay on the bed, unable to sleep yet fatigued. The concept of day and night had slipped away. She couldn't be sure how long she'd been imprisoned. She didn't dare think about her mother or her former life. If she hoped to survive she had to deal with the present.

There was food in the refrigerator: bread, cheese, turkey slices, mustard, soda, even a few ponies of whiskey. Unable to stay on the bed Carla began prowling the apartment. She stopped in the kitchen and helped herself to a shot of bourbon.

The whiskey helped settle her nerves. She returned to the bed and clicked the remote. Biography—the Pam Andersen story. She watched without seeing, brain unable to differentiate between Pam and reality. Hot bodies, expensive toys, the Hollywood dream.

But she never wanted that, Carla reflected. For her it was always family, education, future. Future. The word drew her back to her bleak prison room. This was her future now.

She saw a smudge on the night table and distractedly began rubbing it with a paper napkin. She went into the kitchen, came back with a soapy sponge and went over it carefully. The TV voices drowned out the knocking at the door until it became louder, insistent.

Carla approached the door hesitantly, heart pounding. "Yes?"

She didn't have to hear an answer. The rancid scent oozing through the door jamb sent her stumbling into the bathroom where she fell to her knees, retching.

Chapter 22

"Take care not to understand me too quickly."
Andre Gide

I t wasn't difficult to negotiate the path and sneak around the side of the house. Guided by the two lit windows we separated, each taking one. David Paul was there inside, face lit by the glow of the computer screen. He was seated on an old fashioned armchair butt naked, features glazed as he masturbated.

We looked at each other knowing what we were thinking. Neither of us wanted to break in on that little scene. But Carla's life was at stake. I signaled I was going to find the rear door. Lowell nodded and followed.

Lowell was good, moving soundlessly behind me, pausing occasionally to survey the area. Deserted.

I heard a dog barking in the distance as I located the kitchen door and jimmied the lock. Lowell produced a small flashlight with a solid beam that tunneled a path from the kitchen along the hall to the library.

David was standing now, still naked, a drink in one hand. "Police."

Shattered glass punctuated Lowell's quiet voice. David Paul stepped forward, empty hands extended as if to push us away.

"Careful, Mr. Paul, don't cut yourself," Lowell said. "There's broken glass on the floor."

His concern seemed to calm David down. He glanced aside as if looking for something and for a second I thought it might be a weapon.

It was a robe, draped over the arm of a couch.

"Don't move, please," Lowell said, again very professional. Naked, the suspect was most vulnerable, most likely to crack.

"Let him get his robe," I said, good cop to the end. Plus, he disgusted me.

Once clothed, David gathered himself. "I know you, officer. Do you have a warrant?"

I walked over to his desk. "The child porn on this computer makes you fair game. Remember me? I came to your house... talked to your mother."

I paused, letting it sink in. In the corner of my eye I saw Lowell shoot me a warning glance but I went on confident, I had David's number.

"I could talk to her again. Tell her what a naughty boy you are. How you used your client's computer for immoral purposes."

He sagged and I thought he was about to fall. He caught himself but he was naked again, robe or not. The blood had drained from his face and tears streamed down his cheeks.

"What do you want?"

"Carla Fuente, where is she?"

"I told you I don't know, I don't know, I just gave her a ride."

"Ride where?"

"I told you, Walnut Park. Goddammit, where's your warrant? You have no right, you have no right..."

"Do we have your permission to search this place?"

"No. You have no right..."

I looked at Lowell and inclined my head. He knew what I meant.

"Stay there, Mr. Paul," he said, "maybe you should sit."

I left the room and began methodically searching the premises. There was no cellar but there was an underground storeroom. Not a shred of evidence suggested anyone but David Paul occupied the place. The layers of dust everywhere attested to that.

I returned to the library and looked at Lowell. David Paul caught it as well.

"I told you," he said, reasonably composed now. His mother's son.

"You know where she is," Lowell said, voice threatening.

"I told you everything I know. You have no right to be here."

"You have no right to exploit children," I said.

"They're just pictures. It's none of your business."

"Could be your mother's business if you don't give us something."

"I swear I don't know!" he said, voice rising to a screech. Rhymes with beseech.

I glanced at Lowell. He believed it. So did I. One suspect down, Carla still out there. Mission unaccomplished.

"I know you, officer," David blustered. "I'm going to sue for damages."

"We have you on a child porn charge," I said, "guess who gets damaged? You know what they do to short eyes in prison?"

The question deflated whatever strength David had left. He seemed to shrink, listing to one side as if faint.

"May I sit down?"

"We'll be leaving now, Mr. Paul," Lowell said, "unless you need assistance."

"No, thank you. I'm fine. Please, just go."

Outside we looked at each other.

"He's a freak but he didn't kidnap the girl," Lowell said. "I know the guy."

Did you know he was into child porn? I thought but let it go. Lowell was right about one thing. David Paul didn't have Carla.

On our way down the hill I called Nina.

"Max, where are you? I want you to meet this guy. Yeah... coming, right away... Get over here, Max..." Out. I hate that.

"So, what now?" Lowell said.

"We concentrate on Shane Hazer. What kind of file have you got?"

"Funny about that."

"Funny ha-ha or funny sad?"

"Somebody deleted his file."

"Verona?"

"Another strange event that tipped me off."

"Give me your cell number," I said, "I'll call you later.

+   +   +

I dialed Nina from my car and got her voice mail. Bummer.

Frustrated, I zipped back to the city. Just outside San Rafael my radar detector beeped. I was forced to take the next exit and circle back to 101. San Rafael to the Golden Gate is nothing more than a fifteen-mile speed trap. Cops lie in wait like bears on a salmon run scooping up everything from DUI's to outstanding warrants.

Once safely on the bridge I called again without success. How busy could it be?

When I arrived at the Lone Palm, Nina wasn't there.

I checked my cell. No message. Not like Nina. I tried calling again. No answer.

The bartender was a willowy blond in a tank top that framed twin bluebirds inked above her white breasts.

"I'm supposed to meet Nina."

"She left about twenty minutes ago."

"Did you see with who?"

She hesitated. I slid a twenty across the bar.

"Some young guy." Emphasis on young.

I looked around. The place was still fairly crowded.

"Any idea who?"

She shrugged and turned her attention to a customer waving at her from the end of the bar.

I pushed another twenty her way. "Perhaps you heard a name? Anything."

She took a deep breath. "Ted or something like that. Long dark hair."

"Ted? Maybe Todd?"

"Maybe. I gotta go."

She moved off and began mixing a drink. What does that leave me with? I asked myself. Suspicion of Todd? A cell phone that doesn't answer? Then it hit me.

Nina's cell phone.

I raced back to Corte Madera where my sensitive equipment was housed. For an hour I honed closer to her cell phone's exact location.

It came as no surprise.

Nina's phone currently resided at Todd Fletcher's address. Resisting a primal urge to charge north I fished around some more.

Shane Hazer, Leroy Underwood: I gave them LeBlue's infra-red scan, tax records, properties, the works.

This time I was surprised. Leroy Underwood owned a motel. The Sunrise Motel in Fairfax. The cosigner on the loan was Shane Hazer. Did you know that if you buy property in California you have to be fingerprinted?

I called Lowell and told him to meet me at Todd Fletcher's house. Within twenty minutes I was back in Petaluma.

"How do we do this?" Lowell asked.

"Todd has Nina's cell phone which gives us probable cause. We sweat the little prick for heavy conspiracy—twenty-to-life... he'll tell us something. He lives at home for Christ's sake."

Lowell looked impressed.

I wished I was as confident as I appeared.

+   +   +

Mrs. Fletcher wasn't looking her best when she answered the door but I could see she had been a real beauty when young. Despite the late hour and stressful circumstances she was attractive enough: trim figure, high cheekbones, same smoky blue eyes Todd had inherited.

They stared suspiciously at Lowell's badge then at me.

"Todd isn't here. What do you want with him?"

I let Lowell handle it and he was superb. He just turned on the "aw shucks" charm and her stony glare melted.

"My apologies, ma'am, for the late hour but we are trying to find a missing girl and were told your son might have seen her,"

She gave him a rueful smile. "My son sees lots of girls. Didn't you know? He's a big rock star now."

She slurred her *r*s a bit and I realized she was a bit tipsy.

"Yes, Ma'am. Would you happen to know where he might be?"

"Out all night as usual. You tell me."

"I see. Well, thank you ma'am. Again our apologies."

Lowell backed off, practically bowing and I did the same. Any mention of a warrant would have caused problems. Especially for him.

"Suggestions?" He said as we walked to my car.

"How many places are still open at this hour? Let's check the Buckhorn."

The place was nearly empty except for a pair of diehards at the end of the bar and Helga. When she saw us she threw her shoulders back and took a deep breath to enhance her already generous bosom. Smiling broadly she sashayed over like a real woman.

"So you decided to have that drink," she said, ever the optimist.

"Helga, this is Sergeant Lowell. We're on the job but I'll be glad to take you up on that drink."

Lowell gave me a "what are you doing" look but I just gestured at the stacked bottles.

"What's your pleasure, Sergeant?"

"Tequila's fine," he said reluctantly.

"Two Patrons."

"We don't carry Patron," Helga said, somewhat miffed.

"Make it 1800 and have one on us." I laid a twenty on the bar just to prove I wasn't there to cadge free drinks and take advantage of her.

When she returned, Helga was her old kittenish self.

"So, you guys still looking for that girl?" She asked, giving Lowell the once over.

"Actually we're looking for Todd Fletcher. You know, the guy you saw with Carla the night she went missing."

"Those rocker bums, lousy tippers, rude, leave a mess..." she trailed off but that said it all.

"You haven't seen him tonight then."

"Only time that crowd comes is when there's a show at the Mystic. Usually Saturday night."

A raucous voice cut through the relative quiet.

"Bobo."

I turned and saw a white-haired dude at the end of the bar peering at us from behind thick glasses.

"Bobo," he repeated. "That's where the kids hang out these days. Bobo, like the clown."

That's Bozo, I thought. Aloud I said, "Thanks for the help, sir." I raised my glass and downed the tequila.

I smiled at Helga. "Thank you, too."

"Don't be a stranger," she called as we left.

As if I could help it.

"She your girlfriend?" Lowell said, deadpan.

"No, your mama is."

"Careful, I'm armed."

I was starting to like him.

$$+ \qquad + \qquad +$$

Bobo's was at the edge of town which is easy in Petaluma.

A few motorcycles were parked in front which made me nervous, especially since I wasn't strapped.

The place was big, low lights, sound booth, pool table and a cramped stage where a punk trio pumped out erratic beats. Todd Fletcher was easy to find. He lolled against the wall at a large table, a lady on either side. Todd ignored the wannabes that made up the rest of his entourage, watching the band on stage with bored detachment.

Maybe it was the tequila or the speed hangover or the fucking stress but a cold rush of anger propelled me through the crowd. It wasn't until I came near Todd's table that I recognized one of his girlfriends: Robin Falker.

Lowell must have sensed my rage because he put a restraining hand on my arm.

"Not here. Let me handle the bastard."

Fists clenched, I stepped aside to let him pass. Just as well for when I scanned the room I spotted a pair of bikers watching us with great interest. They were both generic, bearded, do-rag hulks so I couldn't really tell if I had met them socially before.

"Police," Lowell said, flashing his badge. "Todd Fletcher?"

Robin looked like she was about to vomit. The other girl scooted away like a tattooed rabbit. Semi-drunk and hollow-eyed, Todd had the aura of debauched royalty as he examined the badge, and us, with bemused contempt.

"Shit, I don't see a warrant, do you?" he said, glancing around the table.

Nobody answered. Then one of his pals snickered.

Without preamble Lowell reached down, grabbed Todd's shirt and hauled him across the table spilling drinks everywhere.

"I'll show you my warrant outside."

Everything went quiet. The band stopped playing to watch the little drama unfold along with the rest of the customers. I kept an eye on the bikers as Lowell dragged Todd to the door. They had circled around to intercept us and now flanked a short, square-cut man with a neatly trimmed goatee who had the knowing smirk of a jailhouse lawyer.

He folded his arms. "You can't take this kid without a warrant. You don't even have probable cause."

I felt adrenaline surging in my veins, ready for combat.

"You own this place?" Lowell said still calm.

"Matter of fact I do. I'm Bobo Olson and you're..."

Expertly and efficiently Lowell whirled Todd like a dance partner, pressed his bony chest against the wall and patted him down. The very first pocket produced a bag of white powder. Lowell dangled it high in front of the owner. "This will get your license revoked, Bobo."

The owner stiffened then gestured at the hulks to back off.

Suppressing an urge to applaud, I followed Lowell and Todd to the exit. I glanced back and saw Robin jabbering into her cell phone. She was noticeably thinner since our last encounter. Everybody in town seemed to be on a diet.

Despite being violently unseated, Todd maintained his royal sneer intact in public. But removed from witnesses his front crumbled like the Berlin Wall.

"What the fuck. I'm holding a couple of grams. It's inadmissible..." he whined as Lowell half dragged him to my car.

He put Todd in the back and got in beside him. As I slid behind the wheel I saw a few people had gathered outside Bobo's to watch the proceedings. Without putting on my lights I backed up and made a U-turn. I checked my rearview but no one followed.

"I want my lawyer," Todd demanded, regaining his bluster. "Where are you taking me?"

Lowell directed me to a deserted stretch away from street lights.

"This gentleman is from the DEA and he'd like to ask you some questions," Lowell said. "Now, I won't cuff you unless you're uncooperative."

"Where's Nina?" I said voice strained. My anger hadn't subsided but had gathered in my chest like a compressed thundercloud.

"Fuck if I know."

"Bad attitude," Lowell said. He produced cuffs and secured Todd's wrists as I left the car.

I opened the rear door and yanked Todd outside. He looked at Lowell as if expecting help. None came. I slapped Todd medium hard and he bounced off the trunk.

"You were at the Lone Palm. Witnesses saw you leave together. Where is she?"

Todd's eyes were rolling as if he couldn't believe anyone had actually struck him. I slapped him again so he'd know it was real.

"She needed a ride back north," he rasped, mouth slack with fear, "that's all, I swear.'

I whacked Todd very hard, against his ear. He fell to one knee.

"Guess what? Nina's cell phone is sitting in your house right now. You can tell me where she is or we raid the place, arrest your mother as a conspirator and put you away for twenty years for kidnapping and drugs. Talk now and we'll cut you a deal. Keep lying and I'll keep trying."

I paused while Todd recovered and stood up, leaning against the car. I had delivered a brain-rattling smack. One side of his face was mottled red and his eyes were tearing. I raised my fist.

"Jesus, stop! Don't hit me! I don't know where she is. I drove her back here and they took her somewhere in a van."

"You piece of shit—who took her?"

"I don't know. Vandals. They were waiting."

I couldn't hold back. The thundercloud flashed white heat and I blasted a hook into Todd's kidney. He crumpled like a soda can, retching his guts out.

"What did you tell her, scumbag—you could take her to Carla?"

The answer came back as a strangled plea. "Yes... oh shit, please. I'm hurt"

I was having none of it. He was my only link to Nina.

My rage electrified the air around me prompting Lowell to grab my arm. I shook him off and lifted Todd's limp, vomit crusted body off the ground.

"Last chance. Tell me where she is or I kill you right here."

Todd struggled to regain his breath. "They said Fairfax. I don't know where. Jesus help me, I don't know where."

Fairfax? I knew where.

I opened the trunk, pulled out my Kevlar vest then yanked Todd by the scruff of his neck and heaved him inside.

"Sunrise Motel," I told Lowell. "Let's move."

"I've got a buddy in Fairfax. Homicide. We work together. I'll call…"

Before he could open his cell it chimed. Mozart.

"Yeah?"

Lowell looked at me as he listened, expression wavering between compassion and reluctance.

"They found a body in the hills," he said, carefully shutting his cell, "up near David Paul's place. A young girl."

Chapter 23

Nina had no illusions.

She knew they would have to kill her.

She could identify Todd Fletcher and the big man in the van.

Not the two who grabbed her when she left Todd's car but the one who put a knife to her neck and told her to be a good girl. To prove his point he ran his blade along the inside of her thigh and laughed when he saw the blood. He looked like an overgrown child with his dumb mullet haircut and pudgy features. But his wide blue eyes were vacant. He gave her a perfunctory search, pausing to fondle her breasts before pushing her into the room and locking the door.

His body odor hung in the air long after he'd gone.

Fortunately, he'd neglected to find the seven inch clasp knife she always carried in her right boot. Sooner or later he'd return, she reasoned, trying to smother her panic. If he came near her again she'd bury the blade in his heart.

Nina prepared carefully. All she had was the element of surprise. She pulled an armchair closer to the door and turned off the lights. Then she positioned herself behind the chair. The instant the door opened she would strike.

While waiting, Nina counted regrets. Why didn't she call Max back? What the hell was wrong with her, going off like that? Why the hell did she trust that little creep Todd?

She knew why. Because the little creep gave her his rock glamour bullshit and she bought it. Sure, of course, she could trust him. He knew Justin, JLo and Jack Black. What a pathetic airhead she was.

Why didn't I call Max? She asked for the twentieth time. He would have known what to do. Even here, facing death or worse, Nina realized Max had become very important to her. More than she had ever expected—or wanted.

I don't even know where he lives, she thought ruefully.

She must have dozed off, crouched behind the armchair in the dark. A flurry of noise woke her: a car horn, men shouting, the flat pop of gunfire. Nina braced herself, knife gripped tightly.

Loud cries, pounding feet... the door burst open.

Light slashed the carpet as a tall figure shuffled into the room, face pressed against his weapon as if in worship.

Nina leaped, blade first.

A nanosecond, an eternity, a clumsy moment later, she was on the floor staring at the smoke drifting up from her chest.

It took a while longer before she realized she had been shot.

Chapter 24

"You're going to need a bigger boat."
Roy Scheider, Jaws

There's an area in the center of Fairfax which is part parking lot and part public square. In a sense it's a time capsule protected by its lack of proximity to the freeway. The town was largely settled by hippies and new-agers and their children hang out playing folk guitar, passing Js or just getting mellow. California happy.

Beyond the health food supermarket and Buy-Rite gas station across the street there are only tall trees and narrow roads. Once you pass a retreat called Spirit Rock where the good people go to meditate there's nothing but isolated houses tucked inside the redwoods. If I hadn't Googled the Sunrise Motel, I would never have found it.

The detective who was waiting in the darkened parking lot of the Buy Rite looked like one of the local kids with red surfer hair and a big, lopsided grin. Lowell had hooked me up with his colleague, Craig Manson, while he covered the murder scene. He assured me that he would be less than thirty minutes behind me but I wasn't holding my breath.

"Craig?"

"Yeah, that's me."

"I've got strong reason to believe my girlfriend is being held at the Sunrise Motel."

"Yeah, so Bob told me." The grin faded. "Got any evidence?"

I opened the trunk. Todd was huddled in a fetal position. "Witness testimony."

"Good enough for me." He shut the trunk.

I liked him already. "What else did Bob say?"

"He's at the crime scene. Said a mutual friend is screwing things up like he's got an agenda."

A flare of anxiety ignited my anger and I opened the trunk. "If she's hurt, I'll kill you here."

"Easy partner," Manson said, gently pushing me back and closing the lid. "Bob said you're DEA, that right?"

I pulled myself together. "Yes. I've gotten close to a major methamphetamine operation in Petaluma."

"That would be the Vandals."

When I registered surprise he grinned. "Hell, everybody around here knows that. About time you feds got involved."

He was so earnest I almost felt guilty. "Drugs, kidnapping, maybe murder..." I paused, fumbled in my pockets for an old Camel pack I carry for emergencies.

Manson caught the tension in my voice. "Bob'll be along soon."

"Suppose we go on ahead, case the area."

He shook his head. "Once we're out of town, cell phones don't work so good and my two-way is noisy. Which reminds me, we should get on the same page."

We exchanged cell numbers. I made a mental note to lose my phone as soon as possible.

It was a nice quiet place to wait, a deserted gas station at the end of a tree-lined street.

Manson told me Bob Lowell had helped him bust a local burglary ring and they had teamed up on a vigilante drug raid near Petaluma,

"Even out here, these small towns, you can't always trust your fellow officers," Craig said.

"I hear that." I thought of Delaney, my ex-wife. It all seemed very far away. But the memory stirred familiar emotions that amplified my worst fears. If anything happened to Nina... I couldn't deal with the thought.

"Can I bum one of those smokes?"

Now I definitely liked Detective Manson.

"Kind of like the Army... hurry up and wait," he said lighting up.

"How long were you in?"

"Three years. Once in a while I think about a re-up but not for this bullshit. You?"

"Marines, Gulf War. Since we're talking military strategy, do you know the layout at the Sunrise Motel?"

He took a long drag and shook his head. "Been by there any number of times. It's set back from the road behind a stand of Redwoods. Never seems to be that busy but the No Vacancy sign is always up."

There was a thumping inside the trunk. I ignored it.

"Doesn't seem like a good investment for a couple of Vandals."

That perked him up. "Which ones?"

"A guy called Leroy Underwood, now deceased, and Shane Hazer."

Manson gave a low whistle. "Hazer's president of the whole Vandal nation from here to Boston. Even got a chapter in Montreal."

"Can't get him on conspiracy?"

"Hell, they got more lawyers than AT&T. Plus they're colorful media favorites. Show up as Paris Hilton's bodyguards, that kind of stuff."

"You've been keeping tabs."

"I've been keeping them out of Fairfax," he said flatly. "That's all I can do. Bob hasn't been so lucky, especially having to deal with a crooked cop." He carefully field stripped his cigarette butt. "You armed?"

Along the way I had liberated my Sig and extra clips. The Colt nestled snug in my boot. "Yeah, What are you packing?"

His police car was parked in front of mine. He opened his trunk and pulled out a black flak jacket with one hand. In the other was an automatic shotgun. He tossed me the weapon while he put on his jacket.

The shotgun was hefty but well balanced with a cut, deadly looking barrel.

"Remington 12A, 3 ½ inch shells," he said, "what about you?"

I took the Sig from the small of my back where it had made an indelible impression.

Manson gave me a sympathetic smile. "Vegas special."

"Undercover," I said as if that explained anything. I neglected to mention the Colt. That might have really amused the troops. Cops, soldiers, Vandals: all vying for the Macho Cup.

A short time later, Lowell won it hands down.

Chapter 25

This was one of the times Lowell hated his job.

The girl had been stabbed, raped while she lay bleeding to death, then dumped out on the side of a country road. Barely ten minutes from the Pechman place and David Paul.

Off duty, out of uniform, he stood on the sidelines and watched Detective Sergeant Verona contaminate the crime scene. Either the bastard was totally incompetent or wanted to make sure the killer was never convicted.

Lowell had only been on to Verona for a year. Until then he had thought the man was a throwback but basically a good cop. Now he knew Verona was cunning, vicious and corrupt. Any number of cases involving Vandals or their associates had been dismissed because of missing evidence, computer errors or witness intimidation. One female in witness protection had been gunned down because someone disclosed her supposedly secret location. But, without a smoking gun, Lowell couldn't prove anything against Verona.

He knew Max was probably getting antsy but it was his chance to watch Verona operate. Craig would keep Max calm until he arrived.

Lowell got the details from a homicide detective he knew and was headed back to his car when he saw Verona leaving as well. After a moment's deliberation he decided to follow.

Verona was driving an unmarked police vehicle and Lowell kept his headlights off as he trailed the red lights ahead back to town and onto 101 south. For a while he thought Verona was headed to the city until he took the San Rafael exit, turned up Fourth Street and headed for Fairfax.

Maybe they would stumble onto that smoking gun, Lowell thought, mood lifting an increment. Then he remembered the dead girl. He called Craig, knowing Max would be chomping at the bit by now. He hoped the DEA agent could play team ball. There'd be only three of them.

At the moment he wasn't worried about Verona. No doubt he was heading for the Sunrise Motel. He was worried about Max. When he broke the bad news, Max might detonate.

His guess was the DEA agent had been undercover too long. He had all the classic signs: hair-trigger temper, reckless decisions. Lowell knew because he suffered the same character defects.

In the army as a paratrooper he had never really fit in but he'd felt compelled to take on the riskiest assignments: night jumps, free fall to specific targets, anything to prove himself. As a Green Beret he volunteered for a hazardous rescue mission in Bosnia. But, after pulling the hostage out of a rat infested barn, Lowell engaged the captors in a firefight instead of retreating directly to the waiting chopper, resulting in the hostage and another member of his team being wounded. He wasn't officially reprimanded but he was passed over for future assignments.

Lowell applied for sniper school where he could work alone. The next sixteen weeks were more intense than jump school or Green Beret boot camp. He was driven past fatigue then required to control his body and breath and hit targets barely visible. He learned how to stay concealed for hours and approach his victim one inch at a time. He learned how to load, sight and shoot an SR-75 rifle, calculating wind, distance and bullet arc within a radius of two inches at two thousand yards. Ultimately he learned as much about patience as about killing.

The loneliness of the long distance sniper, Lowell brooded. Sitting out there invisible, like a buried land mine. All that patience coiled around his repressed anger like detcord primed to blow.

That's what he sensed in Max, lonely, deeply angry, something of an adrenaline junkie. We share character flaws and deep personal secrets, Lowell observed ruefully, which are dubious reasons to risk my career and my life.

At the edge of Fairfax his headlights picked out Craig's police car. Max's vehicle was harder to spot. He parked next to the gas station then walked slowly to where they stood, dreading what he had to tell Max.

Chapter 26

"If you're brave and honorable and your enemies can't destroy you personally, they'll seek to destroy what you love."
James Lee Burke, In The Electric Mist With Confederate Dead

Lowell's face was grim. I braced myself for the worst. "Did a car go by a few minutes ago?" he asked Manson.

"Yeah, why?"

"That was Verona. He came directly from the site."

"Goddamnit," I blurted, "who is she?"

Both of them looked at me with guarded expressions.

"Victim is Tami Pratchett. Dairy worker found her body about two miles from the Pechman place."

I exhaled slowly. "Tami Pratchett," I repeated.

Then it hit me. David Paul had nothing to do with Tami. Todd had everything to do with her. I whirled and half-trotted back to my car.

Lowell seemed to know my intentions. As I opened the trunk he yanked me back.

"Don't be stupid. The little prick is just a Judas goat."

"Oh, shit."

Manson's alarmed voice brought us back to reality.

"What?" Lowell asked, still holding my arm.

"He's going into convulsions."

I looked inside my trunk and saw Todd shivering violently, face rolling in a pool of vomit.

"Get him up," Lowell said.

I helped raise Todd out of the trunk but he couldn't stand, body shaking and knees collapsing beneath him.

"Don't put me back in there," he rasped, "I'll die in there."

The vomit was enough to convince me.

"Put him in my vehicle," Manson said. "There's a perp cage."

Lowell and I hauled Todd to Manson's police car. Lowell uncuffed him and attached one hand to the door handle. Todd slumped to the floor, arm raised as if accepting an ovation.

Manson found a blanket in his trunk and threw it over Todd's trembling form. While he locked the rear door, four motorcycles rumbled past closely followed by a large van with off-road tires.

We looked at each other.

"Time to roll," Manson said, "I've got a plan."

It was a good plan. We would take separate vehicles, Manson leading the way. He would pull off road about fifty yards from the motel. We would park behind him. Manson and I would proceed on foot to the entrance. Once we made sure the area was secure, Manson would signal Lowell who would block the entrance with the police car and cover our assault with his heavy caliber weapon.

It sounded logical. Except war is chaos.

Lowell left his car carrying the largest rifle I'd ever seen. For a moment I thought it was a Stinger missile launcher.

"Custom Special SR75," he said tersely. I had only heard of the weapon. In fact, until then, I thought it was a legend like the Abominable Snowman. I shut up and let him go ahead, my Sig feeling like an air gun.

Manson was good.

He blocked the narrow road leading to the motel, motioned us into position and moved silently to the courtyard which was hidden behind the trees.

The van and seven motorcycles were parked in the courtyard. The two story motel was small, six units on each floor facing an office across the way which showed light behind closed blinds. Verona's car was parked near the office next to an oddly-small, sleek motorcycle.

The van stood backed against a stairway at the near end of the motel, waiting to load something. The Harleys were bunched at the far end.

Manson took point moving from side to side with practiced efficiency. No noise, hardly a shadow, just sheer cobra skills. Can't teach those.

Lowell wasn't far behind. He coasted down the driveway, parked, and snaked his way to the other side of the office while Manson crawled toward the van. So far not a sound, either of them.

Let the game come to you. For some reason the old mantra learned in CYO basketball came to me as I followed Manson. If Nina was anywhere she'd be in one of the motel rooms.

Abruptly a door on the second level opened, spilling light. Manson froze, so did I.

A giant, mullet-haired biker escorted a disheveled but still striking young female to the van. From where I sat it looked like Carla Fuente. Her escort was a monster, at least six-six and about four hundred pounds of bad karma. Carla looked sick, stumbling after the hulk who dragged her down the stairs by one arm.

That's one, I thought, more certain than ever that Nina was nearby.

The hulk put Carla in the van and shut the door. Then he plodded back upstairs. At the same time a trio of men emerged from a ground level unit at the corner of the motel where their Harleys were parked. They carried taped bricks, probably kilos of crank. Each man stuffed the bricks into their saddlebags. They had left the room door open and a noxious odor tainted the tree-minted air. A blend of sulfurous fumes infused with kerosene, obviously a meth lab. Equally obvious was that they were about to distribute their product. By morning, half of

California would be grinding their teeth, scratching their arms, and bypassing lunch and dinner.

Two more Vandals came into view carrying product, which left two bikes unaccounted for. Most likely the hulk would drive the van which left two more somewhere, maybe inside the lab. I didn't know how many in the van. I had to assume at least one to guard Carla.

As the hulk climbed the stairs, Manson crept to the left side of the van and knelt behind the front tire. This afforded a clear quadrant of fire that covered the lab and office as well as the Vandals still packing their saddlebags with a fortune in methamphetamine.

The hulk moved his great mass slowly and had just reached the top of the stairway when the silence snapped like a power line spitting fire and death indiscriminately.

Chapter 27

Todd Fletcher believed he was in hell.

It was oppressively hot inside the trunk. What little air was available stank of piss and vomit. His blistered, swollen brain throbbed with incessant pain and his back teeth were loose. Agony stabled his bruised kidney with every breath and he was having a massively depressing meth crash.

If he had the balls he'd off himself right here in this stinking trunk, he thought. He still couldn't grasp how fast it had all collapsed. The band, the money, the bitches, the drugs, more money: he'd been ready to drop his new album when this asshole appears out of nowhere looking for Carla.

Should have bugged out the first time the asshole showed at the door, Todd ranted inwardly adding to his crushing despair. Why the fuck had he agreed to lure Nina to Shane? He knew the answer to that one, two ounces of pure blue flake.

That was the price for every bitch he delivered to Shane's stable.

The first time he sold both ounces. Lately he'd been keeping one for personal use.

Dimly he heard voices above the trunk lid. That fucking DEA pig. Where did he come from? Shane had the cops in his pocket. Todd suddenly realized he'd probably get prison time, the prospect causing him to vomit again. Then the chills came back.

The voices above got louder and he heard a metallic scrape. A rush of cool air intensified his chills and he began to convulse, muscles twisting.

"Get him out of there," somebody said.

Shivering violently he felt himself being lifted out of the trunk. "Don't put me back there," he pleaded hoarsely, "I'll die in there."

He collapsed into a fetal position while they talked. Again they lifted him and dragged his spastic body to a police car where they tossed him in the back and cuffed him to the door handle. He slumped to the floor, one arm raised as if half-crucified.

Todd remained on the floor as the cop drove for a while then parked. Then he drove very slowly for a couple of minutes, parked and left the car. For long minutes it was dark and quiet.

Fuckers had him for kidnapping and drugs if Shane didn't kill him first, Todd calculated darkly. Ragged fear tore through the pain and nausea, his brain clawing frantically against his skull like a trapped beast. He couldn't do jail time. He had to get out somehow but he was too drained to move. It was a fucking tweaker's hell crashing cold turkey in the slam. They'd kill him in there or worse.

Then his feverish thoughts found traction... and he remembered.

They hadn't finished searching him. There was still more than a gram of crank in his jeans.

A gargled sob of relief flushed his burning throat when his free hand dove into his pocket and closed on the tiny glass vial. Too impaired to even consider snorting he took the cap between his teeth and very carefully twisted the vial open. Then he spit the cap aside and with trembling fingers tapped some speed into his mouth.

Its bitter taste almost triggered a fresh wave of nausea but he fought it back and let the gritty powder dissolve under his tongue. It took longer than he hoped, huddled in the rear cage for long, tortured minutes, hand clutching the precious vial, but it came on like a clear, sunny day after a hurricane.

Immediately, his contracted ribs expended and he took deep breaths that blew the offal and rot from his skull. The pain in his kidney became bearable and a rush of energy surfed from spine to brain.

A few more breaths and his body spasms ebbed. Another wave, stronger than the first cleared his thoughts. In control now, he sat up next to the door handle, tapped a mound of powder onto the back of his cuffed hand and snorted it.

Another of those and he was beyond fear. Yeah, mother-fucker, he exhorted, time to find a way past this.

Methodically, he picked up the cap, secured it between his teeth and screwed the vial shut. Most important, don't lose the crank. That task accomplished he concentrated on the cuffs binding his wrist to the door handle.

Using his free hand he began to yank on the handle until he felt it give. At that point he paused, gathered himself, reveling in the surge of confidence driving him. He took a deep breath, grabbed the handle with both hands, braced his feet against the door and jerked back hard.

The handle bent and snapped off giving him two free hands. The first thing he did with those hands was snort more meth. The blood surged through his veins like a tsunami, threatening to burst the walls of his heart but he didn't give a shit. Better to blow his aorta than get old behind bars. Oh, yeah, he was a rockstar. Either way he'd be in the headlines, *VH1*, *Biography*, *People*, *Star*, *National Enquirer*: shit they'd be visiting his grave like Jim Morrison.

He replaced the cap on the vial and considered his options.

The locked rear doors were too strong. Only one way out. But there was no hurry. The pigs who dragged him out of Bobo's were pulling a raid on the motel. Todd had only been there once but knew it housed Shane's latest stable and the lab. So he had two ways to play it.

One: Escape back to Petaluma, lose Nina's goddamn cell phone and deny everything. Only problem there, the Vandals would assume he ratted them out and kill him slowly, with extreme cruelty.

Two: He could bust out of this cage and warn the Vandals it was a raid.

He liked Two. It was heroic. Anyway, one was out of the question.

Yes, everything was clear and he had never felt better in his life.

Fuckin' A.

With exaggerated care Todd braced his back, gripped the edge of the seat kicked the cage methodically with his Doc Martens boots. The exertion seemed to enhance the crank whistling through every vein and capillary. His thin muscles expanded with blood and sheer will as he kept kicking.

He would not remain caged, oh no, no, no, no, NO.

The wire netting sagged. A few more kicks ripped it aside.

Yes. He was free.

Todd eased his skinny body through the damaged netting and into the front seat. He was about to jump out when he thought of something. There might be a weapon.

He ransacked the glove compartment in vain, there was nothing up front but a billy club. On impulse he popped the trunk. Yes.

Nestled behind door number two was a Colt .45.

Todd racked a round into the chamber and slipped the safety. The weapon endowed him with a power far greater than drugs. The power of life and death. The power to turn defeat to triumph.

The power to blow that bald motherfucker's face off.

Oh yeah. One bullet in the right place and he was back on top.

Grimacing with boiling emotion Todd stood in the cool silence breathing deep. Then he sprang into action. Moving at a measured trot he came onto the courtyard and saw him crouched behind the van. He kept coming, eyes fixed on the bald skull a few yards away.

Right there in his gun sight was the bastard who started all this. *With his back turned.*

Deliberately Todd took careful aim at his tormenter and squeezed the trigger.

Chapter 28

"Relax, Walter, this is what we've all been waiting for." Verona sipped his scotch. "I say we hold back a week or so."

"We can't. Everything is in motion. Clockwork, Walter. Clockwork."

Verona shook his head and stared into his glass as if looking for an answer.

"Fact is, Shane, there's talk the DEA is sniffin' up here. You know that shit went down at Molly's tonight? Who is that son of a bitch? Tell me that."

Shane Hazer was finding it difficult to restrain his temper. Fortunately, tonight's run would complete their business and end Sergeant Verona's usefulness. He knew Verona would crack like an egg if anything went down.

"Tell you what, Walter, after tonight we all go on vacation. As a bonus, I will personally show you around Vegas. On me."

Of course you won't be coming back, Shane added silently. What happens in Vegas stays in Vegas.

"I do need a vacation," Verona said, somewhat mollified. He knew the Vandals had a string of hookers on the strip. He could use a party.

"We're ready to fly," Shane confided. "By tomorrow afternoon our crystal will have turned into more money than we can haul in our jet. Plus, all the hardware we'll need to blow away any problems."

Shane hadn't told Verona everything. The girls for example. Each of them was worth one hundred fifty thousand. But more importantly it was the reason his client was so anxious to trade. His weapons for my girls, Shane gloated. Pure California bred beauties that would fetch over a million in Oman and Yemen. Oh, yes, this was much better than running hookers with their endless ailments and complaints.

And the return was enormous. A bazooka, two stingers, fifty AK-47s, fifty Uzis, four 50mm machine guns, thousands of rounds: enough armor to eradicate all rivals.

"Here's something that should cool you down," Shane said tossing a fat, white envelope into Verona's fat, white lap. "Count it."

"Always." He ripped open the envelope and riffled through the stacks with practiced ease. He looked up scowling. "There's only twenty-five thousand here."

"You'll get the rest at the other end."

Verona carefully placed the bills on the table beside his armchair. "No way. Our deal is cash up front."

Shane heaved a theatrical sigh and tossed another envelope on the table, spilling some bills. Verona was quick to scoop them up. He eagerly counted the bills then stuffed them into a money belt beneath his black flak jacket.

Shane refilled his glass. "So now—feel better? Let's go over it one more time."

Verona drained his scotch and shrugged. "I know what I have to do. Just make sure your boys don't fuck up."

Shane spread his arms. "Indulge me, Walter. So I know we're on the same page."

"I follow the van to San Francisco. Your boys follow me. Anybody stops the van or your men I step in, show my badge, explain we're on official business."

"Very good, Walter. As soon as my soldiers load the merch, we'll be ready to roll."

"Where are you taking the girls?"

The question surprised Shane. He didn't think Verona was capable of speculative thought. But of course it did concern pussy and money.

"The girls go to Vegas via Cisco," he lied. "You can have one when we get to the strip."

"How do they get there?"

Shane paused. He could tell Verona was getting greedy. But it made no difference. By the end of the week Walter would reside beneath the Nevada desert.

"We have our own private shuttle service," he said. "Tomorrow you fly with us,"

"Damn," Verona said, impressed. Shane could see he was already calculating how much he could skim.

A lewd smile spread across the detective's broad face. "How many chickens we haulin' tonight?"

Shane tried to mask his contempt. "Three," he said, thinking.

Carla Fuente was the prize of the lot but she had to be eliminated between here and the drop point. Slow would handle that. Janis Hopper, the tall blonde, needed motivation in the form of drugs. Otherwise she was top shelf. The third was problematical. He'd grabbed Nina Fuente to teach her—and her boyfriend—a lesson. A few hours with Slow Pain and she'd tell them everything about the bastard. Then they'd ship her to the Middle East. It would make up for Carla.

And there would be others. Many others.

"Only three?" Verona refilled his glass. "You're slowin' down."

Actually I'm just getting started, Shane thought.

"Next run I'm gonna need a bit more money."

"Of course," Shane said smoothly. "Everyone will get what they deserve."

He couldn't wait to get rid of this slime.

His mind leaped ahead to next year when he would have total control of the drug trade in Northern California , Vegas and Montreal. By then he would be nearly legit and in show biz. Suge and Diddy proved the Aryan Brotherhood had a lot to learn.

The sound of a gunshot shattered his reverie.

Verona half-stood, bug-eyed. "What the fuck..?"

Shane yanked his Glock from the desk drawer and pointed it at Verona.

"Get the fuck out there."

Reluctantly, Verona unsnapped his own Glock and lumbered to the door. When he cracked it open all hell broke loose.

The flat clap of gunshots skated above roaring motorcycle engines. Shane glimpsed Slow Pain across the courtyard.

"Five-O!" Someone shouted.

Shane dashed out of the office and across the courtyard. He knew what he had to do. Kill all witnesses, starting with the new bitch.

Chapter 29

"We all have it comin' kid."
Clint Eastwood, Unforgiven

A single shot set it off.

The bullet punched the roof of the van behind me. I whipped around and saw Todd Fletcher lurching into the courtyard Somehow he'd managed to break out of Manson's perp cage and find a gun.

I glanced back. Manson was waving his weapon from side to side, trying to locate the shooter.

Too late. Three or four Vandals revved their engines and rolled across the courtyard, guns bristling. They saw Manson and fired.

Nothing works like a shotgun. Manson's first two blasts dropped the lead biker and forced the others to retreat.

A bullet spat past my ear and I saw Todd staggering wildly toward me, handcuff dangling from one wrist. He was trying hard to kill me but every shot bucked him sideways. I looked up and spotted the hulk at the head of the stairs, pistol raised defensively.

"Five-O!" Todd yelled.

The hulk turned, heaved his bulk across the second level and disappeared inside one of the units. Behind me, Manson fired at the bikers and I did the same trying to keep them cornered.

Suddenly the hulk emerged and waddled quickly along the walkway, gun in hand. I had a bad feeling. He wasn't playing defense. He had another agenda.

I slid back along the side of the van. "Going up!" I shouted, pointing to make sure Manson didn't mistake me for the enemy. I hoped Lowell would hold his fire, wherever he was.

The hulk was shouldering a door as I scrambled up the concrete stairs. His next charge nearly ripped the door off its hinges. Without hesitation he fired blindly into the room.

I didn't hesitate either, peppering the wall with three quick shots all of which missed.

The hulk lunged into the room out of sight.

Just then the Vandals at the end of the courtyard mounted an attack, bikes thundering guns blasting. Manson's shotgun got one but the others bore down on him. I sprayed rapid fire to provide some kind of cover. As the bikers closed to within ten feet of the van I heard a boom that was closer to artillery than a shotgun. I saw the lead Harley literally disintegrate, front end, wheel, handlebars, everything, its rider hurled backwards. The rest screeched to a halt and retreated, rumbling back and forth like trapped tigers.

My focus was still on the hulk. I pressed flat against the wall slipping a fresh clip in my Sig. With short, sliding steps I edged closer to the partially open door.

A limp figure floated into view. My brain teetered drunkenly.

It was Nina, bleeding.

Hulk's beefy arm circled her waist holding her aloft, her blood soaked torso shielding him.

I couldn't shoot but he did. His bullet hit my Kevlar vest like a pile driver swatting me to the concrete. When I got up Hulk was slowly making his way down the stairs.

Afraid to fire for fear of hitting Nina I scurried to the railing. I waited for the sound of Manson's shotgun but he must have been holding fire for the same reason I did.

Abruptly, Verona popped up on my right.

He shuffled around the far corner holding a Glock at high port. He fired the moment he saw me and missed.

My bullet whined off the stucco wall punctuating his retreat.

An instant later someone stepped around the same corner blasting away. Shane Hazer stood in the open, calmly firing at me as if on a practice range.

Again the Kevlar saved my ass. He hit me square toppling me backwards. My neck bounced off the concrete and I blacked out, brain whining like a shrill tuning fork Dimly, I heard two quick shots. When I lifted my head, everybody was gone.

It wasn't easy getting back on my feet. Ribs screaming in pain I crawled over to the railing and pulled myself up. Where the fuck is everybody? I thought insanely.

Where's Nina?

From my perch on the second floor I spotted Shane's silver grey hair streaking across the courtyard. He donned an oversized black helmet, hopped onto the oddly-undersized motorcycle and zipped across the courtyard dodging shotgun pellets and my own erratic fire to rejoin his men at the rear of the motel.

A shuffling sound below caught my attention. Hulk edged out into the open still holding Nina as a shield. She was unconscious, blood soaking her shirt down to her jeans.

I took a step back and moved to the stairs knowing I couldn't shoot. Frustration escalated to rage as I watched him carry Nina into the open courtyard area one labored step at a time. The longer they remained out there the more likely she'd catch a stray bullet.

Hulk didn't care. Nina was just a piece of body armor to him.

At that moment I saw Verona lumbering across the courtyard to his car. I half-expected someone to cut him down but he made it without a shot being fired.

I had lost track of Manson and Lowell. Fuming I shoved a fresh clip in the Sig and moved to the top of the stairs only to see the hulk dump Nina into the back of the van.

I ducked out of sight to give him time to come in my direction then lunged into the open, gun dowsing for a clear shot.

He never saw me. I had him cold in my sight as he clumsily mounted the driver's seat.

A ghostly shadow entered the corner of my vision.

I turned and saw Todd standing there, mouth caked red with blood, nose pasted with white powder and eyes like blue neon pinwheels. The All-American boy, wired to the base of his spine.

He was also aiming a .45 directly at my throat.

No Kevlar there.

No way he could miss.

I heard the van start up and thought of Nina.

Chapter 30

Craig Manson had endured ribbing about his name for as long as he could remember. He had grown up in Los Angeles not too far from where Charlie's angels had done their evil work.

Not far in distance but light years from the gated estates and sleek canyon homes. His father was a drunk and his mom held two jobs to keep Craig and his little sister, Wendy, together. He was a good student but early on became hooked on surfing. Before and after class he would bike down to the pier and surf with a group of older boys.

Craig loved the cold, brackish Pacific waters where he could figure things out on his own and just be. Out there, waiting for the next swell, feeling it rise, feeling the ocean, everything made sense. Nothing much else did.

Whenever his father managed to get sober and find a job he usually lost it by the second month. A few times his old man had held on for over seven months and he'd collected unemployment. That was as close to stable as things ever got.

Otherwise it was the drinking, the rages, mindless destruction... Once or twice Craig had to stop him from hitting his mother. After the second incident his old man never raised his hand to her again.

It happened when Craig was fourteen.

He was tall for his age and strong. He threw one reflexive punch that broke his father's nose. Nobody ever talked about it again and things went on as before except Wendy and his mother no longer feared the old man's fists.

From then on he became the de facto man of the house helping out with odd jobs all through high school, He enlisted in the Army after graduation to get enough money for college tuition. The army trained him as an MP and, eventually, he was based in Germany. When his second tour was up, Craig went back to civilian life.

While attending UCLA, studying marine biology, he got a night job as a security guard. He learned that by taking courses at the Criminal Justice school he would qualify for a higher pay scale.

He kept working security through the summers, taking extra credits during the day and graduated early with a minor in Criminal Justice and his coveted major in Marine Biology. Craig hoped to work close to the sea he loved. However, his father had long since died and his sister was about to enter college. His mother could only handle one job these days and for many years Craig had been a prime support of the family. When an opportunity came up for qualified graduates to join a special unit of the LAPD he applied and was accepted.

The pay grade was higher than a rookie cop and the duties more challenging. Homicides, large drug busts, white-collar crimes, errant celebrities: anything the press was likely to seize on that day. The LAPD needed smart, college educated officers to deal with the victims, perps, their lawyers, and the media.

At first, Craig thought he had lucked out but the toxic corruption all around them soon seeped into their privileged unit. Craig learned a few of the officers were tipping off lawyers in exchange for payment. Others were tipping off the media. In one case a male TV star charged with murder managed to have crucial DNA evidence vanish.

It was that case that convinced Craig to quit the LAPD and find a nice, quiet little community where he could be a real cop. He settled in Fairfax, a charming village in a remote corner of Marin County. He moved his mother there as well. For a few years things were just fine. He solved crimes, arrested bad guys and got married to a local girl.

Then methamphetamine came to town. And with it cash, corruption and violence.

Everyone knew the Vandals were the main players. The gang had even gotten to one of his colleagues, Sergeant Jeff Toomey. Instead of trying to expose him, Craig used him to extract information.

However, in Petaluma the Vandals had Walter Verona on their payroll, a veteran officer with ties to the DA who was much more difficult to deal with. Meeting Bob Lowell had made all the difference, Craig thought. The rugged detective had covered his back during more than a few unauthorized raids on drug houses. Some they just hit and trashed, some led to convictions. He managed to keep the dealers and labs away from Fairfax and had recently received a promotion to Lieutenant.

Problem was, the drugs kept coming.

Lowell wasn't treated as well in Petaluma, still stuck at Sergeant rank, largely due to an inept bureaucracy that spawned Verona. But he hung in and Craig was grateful he did. The cannon he carried had been the decider in a few gun battles with meth-crazed dealers.

Although they had become close, Craig didn't really know much about Lowell. Over time he learned that Lowell had been part of an elite military strike force and trained as a sniper. Lowell didn't volunteer a whole lot more but Craig got the impression he left the service under a cloud.

Most likely pissed off his superiors by telling the truth, Craig speculated. Way of the world.

The new player Lowell had brought in was a wild card. He looked like a rough customer with his shaved head, deep set eyes, kind of a reckless look about him like the big wave surfers at Mavericks. But Craig liked the way the DEA agent conducted himself. Going up against the Vandals they would need to be totally professional. The bikers were deadly shooters and had advanced weaponry. Rumor was they had acquired a Stinger.

What worried Craig was that Max had a personal stake in this raid. He hoped he would keep his cool. If what happened earlier with the kid in the trunk was any indication it could put them at risk.

Hell, this whole thing was risky. Sooner or later the Vandals would target him, Craig knew. And when it happened he didn't want his family around. He and his wife, Ivy, had a two-year-old girl, Sara, and a second due in three months. They still didn't know what sex the new one was. That's the way Ivy wanted it. She was old-fashioned that way.

Craig was still thinking about Ivy and Sara as he neared the Sunrise Motel. After this he was through playing vigilante hero. They needed legitimate backup. The Vandals had a damned army out there. He hoped they weren't all at the Sunrise Motel.

The sign outside read, No Vacancy.

On foot, coming around the trees he could see there was some activity on the seemingly deserted property.

The van puzzled him. The Vandals usually conducted business on their Harleys: fast, mobile, hard to catch. Then he saw Verona's car parked near the office.

Even though he knew Verona was dirty, it saddened him. It also made him angry. It tarnished everyone on the job. A cop with no honor, no shame, a damned scumbag. He controlled his anger as he wove in and out of the shadows, working his way closer to the motel.

It was a typical U-shaped property with a two-storey efficiency on one side, an office cottage on the other. There were connecting stairs at each end of the motel. Manson counted five doors on each floor, probably two or more around the corner. He could see seven Harleys clustered at the far end of the hotel. He was about to move closer when a door on the second level opened and a giant biker came out holding an extremely pretty girl by one arm. The girl looked tired and scared. The giant looked mean and stupid.

Manson ducked back into the shadows as the giant came downstairs, put the girl in the rear of the van and returned upstairs. At the same time, two Vandals walked into view at the other end and began packing bricks into their saddlebags.

He waited until the giant was well gone then quickly moved closer to the van.

Three more bikers appeared bearing taped bricks. Judging from the odor of rotten eggs drifting in the air, there was a lab on the premises. Using the van as cover he moved into position, hunkered down behind the rear tire. He got a glimpse of Lowell circling the tree line behind the cottage.

Manson was also comforted to see Max was exactly where he should be, seven feet back, crouched behind the front tire. He was just about to disable the Harleys when the shit hit the fan.

A bullet creased the roof of the van and he whirled. The kid they'd secured in his perp cage had gotten loose, found a gun—probably the .45 he kept in his trunk—and was staggering toward them shooting erratically.

At the rear of the courtyard, three Vandals mounted their bikes and charged. Manson calmly blew one Vandal into the air. The others retreated. He lost sight of the kid but saw Max firing. The giant came down the stairs, fired a few rounds in their direction then hustled back upstairs.

Again the Vandals attacked. His shotgun brought down the lead man, the others turned away. Everything seemed to intensify. He saw activity on both floors. He glimpsed the kid fire his way then duck under the stairs. Then he spotted the giant sliding along the second level using a wounded female as a shield. He held his fire as the huge biker came down and shoved the bloody female into the van.

In the corner of his eye he saw Max creeping down the stairs gun fixed on the giant. But he never fired. Manson glanced back and saw Verona stumbling across the courtyard to his car. For some reason, Manson couldn't pull the trigger.

Then it all unraveled. A phalanx of Vandals appeared as the van pulled out, leaving him exposed. Pissed at his failure to bring Verona down he stepped out blasting his shotgun. He dropped two but the lead biker squirted past with the van. The other Vandals split ranks. Lowell's rifle sliced one Harley in half.

Manson turned in time to see a MAC-10 spitting in his direction. The shooter aimed low sending up a thick cloud of gravel and dust. Manson calmly kept moving forward and when the dust cleared enough to acquire his target he blew the MAC-10 away.

What he didn't see was the bullet that smacked him down.

Manson saw the blood and knew he'd been wounded somewhere. He tried to get up but couldn't. Vaguely aware of gunfire popping around him he closed his eyes.

When he opened them again he thought he was hallucinating.

A hellish demon galloped toward him, fangs bared in savage fury.

Chapter 31

"If a gallows is cleanwhat more can a criminal expect?"
Alexander Trocchi, Cain's Book

Clack!

Misfire.

Todd had no bullets left.

He gave me a rueful really-didn't-mean-it shrug and dropped the .45.

"Okay, I give up, okay?"

A sharp smirk skipped across his vomit-streaked face. "Shit, I forgot, you assholes don't have warrants do you?"

Battle adrenaline and raving fear for Nina transmuted my blood to a double helix of primal ferocity. Heart battering my cracked ribs I heard the van backing up and jerked my weapon after it. I had to get to Nina.

"Yeah, sure, arrest me. You can't make it stick," Todd said, seemingly unable to shut up. "I'm walking. We're all fucking walking."

I could see the cranked-up triumph lighting up his corroded brain. He scratched his arms, knowing I wouldn't shoot.

The van began moving forward.

"You taking me in or what?" Todd said.

I didn't want to arrest him. I wanted to pull Nina from the van rolling out of the courtyard.

"You dumb bastard, you'll be lucky if I don't sue," Todd said.

Then he laughed.

And I saw *the preacher.*

Long ago, after some childhood episode, my mother sent me to a cleric for a disciplinary chat. First, he took my confession then he beat the living shit out of me.

Later in life I discovered that adrenaline snaps a button in my psyche, unleashing a murderous jolt of electricity. The only way I could explain it to myself was to conjure an image of a tall, stern preacher with two six-guns strapped beneath his black coat, striding out of the sky to wreak God's vengeance.

Another explanation? Maybe I'm psycho.

When he laughed, I pulled the trigger.

The bullet pierced the Sacred Heart tattooed on his chest. He gaped at the spurting blood, surprised.

Before he collapsed I was stumbling after the van. Ribcage screaming with each breath I lurched down the stairs firing wildly at the bikers who trailed in military formation..

As the van left the courtyard I saw Manson step into full view and blast two of the Vandals into the gravel. The lead bike skipped past after the van, the other two reared up like spooked horses. Instead of finding cover, Manson advanced. Meanwhile the van was well out of sight.

The two bikers peeled off in opposite directions. One swung toward Manson, the other to the rear of the courtyard. Dimly, I realized Shane Hazer had followed the van on that small, speedy bike. .

Torn between chasing after Nina or covering Manson, I did the right thing, wrapping him with rapid fire as he kept advancing. Crazy Motherfucker.

Caught in our crossfire the Vandal paused, wedged his weapon between the handlebars and slowly rolled at Manson, shooting all the way. His MAC-10 ripped up a cloud of gravel and dust.

Manson emerged from the smoke and blew the shooter off his bike.

I turned and saw the remaining Vandal taking aim with a long-barreled rifle. Before I could fire he did.

Manson went down hard. I sprayed a few bullets in the biker's direction but he was already nearing the safety of the motel.

A loud crack reverberated in the courtyard and his bike snapped in two like a pencil. Miraculously the man managed to get to his knees, grab his rifle and crawl to the motel as two more heavy-caliber rounds gouged large chunks out of the stucco walls.

I heard an ominous pop. Seconds later a white-flash explosion barbecued the trees behind the office.

I was impressed. The bastards had a fucking grenade launcher.

But I wasn't ready for what they threw out next

Three famished pit bulls tore around the far corner of the motel, their jaws yawning for fresh meat. One leaped in the direction of the office, another raced toward Manson's inert body.

The third beast bounded directly for me.

It closed the gap with astonishing speed. Before I could point my Sig the dog jumped, sharp teeth digging for my flesh.

I love dogs but didn't hesitate. I ducked aside and fired.

My loud shot shredded one of his ears. He squealed and ran off. Lucky pup.

I turned in Manson's direction and saw him fighting off a slavering beast with one arm while his free hand pawed the ground for his shotgun. Desperately trying to survive would be better way to put it since the put bull had his forearm in a canine death grip.

My first shot missed and I ran closer aiming for the dog's flank. Before I got there Manson's free hand found his shotgun, gripped the barrel and whacked the pit bull's skull. The dog collapsed, jaws still clenching Manson's arm. Gingerly I pried them loose. As I did the ragged puncture marks oozed oily red.

"Max, help me up."

I started to do that, then saw a small lake of blood beneath his thigh.

"Stay down... I'll be right back"

I crept quickly across the courtyard, foraging for supplies by the eerie light of a tree set ablaze by the grenade. I took two do rags and a pint of bourbon from fallen Vandals. By now Nina and Carla were four or five minutes away but I couldn't leave Manson. When I returned to his side I soaked the do rags in Jim Beam and tied them together to make a crude battlefield bandage.

I gave the bandage to Manson. "Can you tie this?"

"Yeah sure... where you going?" He said as I turned.

"To get us a ride."

During my supply run I had heard one of the motorcycles still running. I hefted it and saw the key was in the ignition. It was a big, old-school Harley that would carry Manson sidesaddle. As I picked it up I heard a now familiar boom behind me. I looked back and saw a man at the far end of the courtyard. He staggered drunkenly in the dull orange yellow flicker of the burning tree, searching for his missing shoulder and arm which lay on the ground beside him.

Lowell had circled back near the entrance and was covering our retreat. I felt better about exposing my back when I hauled the Harley upright. Rolling back to Manson's side I spotted a MAC-10 and scooped it. I paused to check the dead biker for a fresh clip and found two in a sling.

Armed and mobile, I helped Manson onto the bike and started out of the courtyard.

A loud crack from Lowell's cannon drew my attention. I paused and saw the heavy caliber rounds had crumbled a corner of the stucco wall at the other end.

A door opened. As two figures leaped into view firing wildly, a third knelt in an open doorway, spraying the courtyard with an Uzi.

Lowell responded with a quick pair of shots. The first knocked the shooter back inside the corner unit. The second ignited a violent fireball that illuminated the courtyard like a lightning bolt an instant before the thunderclap shattered windows. I felt Manson grip me tighter as a hot wind almost lifted the Harley off the gravel.

Meth labs are notoriously volatile.

Lowell emerged from the trees at my right waving frantically, his battle-wide eyes gleaming in the flames.

"Take a left," he shouted. "They're going left!"

"Craig's hit," I shouted back. "Call emergency!"

I didn't hear his answer against the roar of the motorcycle as we headed for the main road. Manson's car had been pushed aside by the van. The dented body sat half on the road.

"You carry a first aid kit?"

"In the trunk," Manson said, voice shaky.

The trunk was already wide open. I grabbed the kit and rode to my waiting car. I carefully helped Manson into the back seat, strapped him in along with the first aid kit. I jumped behind the wheel and tossed my new MAC-10 on the seat beside me, bringing fresh meaning to the term riding shotgun.

By now the van was a good ten minutes ahead. There were only two ways out of the Sunrise Motel. Right led to Fairfax, left to back country roads and remote beaches. A ten minute head start might be all the hulk needed, even driving the unwieldy van around narrow curves. He could turn off anywhere along the wooded area and once he emerged there were three roads to choose from. My headlights stabbed the darkness, my hands tight on the wheel when, incredibly, my cell phone rang.

It was Lowell.

"I'm behind you. Roads are sealed west and south. Ambulance waiting both ends. East still open—out."

That was comforting.

I leaned hard on the pedal, the weighted suspension hugging the curved road at high speed.

"It was Lowell," I said over my shoulder, "you okay back there?"

"Good. Got a tourniquet on my leg., poured peroxide on my arm... fucking pit bulls, can you believe it?"

"You know this neck of the woods?"

"Pretty well."

"Where would you run?"

"East probably."

Great. The one road not sealed.

"Can you navigate?"

"No problem. Unless I pass out."

"There's an ambulance at road block west."

"They sure aren't heading for any roadblock. Bob knows it too."

"Your call. You're the one caught a bullet."

"East. I'll tell you when."

I admired him but was worried. Leg wounds can be fatal. There's a major artery behind the thigh that can spring a gallon in minutes. If he faltered I resolved to head for the ambulance and trust Lowell to chase down the van.

"Turn right here."

I turned onto open farmland, hit a rise and there they were. The van, the motorcycle and Verona's car: a skeleton caravan moving along a long shallow valley.

"Call Lowell," I said, "they're up ahead."

"He's right behind us."

I glanced at my rear view and saw the headlights. All I needed now was a plan. What would I do if I caught the bastards? A gunfight might wound Nina or Carla.

For the moment it was enough to have contact. I stamped the pedal and held on. The Merc responded, eating up the distance between me and Nina. Still it was imperative that I come up with a damned plan before Nina and Manson bled to death.

"Can you handle the shotgun from here?"

"Sure."

He didn't sound convincing.

"How's the leg?"

"Bleeding's under control but it burns like a sonofabitch."

"Take a painkiller."

"Not yet. Need to stay alert."

From the Marines to the NYPD to the DEA I hadn't met many like Craig Manson. But even with him and Lowell at my back I was losing hope.

Then an astonishing thing happened. I was midway down the long sloping road, the caravan still within sight, when the lead van fishtailed violently and came to a skidding halt sideways which caused the motorcycle to crash into the van, throwing the rider.

The sudden boom echoing over the valley wasn't due to the collision. It was Lowell's SR75 wreaking havoc on the van's rear tire. In my side mirror I could see him stopped on the crest of the hill where he could get a clear shot.

Still, it was over a thousand yards, in the dark, on a moving target.

Properly awed but angry because Nina was in harm's way I rushed to the now stalled caravan. Verona's car was stopped on the side of the road as if prepared for a quick U-turn.

As I neared the vehicles, I glanced in my mirror and saw Lowell's lights coming closer. Up ahead the biker was still sprawled on the asphalt but the hulk had remained inside the van.

I closed to within thirty yards and stopped. Lowell's car paused on the other side of the road about twenty yards behind me. Essentially we had the fallen biker and Verona trapped. The only wild card was the big man inside the van.

I didn't want to spook anybody. Nina was in that van. I needed to get her out before she bled to death.

Suddenly I had a moment of clarity. The hulk didn't care about Nina, me or the damned raid. He just wanted to escape. I resolved to give him that opportunity. I checked the seven bullets in the Sig's mag, grabbed the MAC-10 and opened the car door.

"Police!"

I pointed my Sig at the voice. Verona was getting out of his car waving his badge in one hand, a Glock in the other.

"Police! Don't shoot!"

He waved his Glock at the biker sprawled nearby.

"This man is my prisoner."

Talk about a fucking turncoat.

"Head's up!"

Manson's shout drew my attention to the van. Lowell's large caliber shell had blown off the rear right tire and part of the axle. The van stood partially tilted, front left tire a foot off the ground. As I watched the tire lifted higher, then lower as if a big man had exited on the other side.

The only way to get an angle was to leave my car and take a wide arc which would leave me exposed in an open field. On the other hand with Hazer down we only had to deal with Verona and the hulk. For all I knew the hulk could be holding a grenade back there.

"Keep Verona covered," I told Manson. "If he looks my way shoot him."

I left the car and took a step away from the open door.

Lowell's headlights illuminated the side of the van as he nosed to a stop next to my car, blocking the road completely. I kept the MAC-10 fixed on the van as I slowly circled off the road and into the open field, expecting hulk to pop out shooting any time, video game villain style.

"I'll take care of this one." Verona yelled.

He was practically warning the hulk I was coming.

Crouching in the darkness outside the circle of light I duck-walked sideways, until I had a narrow view of the space behind the van. The thin slice afforded me a split-second warning if the hulk came my way.

For long moments it was quiet. The low drone of car engines dropped a curtain over the night. Lowell had left his vehicle and knelt behind the front tire, SK75 poking out like a howitzer.

The soft scrape of leather on asphalt jarred my focus. Not sure of the direction the sound came from I crouched lower, acutely aware I had never handled a MAC-10 before and that Nina and Carla were inside the van.

Let the game come to you I reminded myself silently.

Then *the preacher* came down and opened the gates of hell.

Chapter 32

Nina and Carla held each other as the van careened wildly, swaying and creaking like a storm-tossed ship. Carla had improvised a crude bandage for the wound in Nina's side using strips torn from her skirt. For the moment it seemed to work. The cloth pad darkened with blood but it stemmed the flow.

Not the pain. It seared her belly like a blow torch, low and intense.

Carla cradled her, cushioning her against the jarring motion of the speeding van. Nina looked up, tried to smile.

"Thanks..."

Carla leaned closer. "You came for me. You're the only one..."

The rest was lost in the screech of metal when a terrific jolt lifted the van off the ground. It slid crazily almost flipping over and came to rest on a tilt, engine ticking like a slow clock.

Terrified both of them held each other tightly. Even the brute guarding them looked scared. Nina was resigned to her own death. More important was protecting Carla. Carefully she opened the clasp knife still gripped in her hand.

The guard didn't notice as Nina pressed the naked blade against her thigh. Her young cousin kept rocking her like a doll.

It was stifling inside the van. The driver's body odor combined with the stench of fear, burnt rubber, and exhaust fumes became overpowering. Nina closed her eyes. She thought she'd seen Max when the thug hauled her outside. He looked so... anguished when he saw her.

Nina was certain he was out there somewhere. Certain he had somehow caused the van to stop. Certain he would come for her.

"Cover me," the driver said. He pointed outside then silently opened his door with remarkable stealth for a man of his bulk. Nina could see the guard's attention was now on the driver but felt too weak. She tried to gather what was left of her strength, vaguely aware Carla was humming a lullaby under her breath.

The song was punctuated by a staccato burst of gun-fire outside.

The guard stiffened and swore softly, pushing his weapon out the driver's side window.

Nina considered cutting him and taking the weapon but couldn't manage to extricate herself from Carla's tight embrace. She fell back exhausted.

Am I dying?

No dying now, Nina told herself, fingering the knife. It would come soon enough. Hot pain sliced her thoughts. Whatever energy she had stockpiled slowly leaked away. *Max, where are you?* She screamed silently.

Chattering gunfire roused Nina from her stupor.

The guard shifted nervously. "Oh, shit."

Carla didn't react, just kept rocking.

The driver's stench filled the van when he leaned inside. "Give me the bitch," he barked.

The guard looked confused then took Carla's arm.

"Not her—the other bitch."

Nina felt herself being dragged across the floor, lifted over the passenger seat and hauled outside like a sack of rice. She also felt the bleeding start again. God, let me live long enough to kill him, she prayed fervently. Her prayer ended with a shriek as the driver roughly lifted her off the ground.

That first brief glimpse of Max jolted her awake. The pain ebbed to a steady throb.

She felt the tension, the fear in the big man's arm as he pressed her against his filthy body. Oh yes, he was afraid.

"Let the girl go... and you go."

Max's voice energized her dwindling reserves. She realized this was it, she was dying. Oh, God, she was so grateful Max was here no matter what happened.

"Fuck you. Bring a car around or she's dead."

"Okay, relax. I'll get the car, just leave the girl."

Nina coiled her arm, knife ready.

"Get the fucking car, now!"

"Okay, okay."

Through half shut eyes Nina watched Max start to get up. She knew she had only one chance. *One chance more than I have now.*

Desperation has its own universe.

Suddenly time slowed. Nina could see each second clearly like crystal beads on a necklace.

Max stood, took a step to the side.

Her captor snorted in triumph and loosened his grip.

Max paused, eyes wide.

The driver's body tensed, ready to shoot.

Without warning she struck, blade slashing his arm.

He bellowed and flung her against the van.

In mid-air she saw Max running at them, his face contorted like that portrait

The Scream.

It was the last thing she saw before a slab of raw agony shredded her body like an iron maiden.

Chapter 33

A large shadow spewing fire lunged from the side of the van. I ate dirt, pressing my face into the damp ground while the field erupted with a hundred killer volcanoes.

We were both exposed but he had a handicap. He was still on his feet. I rolled and aimed for his right side well away from the van. The short burst drove him back out of sight.

I crawled nearer and took a position. Anything that came around that corner again would be mine.

Not really.

I heard a cry. My stomach tightened. The voice sounded familiar. When hulk next appeared he had Nina in front of him. Someone had put a crude compress on her wound but everything from shirt to jeans was soaked with her blood. I struggled to control myself.

"Let the girl go and you go!" I yelled with as much calm as I could muster.

"Fuck you. Get a car over here or she's dead."

So much for diplomacy.

Still I was in no position to bargain. I had a crazy idea... I deliver the car, Manson hidden in the back... I couldn't even suggest it.

"Okay, relax," I said inanely. "I'll get you the car. Just leave the girl."

"Get the fucking car, now!"

"Okay, okay."

Nothing like a crisis to reduce one's vocabulary to bare essentials.

Confident that Lowell and Manson had my back I got to my feet and began edging to my car, eyes fixed on Nina. She appeared to be unconscious.

A twitch of movement caught my eye. In the corner of my vision the hulk was extending his gun hand in my direction, plump features suddenly alive with the malevolence of a child ripping wings off a fly.

For a millisecond I stood transfixed, unable to move.

Abruptly Nina cried out. I saw her lash her arm back, swatting blindly with a small blade. Hulk's gun hand jerked spastically.

Roaring in pain hulk threw her hard against the van. Nina shrieked when she hit and crumpled lifeless, one leg awkwardly splayed.

Snap. Before the hulk could lift his gun I was up and running firing thirty rounds a second at his exposed midsection. At least half those rounds found their target. Later, they told me I was screaming as I ran.

Hulk lurched back a few steps staring at the slimy intestines spilling from his torn belly. He tried to stuff them back. He was still trying when he collapsed.

A bullet cracked past my ear. The flash came from the van's open door. Unable to fire back because of Carla, I dropped, rolled, grabbed Nina's knife and dove inside the van. A bald biker with Nazi tattoos blasted point blank catching my shoulder. Howling in pain and primal blood lust I didn't stop. Eyes bulging with terror he twisted away but I buried the knife behind his ear. He stiffened violently as if shocked by ten thousand volts.

In the numbed silence I heard a crooning voice. I peered into the interior and saw Carla

She sat huddled in a corner rocking back and forth while she hummed the refrain of some Latin lullaby over and over. Her eyes were closed and she seemed unaware of my presence, shut inside her own world.

She didn't even react to the sudden burst of gunfire outside. I heard the growl of a motorcycle and jumped outside in time to see Verona on the ground, Shane Hazer astride his bike and Lowell nowhere in sight.

Manson fired as Hazer swung his bike around and revved the motor but he was leaning precariously against my car and the shotgun kicked him off balance. My dropped MAC-10 was at my feet and my Sig was tucked inside my belt.

I didn't have a chance to use them.

Hazer revved his engine to its shrill limit and raced directly at the two vehicles blocking the road. Astonishingly, his motorcycle lofted high in the air, wheels clearing the space between cars by inches. He landed neatly on the other side and zoomed off toward Fairfax, the frantic whine of his motorcycle receding into the night.

Suddenly it was quiet except for the ticking of the car motors. The air was thick with the smell of cordite, blood and death. I heard the muted rasp of a police radio. Dazed by the abrupt adrenaline comedown I walked unsteadily toward the sound.

It came from Lowell's car. He was lying on the ground. He'd been hit in the thigh, the bullet having pierced the front door.

"I'm alright," he said, teeth set, "paramedics are on their way."

"What happened?"

"Hazer was playing dead. When the shooting started he killed Verona and hit me. I couldn't get a shot." He looked at me. "Can you believe he did that... that jump?"

Manson limped over. "You guys hit? You're bleeding, Max."

"Nothing serious."

I heard sirens wailing in the distance.

"Listen up. It's extremely crucial nobody knows I was here. It's your call, but I'd be grateful."

Both stared at me.

Without waiting for a response I ran around the van to Nina. She was still breathing. I fastened a fresh compress over her wound with my belt as the sirens got louder. My trembling fingers made it difficult.

My numbed shoulder pulsed with pain as I staggered to my car half fell inside and grasped the wheel with shaking hands. Heart rapidly hammering my sore ribs I swerved around the tipped van and sped east into the empty darkness of rolling farmland.

Chapter 34

David Paul's world was disintegrating hour by hour, bit by bit, photo by photo.

Although he'd deleted the evidence he knew they could pull it out of the hard drive. And even if he destroyed the hard drive they had probably stored the evidence on CD. He brooded. He would lose his only client, his sanctuary, his income, his career, self-respect, freedom—and eventually his life—when his special secret was uncovered. And he had no doubt it would come out.

The two cops had let him go because they had no warrants and they were looking for someone else. But they would be back. Of that he was certain. And once they started to investigate and identify the ladies in his forbidden harem his special secret would condemn him to death row.

And then there was his mother.

The old bitch would gladly, no, *gleefully,* help the authorities skewer him. It was the only reason she had lived so fucking long.

It wasn't fair. One mistake, *a good deed,* a lapse in judgment and his life was about to be squashed like vermin. He knew they'd be ruthless when they discovered his connection to the Vandals.

When they found out about Slow Pain and the girl.

David was a realist. The biker would turn against him in a heartbeat if his back was against the wall.

He rarely drank but tonight was an occasion. He had selected scotch, Glenmorangie to be exact, a fine spirit. After deleting his forbidden file, David turned his attention to his manifesto of defiance, his testament.

Fueled by alcohol it went well. He felt vindicated as he read it over, made his corrections.

Satisfied finally, he printed three copies and signed them. By then he was starting to feel more than tipsy. He knew he'd be unable to ride his motorcycle. Even if he could, chances were good he'd be stopped.

David remembered something. The little gift Slow Pain had given him when they closed their deal for The Princess. It had been just over a year ago that Slow had given him a vial of white powder and introduced him to the power of methamphetamine. The first eight hours were exhilarating followed by a hellish nightmare. He hadn't touched it since.

But he knew the meth could cut through the alcohol and make him fit to ride. As for the consequences, they no longer mattered.

He was already living in a hellish nightmare.

The first hit woke him up, alright. Perhaps he overdid it but it worked. He felt sober, alert and eager for the act that would seed his metamorphosis. Just to be sure he inhaled another line.

That did it.

Brain sizzling like a hornet's nest, David went about his preparations with precise efficiency. In a final act of defiance he had another scotch.

The alcohol flared in his consciousness like a gasoline fire. He could literally feel the heat as he unlocked the gun case and removed the engraved shotgun so highly prized by his client.

He began to sweat. He carefully shut down the computer, turned off the lights and locked the door. He would exact his vengeance. He would make them all pay for what they did to him. On his way out he saw a small axe leaning beside a woodpile. Without pausing he snatched it up and marched to his destiny.

The night air was invigorating. He breathed deeply as he rode, trying to slow his accelerated heartbeat. It was essential he remain calm.

Dave exulted in night riding; the cool rushing wind, the open sky, the power between his legs. He saw everything in clear detail, the moonlit road unrolling before him like a magic carpet as it had that night a year ago when he first met The Princess.

But she never understood.

Just like his mother.

Slow Pain had brought her to him for a twenty thousand dollar finder's fee. She had not been sold she had been brought to him. But she never understood that.

He did everything to make her happy, to make her feel she was special but it was never enough. She cried, complained, fought him and demanded the impossible. After a few months all that morphed into pathetic pleading. She never understood the joy, the potential ecstasy of being his Princess.

She began to belittle him.

Just like his mother.

That was the last straw. He lost his patience. The Princess had become an expensive burden. So he eliminated her from his harem. And after tonight they would find where he'd left her.

So what, he told himself. It didn't matter anymore. All that mattered was his vengeance.

When he reached the outskirts of town he slowed to a crawl. At night, the police had little to do except harass drivers. They didn't have the imagination to see what was happening right in front of them.

David chuckled at that. He was still chuckling as he walked to the house, shotgun over his shoulder and axe in hand like a pioneer home from the hunt. When he entered the kitchen his mother was there, sitting at the table reading a magazine.

She looked up, squinted at him with her usual disapproving expression.

"What's all this nonsense?"

"Hello, mother," he said.

He swung the axe hard, severing her carotid artery and jugular. Oily red jets of blood sprayed the small kitchen as he walked around the table to where she lay slumped and finished the job, severing her trachea.

He set her head neatly in the center of the table where she could watch him.

Then he sat in a chair facing her, propped the shotgun against the table and blew off his own head.

Chapter 35

"Behold, someone greater than Solomon is here."
Luke 19:31

Nina stayed in intensive care for ten days.
For five of those days she was unconscious.
During that time I patched up my shoulder with some help from Jimmy Shu then flew to LA and took a room at a Venice Beach motel that didn't require a credit card. I also bought a prepaid cell favored by out of work actors, dealers, and prostitutes. I phoned Lowell and the hospital daily for updates on her condition. As requested he had kept me out of his report. So had Craig. The official story was that Verona died in the line of duty. Not surprisingly, Shane Hazer was still at large. The gang leader could find safe haven in a hundred Vandal chapters.

For the next few days I hung out in Venice, running on the beach, sitting in the sun watching the sea, drinking vegetable juices, the whole rehab trip. It helped heal my body but my soul needed a thousand step program.

Lowell was the first to visit Nina when she recovered consciousness, ostensibly to get her official statement and to mention it was important I stay anonymous. He also mentioned the reason.

"Why didn't you tell me you're DEA, Max?" Her pout was both reproving and sexy. She was still in intensive care. I was back from LA, somewhat recuperated.

"Need to know," I said, mock serious. I bent closer. "I would have... eventually."

"No wonder you wouldn't tell me where you live."

"Get better and I'll tell you anything you want to know."

She smiled weakly. "Gonna hold you to that Max."

Len Zane was less forgiving.

"You can't keep bangin' up my work Max. It ain't a matter of money." He regarded the bruised, bullet-pocked Merc sadly. His expression became indignant when he inspected the fetid trunk.

"Sheeit. Somethin' die in there?"

I tried to think of something clever, couldn't.

Sensing he had touched a nerve Len backed off. But not much.

"Alignment's fucked up. This ain't no off road vehicle."

"All in a worthy cause, I swear."

"Word is there's a hundred grand bounty on a guy who looks a lot like you."

"I'm growing out my hair."

He sniffed at that. "Those cops did a damn good job. Vandals are broke and disorganized. But that won't last long."

"Hear anything about Shane Hazer?'

Len shook his head. "He'll be back. That's for damn sure."

I took a puff on the joint he proffered, knowing he was right.

After leaving the hospital Nina recuperated at home. She had convinced her aunt to take Carla to stay with relatives in San Diego. Petaluma would never be safe for her again.

Or me.

I stayed holed up in my apartment in North Beach for the next few weeks trying to stave off a massive depression that kept spreading like a mushroom cloud. It became a daily struggle to get out of bed. I made myself go down to Curley's for breakfast every day but it was like walking beneath the sea. I plodded on, surrounded by exotic life forms not of my species, which, by the way, was fast becoming extinct.

There I was again, a fugitive in my own safe house.

No doubt, freeing Nina and Carla was justification enough without adding the host of heinous crimes perpetrated by the recently departed. However, I couldn't get out from under that dark, toxic cloud. They say depression is anger turned inward. In my case it was anger turned upside down.

I tried to keep it light and bright with Nina but she saw right through me. She had resumed working a shift at the Lone Palm and I would watch her from the end of the bar as usual.

Except now it was different.

Nina moved a bit slower behind the mahogany. Her grace was still intact but there was a minute hitch in her moves, a hesitancy where once she enjoyed a fluid confidence. I was probably the only one who noticed.

For her part, Nina noticed plenty.

"Max, you're drinking way too much these days," she said, serving me a fresh scotch

"Just one or two more than usual."

"It's not how many you drink. It's the way you drink."

"How do I drink?"

"Hard and unhappy."

Couldn't argue there.

"Is it me?"

Behind her Bruce Springsteen was singing my anthem, Born to Run.

"You kidding?" I took her hand. "You're the only thing I believe in."

"You should believe in yourself, Max. You're a real hero, you know?"

I didn't.

She leaned closer, ignoring the thirsty customers calling for their drinks.

"I'll never forget what you did for me—for us."

Her kiss went a long way to heal any doubts about us but the toxic cloud clung tight, shrouding me like Eastwood's serape in *A Fistful of Dollars*. Wherever I went, whatever I did, it stayed with me: thick, heavy, stinking of death.

Later, holding each other in the darkened motel room I'd rented, Nina presented me with an unforgettable gift.

"You don't have to tell me anything Max," she whispered, mouth close to my ear, "not where you live, not what you do, not where you've been because I trust you, Max. And to prove it..."

She gently pulled away and turned over. There, inked in three colors on her world-class ass were three flaming letters:

MAX.

I was overwhelmed. "This is truly the highest award a man can receive. I am honored."

She came close. "Then prove it."

I did my best.

Afterwards, smoking cigarettes in the non-smoking room hoping the alarm wouldn't go off, she said, "Max?"

"Yeah?"

"How come you never got a tattoo?"

I took a drag and thought.

"Why make it easier for them to identify me?"

She laughed but I was serious. A stray image of Todd's Sacred Heart gushing blood drowned whatever sense of well-being I'd managed to conjure.

"Max?"

"Yeah?"

"You're drifting away again."

More like lost at sea.

I gently rolled her over and kissed the new scar on her side. The bullet had missed her vital organs but nicked an intestine. Peritonitis complicated her recovery.

"I'm right here," I said.

"I hope so, Max."

"Guy in my so-called career can't promise much."

"I'm not asking for promises. Just that you be here while you're here."

Sound advice. Whole religions have been founded on less.

"Maybe we should take a little vacation together," Nina ventured.

"Like where?"

"Mexico, maybe? I hear Zijuatanejo is nice."

"Sounds good," I said. "let me clear up some work first. When can you get free?"

"Anytime.'

I smiled but I was dubious, extremely wary of airports in the post 9/11 hysteria. My identity was bulletproof but why keep shooting at it? Everything breaks down eventually, Look at me.

A week later I met Lowell and Manson at the 2AM club in Mill Valley. We were celebrating Lowell's long-overdue promotion to lieutenant. Lowell's leg wound had healed but Manson's hadn't quite mended. He walked with a cane and he had one of those decisions to make that would give Solomon pause.

"I can keep the lower leg but it may not work so good. Or they can amputate and I can get fitted with a prosthetic that will qualify me for the Olympics."

I looked at Lowell. He shrugged.

"Will they give you disability?"

"Shit, yeah. Question is what does my little girl think?"

"What does Sara think?" Lowell said.

"Actually, she's too young. But my wife would like to see me mobile. Gotta be able to play a little ball with my daughter.'

"What about the job?"

"Well, this injury will restrict me to office duty. So I was thinking, I could retire with my disability and a small pension, go back to school and get a degree in Marine Biology. Hell, in the water my bum leg won't be a handicap. I might even start surfing again. At least my kids will learn how to swim."

He drained his glass and gave us a sheepish grin. "Hell, that was just bullshit. I mulled over retiring, starting over someplace else but then I thought of my family. I want my kids to grow up in a town where their father has respect. And where you guys have my back."

A real optimist despite the real possibility he'd lose a leg. Perhaps it was the benefit of family life. Suddenly, I felt like a pussy.

"When do you decide?" Lowell said.

"End of the month. Final say is up to Ivy." He glanced at me. "My wife."

Lowell turned to me. "How have you been holding up?"

"I've been better."

"Me too. Post traumatic stress. It'll settle eventually."

"You sure?"

"No, but I'm trying to stay positive. Have to be in this game."

"Congratulations on the promotion. What took so long?"

He looked at Manson. "Verona was a real stumbling block. "Now his plaque's on the wall of fame."

Lowell shrugged, square jaw, the All-American straight shooter.

"The real story would hurt a lot of innocent people. Better that way."

"Unfortunate fact is, Verona's being in on the raid gave us legal credibility," Manson added. "He was senior officer."

I nodded. They were probably right. "How the hell did Shane Hazer get through the road blocks?"

Manson and Lowell glanced at each other.

"We got a dirty cop in Fairfax," Manson said finally. "I've known for some time. He was out on duty that night."

I shook my head in resignation. "Hazer's coming back. Bet on it,"

"When he does we'll know what to do," Lowell said.

It was scant comfort.

"What about you?" Manson said. "Can we get some help from the DEA?"

I was ready for that one. "Not while I'm still undercover."

Lowell watched me knock back my third tequila. "Maybe you've been out in the cold too long."

"I was born out in the cold."

Both laughed but I was serious. I wouldn't know how to handle civilian life. Which left me nowhere. Suppose I settled down with Nina. We'd be looking over our shoulder for the next five decades. Me, I was resigned, but Nina deserved a lot better.

"How come it took so long for you to get promoted?" I asked Lowell, anxious to change the subject.

It was his turn to get serious. "Verona," he said carefully. "As senior officer, he enforced every rule in the book and made sure I didn't get access. So I made my own access. Even with my arrest and conviction record I was always one fuck-up away from permanent desk duty."

He drained his glass. "Verona was too chicken-shit to off me. He needed Hazer for that."

"Sounds like he had something on you."

Lowell gave me a shrewd glance. "You're one smart dude, Max. How come you're still on the street?"

"Politics."

They both nodded in solidarity. We all knew that good street cops don't fit the new corporate image of law enforcement. If anything, guys like us are dangerous. Manson and Lowell achieved their celebrity cop status by operating outside the rules. One mistake, one botched raid, one dead civilian and their careers would be finished. They'd be lucky to stay out of prison.

Funny. The two finest lawmen I'd ever encountered and they were considered untouchables by their fellow officers.

Me, I had nothing to lose No rank, salary, pension, family, security... or power. Anything happened, I got swept under the sidewalk.

Except for Nina. She would never let me be ground down to become society's slider, a convenient snack for the powers that be. Her belief in me elevated my game.

Problem was I didn't share her vision. I knew who I was: drinker, drugger, failed husband, needy lover, fugitive, adrenaline junkie... killer.

Todd Fletcher haunted my waking thoughts and most of my dreams.

He surrendered. He was unarmed.

I executed him in cold blood.

Lowell pulled me out of the pit.

"Remember David Paul?"

"What about him?"

"Beheaded his mother with an axe then blew his brains out."

"Jesus is that supposed to make me feel better? Poor pathetic bastard, all he did was look at kiddie porn."

"I'm afraid he did a lot more, Max. He left a confession."

"To what?'

"David Allen Paul purchased an eleven-year-old girl from a member of the Vandals. Then he killed her. The details are in his suicide note."

"Purchased? You mean she was sold?"

He nodded, expression tight with pain.

I couldn't wrap my brain around it—and I'm a professional cynic.

"Purchased?"

"Then he killed her. He left the location of her grave."

Where are we? Who are we? What are we? This tiny planet oozes evil. No wonder UFOs won't land here.

"We did the right thing, Max," Lowell said, sensing my angst. "Nina and Carla were doomed. No appeal, no retrial. Dead... or worse."

I tried to believe it.

During the next few weeks, I began drinking heavily. I would find myself walking Valencia Street in the Mission late at night, peering into the alleys where the coke and heroin changes hands. Don't let anybody kid you, alcohol is the real gateway drug.

I was trapped in a perfect storm of rage, violence, and repentance which generated brutal gusts of self-immolation. Nina didn't say much but I could see she was rethinking her tattoo.

I tried to act more like a boyfriend, take her to dinner, the movies, go for long walks. She seemed to enjoy those occasions until I was well past my fourth drink. For that reason she steered me to neighborhoods that had few bars, such as Dolores, a wide gracious avenue divided by lush palm trees.

One such an occasion followed two exhausting nights of sleepless dreams, vivid images of charred corpses jutting like withered black flowers from the hatches of burning tanks, screaming women, their hair on fire, blood gushing like oil from a pulsing black heart... you get the drift.

We stopped for two drinks before dinner which melted my weary depression for a short time while I concentrated on my lovely Nina. Aware that I had been a major pain in the ass for way too long I tried hard to please her. So I went quietly when she declared last call on the margaritas and truly enjoyed our whispered talk as we strolled past the stately homes lining both sides of the street.

We turned off at Eighteenth to get a bite at Delfina's, a superb Italian establishment. Normally, you need to book a table weeks in advance but they have a counter and later at night seats are available. The spaghetti alone is worth the trouble and I confined my drinking to wine.

However, after dinner we left the restaurant still wrapped in each other and wandered a few blocks until we were in the Castro, the city's openly gay district. It's a bit more flamboyant than Christopher Street in New York and features more bars per square foot.

The neighborhood hangouts were packed with single men but all I saw were the bottles stacked behind the bartenders. Still buzzed on dinner wine I could smell the booze from the sidewalk.

Nina could tell I was getting thirsty. "Let's go back to Valencia, I need a coffee."

I didn't argue, having realized in a moment of semi-alcoholic clarity that drink did nothing to ease my pain. Or my fear. It just wasn't time to admit it.

We walked past a bar with a monolithic façade and one small, tinted window. The place was aptly named Midnight Sun. The door opened and a male couple emerged, one with a hand on his "friend's" shoulder. The man in front was dark, slender and his forearms were carpeted with green and red tattooed fish. For a sick moment I thought he might be a Vandal.

The man behind came into focus. At first glance he had the rugged Marlboro Man features idealized in gay culture. At second glance I realized I knew him.

Knew him well in fact.

Lieutenant Bob Lowell of the Petaluma Police Department.

He seemed delighted to see us.

"Great to see you guys out and about," he said giving Nina and me a hug. "This is my partner, Steve Kooper, with a K."

We made small talk for a few minutes then said our goodnights. I thought I'd been perfectly cool but as Lowell shook my hand he leaned closer.

"Nobody's perfect."

Thank you, Billy Wilder. Suddenly I understood why he had left the military and how Verona was able to keep him in check.

"Did you know Bob was gay?" Nina asked over coffee.

"Never gave it any thought. Tell you one thing, though."

"What's that?"

"Bob's aim sure is straight."

We were both quiet after that.

A few days later I was out on the town. Tony Nik's to be exact. It was late, the place was empty and I was seated alone at a rear table trying to burn off my guilt with overproof bourbon. The bartender kept looking my way as he rinsed glasses, hoping I'd leave so he could close early. But I was still obsessively going over it fact by fact.

Fact: Todd was directly responsible for the kidnappings of both Carla and Nina, fully knowing what would happen and caring not a shit.

Fact: Todd would have blown me away had he not run out of bullets. Buried somewhere deep inside my regrets was that sharp *clack* that punctuated the thin line between life and oblivion.

Fact: If I had tried to leave him and follow Nina he would have picked up one of the fallen weapons strewn everywhere and shot me in the back.

Fact: Any decent lawyer would have gotten him off with less than a year, if that. The prison time would make great publicity. By the time Todd got released he'd be a star. That all-knowing smirk was based on a lifetime of getting away with it.

Was I right to kill Todd in order to save Nina?

Was Jesus good?

That night I resolved to stop drinking.

Chapter 36

"Why, ninety five percent of the information that reaches us has already been preselected and paid for."
Haruki Murakami, A Wild Sheep Chase

On the seventh day of my sobriety I was sitting in Mario's, unable to believe what I was reading in the New York Times and what I was witnessing every day. Truly we live in a Swiftian age.

From the day our prez landed on a carrier dressed in a genuine flight suit and blithely declared "Mission Accomplished," the grotesque absurdities have mounted. No bid contracts for administration cronies, dumping twenty billion dollars a month on a never-ending war with shifting goals, complete indifference to the fact that we invaded a sovereign nation under false pretenses, the politics of fear, the disdain for the Geneva Convention, the suspension of Habeas Corpus, the distortion of science to suit political agendas... the hits keep coming.

Granted, I'm old school. Roy Rogers, Captain America, Indiana Jones, Jimmy Stewart bucking the machine in *Mr Smith Goes To Washington*, George Clooney bucking the corporation in *Micheal Clayton*—that's me. In the abstract, of course.

Through it all I've always kept faith in the innate common sense and decency of the ordinary citizen. It never crossed my mind that our democracy could come so close to collapse. But face it, so long as America stays attached to a PlayStation it will happen. We are a society that is entertaining ourselves to death.

These days, Miss Liberty has a credit card in one hand and a lottery ticket in the other.

Meanwhile, a significant segment of the local population was keeping itself amused with real-life gun wars in various hoods. At the moment MS13 was in a serious rumble with the Sureños and elsewhere the Vandals were in a hot war with the Hell's Angels.

At least it keeps the heat off Lowell and Manson I reflected. It was a lovely day, why waste it ranting? Encouraged by the slim shard of reason cutting through the cloud I moved to an outside table for a cigarette. You can't give up everything at the same time. But my cigarette consumption dipped way down when I quit drinking.

A sunny day in North Beach is an impressionistic painting. The passersby all had colorful style, even the tourists, and I clocked them all as I enjoyed my coffee and cigarette—one of life's fading pleasures in the wheatgrass era. I might have been sitting with Fellini in Roma.

A moment later I wished I was.

Walking along Columbus Avenue wearing a smart black blazer and designer jeans was my friendly heroin dealer from my past life—Byron like the poet—lightning scar and all.

I kept my cool. He's a tourist like millions of other tourists I told myself. Or he's in town for a sit-down with the Chinese Tongs. *Whatever the fuck the reason it had nothing to do with me.*

Comforted by my ability to place logic over emotion I returned to my coffee. But Byron's walk-by had me rattled.

Always notice when you light a cigarette, said the wise man.

I lit another. Paranoia is nitro to depression's glycerin. I kept working it out methodically, odds in the multi-million etcetera. But I couldn't help recalling old Bill Burroughs: "There's no such thing as coincidence."

I took a deep breath, wondering if it was an omen.

Less than four minutes later, all my omens imploded.

Long legs in tight black jeans floated into view. Striding purposefully across Union Street, clad in dark glasses and long leather coat, like some latter day Mata Hari, was Lady Brett.

That was no coincidence.

After deep meditation, I extracted my cell and called Nina.

"Max, I'm kind of busy—what's up?"

Not what I'd hoped for.

"I've been thinking, do you still want to take that vacation?"

Her tone softened considerably.

"Whenever you say."

"How about tomorrow, can you get away?"

"Sure. Are we flying somewhere?"

"No. Rent a car and we'll drive to Mexico. I'll cover expenses."

"Perfect. I'll do it right now."

"Good."

"Max?"

"Yeah?"

"I love you."

I took a deep breath, held it.

Nina stepped into the silence.

"Well?"

"That's a loaded word."

"Unloaded words don't mean anything, Max."

She had me there.

It was going to be an interesting ride.

37483657R00162

Made in the USA
Charleston, SC
07 January 2015